Final Grains
OF SAND

Final Grains OF SAND

a novel

DAVID HARDER

AMBASSADOR INTERNATIONAL
GREENVILLE, SOUTH CAROLINA & BELFAST, NORTHERN IRELAND

www.ambassador-international.com

Final Grains of Sand

ISBN: 978-1-62020-611-9
eISBN: 978-1-62020-685-0

Cover Design and Page Layout by Hannah Nichols
eBook Conversion by Anna Riebe Raats

Printed in the USA

AMBASSADOR INTERNATIONAL
Emerald House
411 University Ridge, Suite B14
Greenville, SC 29601, USA
www.ambassador-international.com

AMBASSADOR BOOKS
The Mount
2 Woodstock Link
Belfast, BT6 8DD, Northern Ireland, UK
www.ambassadormedia.co.uk

The colophon is a trademark of Ambassador

To Dr. Emily Weinacker,
an amazing, loving wife & a gift from God.

Dedicated to Roy Kreider Woods II

February 6, 1936 ~ March 14, 2013

Although I never personally met Roy, I discovered through his daughter the truth concerning this brilliant man. A wonderful husband, terrific father, and loving grandfather, Roy instilled in his children appreciation for classical music and the ballads. A member of Kappa Sigma while attending the University of Illinois, Roy served four years in the U.S. Navy as a pilot. He enjoyed and continued flying as a civilian. A man of inspiration and character, Roy was an adventurous spirit, participating in every sport, including skydiving, racquetball, boating, traveling, and studying. Roy appreciated and loved traveling the world. Roy was also a wise business investor, and he worked as an industrial engineer for Northwestern Steel and Wire Company for more than thirty years. I wish I could have met Roy because this loving man was a tremendous influence on his family and many other people. Plus, he crammed an enormous amount of life into the limited time he had on this earth. The life of Roy Woods provided the inspiration for this book.

PREFACE

BIRTH AND DEATH ARE NATURAL parts of life. No one gets to choose who his or her parents are or where they are born in this world, yet our character determines how well we handle our journey. From adversity, one person rises to become a national leader, and another, whose life seemed perfect, develops into a living monster. Our journey is littered with peaks and valleys. How we deal with our challenges reveals our true selves.

Cancer is one of the most malignant and destructive diseases known to man. It is no respecter of persons and kills 8.8 million people every year. Almost every one of us is familiar with someone—a friend, relative, loved one—whose life was cut short because of cancer. I've never survived cancer, but I have close friends who've beaten the odds. Whether they survive or succumb, their stories are eerily similar. If nothing else, it causes us to pause and appreciate this moment, this day, as a treasure.

Although *Final Grains of Sand* is fiction, the story is one with which many folks can easily identify. The main character, James Kreider, has everything in his favor until, unexpectedly, he is diagnosed with a rare form of cancer. Married with three grown children, his estranged wife was involved in a tragic car accident many months before his diagnosis. Alone and struggling with his personal legacy,

Jim eventually plans his funeral and, for his friends, a unique experience. He selects five individuals to represent his life at the memorial service. None of these people know each other nor are they prepared for the revelations resulting from their participation. Jim selects his boss, Nathanial; his neighbor, Joe; Michael, the pastor of his church; Tom, his physician; and a woman James was involved with for many, many years—Arleen. Each individual has a unique perspective on the man they knew, and like a diamond in the rough, they must chisel at the edges of his story until the gem of their friend emerges.

The story of James Kreider concerns relationships. Not all of Jim's friends are Christian, yet how he lived his life imparted a message of God's love and forgiveness to friends and strangers alike. Like a mirror of reality, learning the information between the covers of a book defines the message hidden in the pages. The life of James Kreider is no different.

We live in an era where churches are experiencing membership decline. All too often, they have lost touch with the message of Jesus—that is, loving our fellow human and bringing God's "Good News" message to everyone. Society, including Christianity, is rampant with quick judgment and doctrinal standards that are many times not biblical. Still, Jesus' message is a simple one, brought to everyday people and delivered in a practical format: Love! Value everyone around you. See the beauty in every individual. Encourage one another. Remember, life is not perfect, and neither are humans, but we can make a difference in the world. Choose love.

CHAPTER ONE

"JAMES, WOULD YOU STEP INTO my office, please?"

At the doctor's appearance, Jim stood up. He had been scanning, but not reading, a tennis journal. Jim flopped the magazine on the side table and followed the doctor down the hallway. He was apprehensive about why Doctor Nolan wanted to meet with him—face to face—on short notice.

During the quick drive from his business office, Jim was distracted as he mentally ran through the various reasons why he might be here. He wondered if it was a mistake to cancel his important sales meeting this morning. He'd had a physical a few weeks ago, but it was routine. Most likely the doctor was following up on test results—perhaps the blood tests or the PET scan. Jim felt confident he'd get a glowing report, since he was in excellent health. Surely there wasn't anything the doctor couldn't tell him in a few days.

"Please have a seat, James."

The office felt warm, and Jim's mouth was dry. He was suddenly thirsty.

"What's the urgency, Doc?" Jim tucked his long legs under the chair and watched Dr. Nolan close the door before walking around to the other side of his desk. Sitting up straight, Jim edged forward in his seat.

Dr. Nolan removed his glasses and rubbed the red spots on the bridge of his nose before speaking.

"James, we need to talk about your lab test results because they're concerning. I ordered so many tests because I wanted to be sure of the results."

"Everything is fine, isn't it?" Jim shifted uncomfortably, his cocksure, business attitude deflating at the sight of the doctor's grave face.

Dr. Nolan looked him in the eye. "James, we've been friends a long time. I'm going to give it to you straight. It appears your body has an invasion of three different cancers that are feeding off each other in several vital organs. Cancer has invaded your liver, pancreas, spleen, and possibly your kidneys. I can't begin to tell you how exceedingly rare your condition is."

"Wait a minute, Doc. This makes no sense. I feel fine, and I've never been sick a day in my life."

"You feel fine now, yes, but I'm afraid those feelings aren't permanent."

Jim shook his head and then ran his hands through his dark hair. This couldn't be happening. But he'd known the doctor for decades; he wouldn't lie.

Dr. Nolan sat back and waited for Jim to absorb the enormity of the situation.

"I have *three* cancers? I . . . I . . . How is this possible? I've always been so healthy." Jim began to pant, his breathing labored. "Okay, wait a minute. So, I'll need to take some time off from work, but you're saying chemo, radiation, surgery—they're an option for me, right?"

Dr. Nolan got up and sat in the chair next to Jim, putting his hand on Jim's shoulder.

"The cancers are fast-growing and widespread. You could go that route. We might buy some time and maybe add two or three months at the most. However, you would have to decide if the side effects are worth it."

Time came to a screeching halt for Jim. Frightened, he inquired in a nervous voice, "What kind of time are we talking about?"

"After seeing the scan images, I conferred with several friends and oncologists around the country. Short of a miracle, the consensus is three to maybe four months. I wish I had better news, James."

Jim shook off the doctor's hand and stood up. "What caused this? Why don't I feel anything drastic?"

"Those are questions I can't answer."

"I know I've felt fatigued a lot lately, but I just figured I was working too hard and not sleeping enough. Everyone has fatigue, right?" Jim paced, rubbing his face. He stopped. "What if I hadn't come in for the physical?"

Dr. Nolan did not sugarcoat his next edict, and his voice was kind. "You would still experience your illness, but you would face it thoroughly unprepared."

Jim suddenly felt faint, like someone had sucked all the oxygen from the room. He collapsed into the chair. He was unprepared for the dreaded word *cancer*. Random thoughts hit him in machine-gun succession. Normally self-reliant, Jim was quickly devoid of immediate answers. He bent over at the waist and placed his head between his knees and slowly began to rock.

Dr. Nolan's hand hovered above Jim's back.

"James, are you in any pain at the moment? Can I get you something?"

Jim shook his head but continued to rock.

"If it's okay with you, I'd like to confirm my findings with a couple more biopsies—perhaps run another PET scan with contrast."

Jim stopped rocking and sat up, staring at Dr. Nolan.

"Doc, I mean no disrespect, but poking holes in sensitive areas of my body, yanking out tissue or bone, and pumping me full of radioactive junk doesn't sound pleasant. Will it help rule out cancer?"

"It will confirm my findings."

"This can't actually be happening. Why now? Why me?"

"James, you're not even sixty and—"

"No, unfortunately, I turned sixty last week."

Startled, Dr. Nolan said, "Seriously, James? Has it been that long? I remember delivering you. I know you have three lovely children, but you should be looking forward to a full life with grandchildren and retirement."

Jim put his head in his hands again, making a wordless, groaning sound.

"I would recommend reaching out to family and getting some support. In less than two months, your organs are going to start to fail, and before the third month is finished, you'll be needing twenty-four-hour care. Right now, while you can, make some decisions by planning and making arrangements."

Jim blankly stared at the doctor.

"Well, I guess that last part is easy. When I'm dead, cremate my body, and scatter the ashes to the wind."

"James. I'm serious. If you want, I could contact your family."

"Please don't! Your information is a lot to digest, and it appears I haven't much time to spend it casually."

Jim stood and turned, facing the door.

Dr. Nolan reached out, grabbing Jim's shirt sleeve.

"If you need anything, anything at all, please get in touch with me. My receptionist will give you my personal cell phone number, and you can call me day or night. If you're in pain, I'll immediately arrange for something at the hospital or your pharmacy. If you don't mind, I would like to see you again in one month."

Resting his hand on the doorknob, Jim stood frozen, staring at the closed office door. His voice was flat, monotone.

"I need a little time to figure some things out, and I appreciate your concern. You've been a terrific doctor, but I think I need to spend some time alone. Please do not discuss my condition with anyone or make any family calls. I beg you."

"Of course. You have my word, James."

Jim walked out of the office to the parking lot. After dropping his full weight into the leather seat of his BMW 540, Jim looked at his watch.

Three o'clock!

In a fit of frustration, Jim yanked the Rolex off his wrist. He tossed it on the passenger side of the car's floor. Clenching his fists, he hammered on the steering wheel with eyes tightly closed.

"I can't be dying. I'm too young."

Peering in the rearview mirror, Jim studied his chiseled face, looking for signs of any sickness. He pulled down on one lower eyelid, staring at the steel-gray iris, and then opened his mouth, inspecting everything with his tongue stuck out.

Jim shook his head. He then started the engine and ignored the seatbelt warning indicators. The BMW screeched backward from the parking stall, and then jerked to a stop. Heading for the exit, the car leaped from the curb like a cheetah. The tires squealed as Jim drove off in a rush, speeding down the boulevard.

* * *

Dr. Nolan gathered the lab reports and various papers associated with his patient. He took his time as he slid the papers into a thick folder. Sitting down, Dr. Nolan let his finger trace out the name, *James Kreider*, printed along the edge.

Dr. Nolan buried his face in his hands and wept. Choking on his words, he began to pray.

"Our Father, Who is in heaven, great is Your Name. Your kingdom come, Your will be done—"

CHAPTER TWO

CHANGING HIS MIND ABOUT RETURNING to work, Jim steered the BMW toward his house. Thoughts and actions were in slow-motion. On the ride home, Jim spent time reflecting on his life.

Of his three children, only Stephanie, his oldest daughter, had showed any promise. Steph, as Jim called her, was in her fourth year at Stanford, studying economics—a degree which Jim and his daughter argued about until they were both blue in the face. It was careless of Stephanie to start college three years after high school just so she and her friends could tour Europe; but her degree decision was incredibly off-base, and Jim saw no future for her now.

All of Jim's logic fell on deaf ears because Stephanie was determined it was the right choice for her. Jim finally conceded, acknowledging she had her mother's stubbornness and her father's tenacity of challenging the norms. Stephanie was dating a medical student, and the two were already planning their future.

Will I live long enough to see them get married? Jim thought.

Robert, the middle child, was in his sixth year of college and studying business law at Santa Clara University—a Franciscan college in northern California. When Jim questioned Robert's decision to attend law school after spending the first four years of college in computer technology, Robert's excuse was more money.

"You mean more of *my* money?" Jim remembered asking his son over the phone.

It seemed Robert had inherited his mother's stubbornness as well.

Staci, the youngest daughter, was the problem child, and it was her mother's fault for spoiling Staci when she was young. Constant trips to the doctor for ear infections, runny noses, and a sundry of the ancillary ear, nose, and throat conditions plagued Staci for her first seven years. Then, as if by some unidentified miracle, she was instantly healed. From that point forward, Staci's rebellion developed.

Now living with some jobless poet four years her junior and in dilapidated section-eight housing, Staci had refused any monetary support. Studying art at an obscure college in Houston, Texas, Staci was also the visual poster child for tattoo and metal piercings. She was a beautiful little girl, and Jim could never understand why she had to destroy her beauty with "body art." Her last Christmas card included a photo of her and what's-his-name sitting completely unclothed somewhere in the middle of nowhere and looking like two circus freaks. Jim tore the picture into shreds the moment it escaped the envelope.

Jim and his wife, Samantha, had been married only ten years when their marriage showed signs of severe fractures. They were high school sweethearts, and everyone had predicted a long, happy future on their wedding day. But starting out at age twenty and nineteen respectively, Jim and Samantha matured along two divergent paths.

They added children, thinking this would improve their relationship, but it only made things worse. As they entered their thirties, it was apparent that their love was lukewarm at best. It never improved, and this frustrated Jim, but he also refused to seek help from an outside counselor. They kept the relationship alive for the sake of the children only.

Jim and Samantha eventually agreed to live separate lives under the same roof—again, for the benefit of the children. Polite and courteous, all external appearances to friends and relatives presented a picture of an ordinary family. Inside the home was the opposite, with Jim and Samantha fiercely arguing over which direction a chair should face in the family room. They regretted the pettiness of their arguments but also refused to yield to one another or find any common ground.

All of Jim's children had spread their wings immediately after high school graduation, leaving Jim and Samantha alone in their four-bedroom, two-story suburban monolith. Meanwhile, Samantha had started quietly dating a younger man from her workplace. Jim knew about it, but at least Samantha was respectful enough that she never brought the kid around the house. As time slipped by, Jim and Samantha worked out their love-hate relationship and agreed to be roommates. At least Jim had someone to talk to at the end of a day, and Samantha had a solid business mind she could bounce ideas off of. With very limited interaction, they made their dysfunction function.

Ten months ago, Samantha and her boyfriend had gone out for dinner one evening. On their way home, a drunk driver plowed into their car at eighty-miles-an-hour and headlights extinguished. The vehicle that Samantha and her boyfriend were driving was immediately reduced to an unrecognizable mass of metal, and their bodies were unrecognizable as well. It was so horrible that even hardened emergency medical rescuers had difficulty maintaining composure during the cleanup process. Despite the carnage, the drunk driver walked away unscathed.

The funeral was simple and attended by Jim and most of Samantha's work associates. Term papers, finals, and sheer laziness prevented any of the children from attending. Staci stated, in no uncertain terms, that it was a sham anyway, that her mother was unfaithful, and that she did not deserve any recognition. Jim sat through the service in a catatonic state; and, in spite of all forced attempts, he could not make himself shed a single tear. Time had evaporated too fast, and he supposed he wouldn't be attending any weddings for his children or meeting his grandchildren.

As he was lost in his thoughts, Jim suddenly found himself parked in the driveway of his home. After a forty-minute drive, Jim had no clue how he had arrived or the journey from the doctor's office. Jim was instantly overwhelmed with regretful sadness. His body felt encased in sludge as he dragged himself into the house.

CHAPTER THREE

FOR OVER FOURTEEN HOURS, JIM sat in his living room easy chair staring at the blank screen of his behemoth, flat-screen television in a darkened house. Seated in the same clothes he went to work in, he sat like a statue. Unmoved, Jim could neither think nor not think. Random thoughts came and went without any processing, and he spent hours sitting in a neutral, trance-like state. Praying silently, he cried, swore at God, and exhaustively ran every possible scenario through his mind.

The telephone rang several times, and the doorbell rang twice. Just before midnight, his neighbor Joe banged with his fist on the front door, calling out Jim's name. Unfazed, Jim never moved his eyes but focused on the blank screen of the television in his pitch-black house. The pendulum of the antique wall clock ticked off the seconds like a metronome. Around five in the morning, daylight was struggling to breach the day when Jim's eyelids felt like lead, and he fell soundly asleep.

The transition to slumber gradually enveloped Jim. One moment, he was blankly staring at the television screen; the next moment, he was relaxed and unconscious.

A reoccurring dream appeared, and the recognizable moments played out like reality inside Jim's brain. The geographical location was different each time he had this dream, but the theme was always the same. In his nightmare, and completely unaware of his surroundings, Jim eventually noticed something was shadowing his footsteps. He would quicken his pace, but who or what was behind him matched each step. Suddenly, Jim found himself running for fear of his life in a full sweat.

Despite efforts to identify his nemesis, Jim could not maintain his running pace and also see the unknown monster over his shoulder. He could feel its breathing just inches from behind him, and he knew it was gaining momentum. The monster produced a wheezing, raspy sound. Jim's blood pumped wildly throughout his body, and he could hear the sound of his heart drumming inside his ears. After an eternity of running, all sounds abruptly stopped. Typically, at this point in his dream, Jim would find he was on the edge of a cliff, teetering and struggling to maintain his balance. The abyss below appeared endless, and Jim would eventually slip over the edge, falling for eternity. Then abruptly, Jim would awake from the terrible dream, drenched in sweat.

This time, though, Jim wanted the outcome to be different. He wanted to identify the monster. In slow motion, Jim lost his balance and started to fall over the cliff's edge, as usual. However, Jim took this opportunity to twist his body and face the monster that had bedeviled him all these years. A look of shock and then amusement crossed Jim's face as he finally saw his adversary. A pair of lungs, liver, heart, stomach, and intestines loomed above. The organs were spotty and disease-infested, making them hideous and black. Tentacles of the intestinal track reached out to grab Jim as he fell backward, but it was too late. Jim watched the scene fade away as he silently dropped into the abyss. This time, for some unexplainable reason, Jim felt relief and closure.

At precisely seven in the morning, an internal clock inside Jim instantly jerked him awake, forcing him from his easy chair. Jim never needed an alarm and stuck to his routine with military precision. After a long, hot shower, a shave, and breakfast—consisting of black coffee and toast—Jim roared off to work.

Jim's day proceeded as usual with business meetings and phone calls as if nothing had changed. Generally, most of the mid-level managers would gather at Charlie's for cocktails and a bite to eat around one in the afternoon. But today, Jim declined. Staring out the glass walls of his office, which faced the interior of the department floor, Jim watched the muted employees move about. People attending to their routine activities were entirely unaware of Jim or his condition. Tired, he dropped his forehead to the desk, dangling his arms at his sides to rest, and he fell asleep in seconds flat.

CHAPTER FOUR

"MR. KREIDER? MR. KREIDER?"

Soundly asleep, Jim felt his body being shaken, and, in the distance, he heard his secretary's voice.

"Did you check to see if he has a pulse?" asked a male voice.

"Oh dear! He's not dead, is he?" asked a female employee.

Jim opened his eyes and slowly raised his head.

An immediate gasp emitted from the crowd crammed into Jim's office.

"All right, people, get back to work. All of you, now! Give the man some space."

Jim's focus finally returned, and he saw his boss, Nathanial Martin, the vice president of sales and marketing, standing in front of Jim's desk.

"Did you have a little too much fun last night, Jimmy-boy?"

Jim frowned, his voice groggy. "What? Huh? No. I had trouble sleeping last night. What time is it?" His last words sounded almost panicky.

Perplexed, the secretary glanced up at Mr. Martin and then back to Jim Kreider.

"A quarter past two, Mr. Kreider, and your two o'clock appointment is already waiting in the conference room."

Jim stared at the sheer walls and could see a crowd of employees with their noses pressed against the glass, watching Jim as if he were a fish in a large aquarium. Mr. Martin followed Jim's stare and yanked open Jim's office door.

"Any employee still standing here in the next two seconds is immediately fired!"

Like a flock of birds resting on a high-tension wire, the employees instantly scattered in various directions, bumping into each other as they scrambled to escape Mr. Martin's proclamation.

"Here, Mr. Kreider, I poured you a hot cup of coffee."

The secretary set the steaming cup on the desk, and Jim could "smell" the caffeine. He looked up and gave her a faint smile.

"Thanks, Michelle. Please let my clients know I'm on a call and will join them in a minute or two."

She smiled. "Already done, Mr. Kreider. They're busy typing away on their laptops, and I believe they forgot the time."

"Thank you."

"Jim, are you okay?" asked the vice president.

Jim stood and sipped the hot coffee, which tasted fantastic. He made a face as the hot liquid scalded the insides of his mouth.

"I'm fine, Nate. Honestly, I am. It was a long night of little sleep, that's all. I'm terribly sorry." Jim stretched his body, which was stiff and achy.

"Well, you look like something the cat dragged in."

"Thanks, Nate. That really helps."

"You scared the daylights out of everyone. Michelle came running into my office, white as a ghost, and said she thought you were dead. To tell the truth, when I first laid eyes on you, I thought the same thing. You're our number one sales executive. Don't go checking out on us like that again. Do you understand me?"

"Got it, Nate. Again, I'm terribly sorry."

His boss headed for the door but paused. Turning, he said, "After your two o'clock appointment is finished, do me a favor and go home for the rest of the day."

"Nate, I said I'm okay. It won't happen again. I promise."

"It's not a request. That's an order! If I come back in one hour, and you're not gone, and the light's out, you're fired." Nathanial turned and walked out.

After watching his boss disappear around the corner, Jim set the cup down and placed both hands on the side of his desk. Dropping his head, Jim shuddered and gave out a long, heavy sigh. What was he thinking? He needed to pull himself together.

Jim looked up and grabbed his jacket from the chair back. He slipped it on and adjusted his tie and shirt collar. Bending over the desk, Jim swilled the remnants of the hot coffee. Snatching a notepad and pen from his desk, Jim darted out the door, heading to the conference room.

* * *

Three weeks later, Jim tendered his resignation, claiming personal matters demanded his immediate attention. Mr. Martin was beside himself and knew the loss would impact the sales figures. He outright refused the resignation but agreed to give Jim three months leave of absence instead if Jim would be available for consultation calls. Most of the employees figured Jim was grieving the death of his wife or that the emotions had finally caught up with the man. Either way, it would be the last time any work associate would ever see Jim Kreider alive again.

Initially, Jim conducted his life at home as if nothing had changed. He shunned his neighbor Joe, and would go shopping at midnight to avoid running into anyone he knew. On Sundays, Jim took Samantha's makeup and colored his face and hands, so no one could see his gray skin. He sat in the back row of the church, and as soon as the service was over, he'd slink out the door and rush home. It was a large congregation, and no one seemed to notice Jim anyway.

By the end of the first month, Jim woke up with pain coursing throughout his body. Fumbling to get the morphine bottle open, Jim would suck down three pills with fresh, hot coffee. His clothes were so baggy, Jim resorted to wearing sweat pants and loose-fitting shirts to hide his sagging skin. Every time he stepped on the bathroom scale, the digits displayed a precipitously lower number. Jim finally called a realtor and listed his home on the market, refusing to allow the agent permission to place any signs in the yard to indicate it was for sale.

After a few weeks, the frustrated, but surprised, agent had a solid contract with a family who had been dreaming about Jim's house every time they drove through the neighborhood. An arrangement was agreed upon, whereby they disposed of Jim's furnishings as they saw fit. The new homeowners were ecstatic and supplied their favorite thrift store from Jim's bounty.

The next week—packing nothing but a toothbrush and paste—Jim drove to the BMW dealer and closed out his lease. He then shuffled two blocks south to Woody's used car lot and cash-purchased a lime green 1967 Dodge Dart that consumed more oil than gas. Motoring to the outside edge of town, Jim arrived at an obscure hospice facility to check himself in. After tossing the keys on the floorboard of the Dodge and locking the car, it required every last drop of energy for Jim to walk from the parking lot to the front door of the facility.

Just inside the lobby were several empty wheelchairs, and Jim lowered himself into the nearest one, sitting askew. Breathing hard, Jim witnessed a sympathetic nurse rushing over to assist him into a seated, comfortable position, for which Jim was immensely appreciative. Earlier, Jim had discarded his wallet and any credit cards through his home office shredder. He had no identification whatsoever and provided the administration nurse with his name, social security number, and the name and number of his attorney.

After paying off all his debts, closing all his bank accounts, and making final arrangements upon his death, Jim had the bank write out a certified check to the hospice for what remained of his investments and savings. He handed the administration nurse the folded check.

"I believe this should cover any expenses. In addition, anything remaining should be considered a donation to your organization."

When the nurse opened the check, she saw that it was for two hundred ninety-four thousand dollars and seventeen cents. Gasping, the nurse quickly located the hospice administrator. Jim was immediately situated into a private room in the far corner of the building with a massive window facing the green space of their grounds. It was a lovely view of a large pond, a huge oak tree, tons of flowering plants, and a meticulously manicured lawn, which would cause most golf course owners to be insanely jealous.

For the first few weeks, Jim relaxed and was starting to feel slightly better, but then the convulsions started. Food and liquids refused to remain in his stomach, so the hospice staff placed Jim on a feeding tube. His pills were replaced with saline and morphine drips that soothed Jim to sleep most of the day. At first, two male nurses were needed to lift Jim off the bed while they changed the sheets. In no time, his six-foot-one frame was so reduced in size that one female nurse could accomplish the same goal alone.

The attentive staff murmured and gossiped outside Jim's room, trying to determine why no one ever visited or called on the man. Two days before his death, Jim had the hospice summon his attorney, who dropped everything and rushed to Jim's side. The lawyer was unprepared for the horrifying sight he beheld when he laid eyes on Jim. He had last seen Mr. Kreider in his office a little over three months earlier, but the skeletal corpse speaking from the bed at this exact moment was entirely unrecognizable.

"For goodness' sakes, Jim," he exclaimed.

The dying man commanded in a raspy voice, "Shut up, Tony, and close the door and those curtains first."

The attorney was aghast because his client was shriveled and emaciated. Despite nearly losing all his muscle mass, Jim, remarkably, was able to move his arms and hands.

How can this man even be alive?

The sight was sickening and almost caused the attorney to use Jim's restroom and regurgitate an earlier-consumed lunch. Slightly more than one hour later, the counselor emerged from Jim's room. Shellshocked, ashen, and crestfallen, the lawyer walked away from the hospice without uttering a single word to anyone watching him leave.

Two days later, the morning nurse arrived for her shift at six a.m. As usual, she started her rounds near Jim's room. Jim slept for long periods of time, so the nurse followed her regular morning routine. In a cheerful, affirming voice, she greeted her patient.

"Good morning, Mr. Kreider. How are you feeling today?"

She didn't wait for an answer because she rarely received one. The nurse opened the drapes, letting in the early, warm rays of sunshine. She performed various small housekeeping chores, humming a soft, religious tune. When she walked over to the bed, she checked on the morphine and saline bag and noticed it was no longer dripping. A look of concern crossed the woman's face, and she stopped humming.

"Mr. Kreider?"

She opened his left eye with her fingers and shined a small penlight into the void and saw nothing. Checking his wrist for a pulse, she found none. Reverently, the nurse then pulled the bed sheet over Jim's body, covering his face completely.

Sometime during the night, James Kreider had slipped from this life into the next in a peaceful process that involved no other human being. Without fanfare or relatives to mourn at his bedside, Jim's life and suffering had ended. For Jim's book of life, there would be no more chapters or pages written.

There, in the solitude of his hospice room, Jim had taken his final breath, and his heart had given its closing, soundless beat. Like other countless souls over the millennia before him, Jim had finished his human journey. Sans any witnesses, Jim had crossed over to a place known only to those who have tasted death.

CHAPTER FIVE

"GOOD MORNING, SIR. HOW MAY I help you?"

An attractive receptionist in her early sixties, nicely dressed with silvery-white hair, looked up and smiled.

The man standing before her redefined the term "big and tall" and was dressed extremely casual, with his bold print Hawaiian shirt hanging out to hide an expanding waist.

"The name's Joe Langley, and someone from here called me regarding an appointment."

The woman typed on her keyboard and scanned the screen. "Mr. Langley, yes, you have a ten o'clock appointment with Mr. Toncetti. Please follow me."

"Can you tell me what this is all about?"

The woman ignored Joe and walked through the large, frosted glass doors, holding them open for her guest. The names Toncetti, Silva, Barnes, and Smith were etched into the glass. As the woman walked down the hall, Joe couldn't help but watch the receptionist. Her body was toned, and she was tall and particularly attractive for her age. Joe suspected the beautiful lady had been a model in her earlier life. She displayed an air of class.

She led Joe into a large, well-appointed conference room. A long table of solid teak, with fourteen luxurious, leather chairs surrounding it, dominated most of the chamber. Two conference telephone speakers divided the center of the table. The room was walled on three sides with teak paneling, and tall, frosted glass panels completed the final enclosure. The woman held the door open, and Joe slipped past her into the room. He could smell her expensive perfume, and his head felt dizzy. Across the far wall on a long credenza was an assortment of pastries, coffee, juices, and a mixture of deli meats and cheeses on silver platters.

"Please have a seat, Mr. Langley. The others will be joining you shortly. My name is Betty Thurgood. Please help yourself to coffee and juice only."

Joe surveyed the smorgasbord of delicious food, and his mouth started watering. "So, can you tell me what this is all about and why I'm here, Betty?" When Joe turned around, the woman was gone, and the large glass door was slowly closing.

Joe looked back at the credenza. "Well, I don't mind if I do."

He grabbed a monogrammed china dinner plate and began filling it up. He helped himself to ample portions of everything, including two juices and a cup of coffee. At each end of a long conference table were two larger leather chairs with arm rests. Joe selected the end farthest from the door and plopped his substantial body down into one of the larger chairs, causing the leather to squeak under protest.

When the glass door opened again, two men walked in and froze, staring at Joe, who had a forkful midway to his open mouth. "Hey, come on in—the food is delicious."

Betty glared at Joe and then said, "You gentlemen take a seat. The others will be joining you soon. My name is Betty Thurgood. Please help yourself to coffee and juice only." Betty emphasized the words *coffee* and *juice* when she spoke. As she walked out, she narrowed her eyes at Joe.

"The name's Joe Langley." Joe stood and stuck out his hand.

"Pastor Michael Richards. Pleased to meet you."

"I'm Dr. Nolan." Tom could not help but notice the telltale signs of obesity and high blood pressure on Joe. "Tell me, Joe, how often do you visit your doctor?"

"Me? Nah, I'm healthy as a horse." Joe patted his fat tummy with one hand. "I come from a family with big bones." Joe's plate was almost empty, so he reloaded it, since he was close to the food.

Dr. Nolan was a slender man, remarkably fit and healthy. His smile always involved pursed lips—almost as if he were grimacing. Although his hair was as white as snow, Dr. Nolan had no less than his youth. He sat in the nearest chair, which blocked half of the credenza containing food. This forced Joe to end his feeding frenzy and retreat to the end of the conference table.

Dr. Nolan was wearing dark pants, a white, short-sleeved shirt, and a tie. Sitting next to the doctor, Pastor Richards was dressed in a nice, tan suit with a crisp white shirt and dark brown tie. He was in his middle-to-late sixties, clean cut, with unusually large receding hairlines that curved on either side of his widow's peak. His face was slightly rigid, and Pastor Richards kept his chin held high. Carrying a few extra pounds, he appeared to be someone who ate well but lacked the exercise to maintain his physique. Pastor Richards got up and poured himself a cup of coffee.

"Would you like a cup, Doctor?"

"No, thank you."

The door opened again, and a tall, distinguished gentleman walked in. With coal-black hair that was turning white at the temples and a permanent tan from his Eastern European heritage, the gentleman was handsome and fit. Standing six-foot-two, his lean frame gave him a healthy appearance. He looked as if he worked out in a gym several times a week. He wore a six hundred dollar, dark blue, tailored suit, and his hand-tailored white shirt with French cuffs was silk. The initials N.D.M. were embroidered in blue on the left cuff, which barely covered an expensive Rolex watch that the gentleman regularly checked.

His blue eyes scanned the room to size up the others. A perfectly-folded handkerchief of white silk was nestled in his jacket pocket. The silk, red, printed tie he wore starkly contrasted the white shirt. When he saw Joe, the gentleman made a face. Clearly, this was a man of importance, with an impatient and commanding demeanor.

"My name is Betty Thurgood. Please have a seat, sir. Two others will be joining you soon. Please help yourself to coffee and juice only." Betty again emphasized the words *coffee* and *juice*. As she walked out, she also narrowed her eyes at Joe, who was still stuffing his face.

Quickly wiping his face with a napkin, Joe, with a full mouth, introduced himself.

"Hey there, the name's Joe Langley."

He stuck out his hand, but the gentleman ignored Joe, who then shrugged and went back to attacking his plate.

"I'm Pastor Richards, and you are?"

"Nathanial Martin" was his firm and direct response.

The pastor nodded.

"I'm Dr. Tom Nolan."

"Doctor" was Nate's brief summation regarding introductions.

Everyone sat back down, except Nate. He paced in front of the frosted glass wall and kept checking his watch.

Pastor Richards asked, "Does someone have a clue as to why we were called here?"

"No, and I don't care. I haven't got time for this, and, quite frankly, in my business, time is money!"

"I'm sure you feel the importance of your responsibilities, Mr. Martin; but I assure you, as a doctor, my duties are no less important. I'm certain the explanation is forthcoming."

"Well, it better be because I'm about to—"

The conference room door opened. "Gentlemen, please have a seat. I'm sorry for the delay, but we are waiting for one more individual."

The man set a pile of oversized, white envelopes on the table and ensured a single piece of white paper covered the stack. He was dressed in a dark business suit with faint pinstripes, indicating the man's intention to dress well, but not in an overstated fashion.

"And who are you, and why have we been summoned like this?" demanded Nate.

"Mr. Martin, please be patient. There will be answers. My name is Tony Toncetti, and I am one of the principals with this law firm. I represent a client of personal interest to each of you." Tony looked at Joe, who was finally finishing his third plate of food. "I see you found the food reserved for lunch this afternoon; please help yourself to *juice and coffee.*" He enunciated the last three words.

"This was lunch?" asked Joe. "Oops." He shrugged.

"Why don't we all take a seat, please? Our last guest will be arriving any moment and can join us."

Nate resisted and continued to pace, while the others sat in their chairs. Ten minutes of grueling silence elapsed with Nate clearing his throat several times. Tony stood and poured Nate a glass of water from the pitcher, setting it on a coaster in front of Nate. Nate bent over and took a sip, then set the glass back down. He refused to sit. Nate's patience was at its limit.

"Look, Mr. Toncetti, I'm afraid I can't wait here any longer. I have a busy day, and I'm afraid I need to leave."

The glass door opened again, and a tall woman with strawberry blonde hair walked into the room. Nothing was out of place. The woman captured everyone's attention. The woman was perfect elegance on display, and she appeared as if she were cut out of a fashion magazine. Her matching, large brim hat complemented her outfit, giving her an air of European influence. Her age was perhaps fifty, but she looked to be in her thirties. Tony offered her the first chair on his right, and then he sat at the head of the table with Pastor Richards to his left. Dr. Nolan sat next to the pastor, and the next six chairs were empty. Joe sat on the opposite end of the conference table, and finally, Nate took a middle seat, leaving two empty seats on either side.

"Excellent. Thank you all for coming today. We will begin with Mr. Richards and introduce ourselves. Please state the name by which you would like to be addressed during this meeting and your nature of business. And please indicate your relationship to James Kreider."

Just the mention of this name caused immediate and varied reactions around the room.

"Minister?"

Tony held out an open palm in the direction of Mr. Richards. Immediately, Dr. Nolan felt a lump swell in his throat. He felt sick.

"Hello, my name is Pastor Michael Richards. I am the lead pastor of the downtown First Baptist Church—the oldest church in this city, I might add. I have been the pastor for thirty-eight years and met Jim Kreider a few years after I moved into the pulpit. Jim is a member of our congregation." He then turned and faced Dr. Nolan.

Racked with guilt, Dr. Nolan took a long minute to gather his thoughts. He spoke slowly and deliberately.

"Good morning. My name is Dr. Thomas Nolan, and I am comfortable being called 'Tom' or 'Doctor.' I think we can dispense with the formalities today. I was present when James' mother gave birth and delivered him, as well as his three brothers."

Nate interrupted. "Excuse me, Doctor, did you just say you delivered Jim when he was born?"

"That is correct."

"But you can't be more than seventy years old. What were you—a doctor at the age of ten?"

Dr. Nolan smiled. "No, sir, I'm actually eighty-seven."

"No way!" blurted Joe.

"Well, Doctor, you look fantastic for your age. I would have never guessed."

"Thank you, Mr. Martin."

"Nate. Call me Nate, please. I have too many employees that address me as Mr. Martin already."

"Okay, Nate, nice to meet you. Anyway, as I was saying, I've known James since he was born and have continued to be his personal physician all these years." Tom paused and looked at Joe.

"Hey, everybody. I'm Joe Langley, but everyone calls me Joe. I'm a retired sixth-grade teacher and a neighbor to Jim. He and I have been buds for thirty-some years. Is that why we're here? Because of Jim Kreider?"

"Mr. Martin, I mean Nate, you're next," said Tony.

Nate leaned forward, making his shoulders seem even larger. Folding his hands on the table, the gleaming Rolex peeked out from under his shirt cuff.

"You've just heard my name. I work for Tynedex Corporation, and I'm the vice president of sales and marketing. Jim is my best sales executive, and I've known him now for almost forty years. He's on a personal leave of absence from the company at the moment."

"Excellent, Nate. Thank you. And now, I guess we saved the best for last, Miss."

When she spoke, her voice was soft, eloquent, with a hint of a French accent. "Good morning, gentlemen. My name is Arleen Chenair, and I am an executive with Chanel S.A. of France. I have known James for less than thirty years. Please, call me Arleen."

"You work for Chanel? Nate interrupted. "You're one of our clients?"

Arleen nodded.

"Excellent, folks. Now, before we get started—"

"Okay, okay, since everyone is being informal, you can call me Michael. No, that's still too formal. Oh, fiddlesticks, Mike will be just fine. I guess for the purposes of this meeting, I'm okay being called Mike."

"That's excellent, Mike. Thank you. I introduced myself earlier, but please address me as Tony. I am meeting with each of you for the first time. In fact, I suspect all of you are meeting each other for the first time as well. I was given instructions to contact each of you and invite you here today. Unfortunately, I have some unpleasant news to share this morning. This past Friday, the fourteenth, I'm sad to report that Mr. James Kreider passed away."

Immediately, the room erupted in soft chatter.

"Tony, did you just say that Jim is dead?"

"Yes, Nate."

"But how? I know I haven't seen him around his house lately, but I figured he was on one of his business trips," Joe interjected.

"He sold his house, Joe."

Nate stood up and slammed his fist on the table, making everyone jump. "Why wasn't I informed about this?"

"You're being told right now, Nate, along with everyone else. Other than me, you folks are the first to know."

"This is the most ridiculous thing I've ever heard of. Who in their right mind dies but doesn't tell anyone?" Nate started to pace the room.

"Please have a seat, Nate. We have a lot of business to address."

Tony waited for the room to calm down. As everyone composed themselves, Tom cleared his throat, raising his hands slightly off the table.

"I'm afraid James was diagnosed with cancer a few months ago. I'm the bearer of the unfortunate information." Tom looked down at his lap. "I called his house several times, and then, eventually, his number was disconnected. I stopped by his house numerous times but received no answer, and he never returned my calls." Dr. Nolan slowly shook his head in disbelief as his voice trailed off.

"I don't understand, Tony. I'm Jim's pastor, and he never said a thing to me. Why?" Pastor Michael rubbed his head in concern.

"I'm afraid I only discovered his condition two days before he passed away. He summoned me to the hospice, where he spent the last month of his life."

Everyone expressed varied emotions, including anger and frustration. Suddenly, the room went quiet. Arleen's gaze was fixed on the opposite teak wall. Unhindered, tears streamed down Arleen's cheeks, splashing on the teak conference tabletop. She was fighting her emotions, but the tears flowed like rivers.

Tony reached behind his chair and obtained a box of tissues from the cabinet. He slowly slid the box on the table, gently placing it near Arleen. The woman looked down and gingerly plucked three successive tissues from the box and softly patted her cheeks and chin. She looked at Tony and gave him a small nod. No one spoke. The tears continued to flow, so Tony stood up.

"Gentlemen, I'm sure all of you must need to use the facilities. Will you please follow me?"

Tony opened the glass door and ushered all the men from the room. As Dr. Nolan passed Arleen, he gently patted her shoulder.

* * *

For well over thirty minutes, everyone waited in Tony's office. Despite their pleading, Tony refused to discuss the nature of the meeting without Arleen. When Betty entered the room, the men immediately jumped to their feet.

"I think she's ready, Mr. Toncetti."

"Thank you, Betty. Gentlemen, this way please."

The group filed into the conference room and sat in their respective chairs. Arleen was now wearing rose-colored sunglasses. Clutched in her hand were crumpled tissues. Tony waited until he had everyone's attention before he continued to talk.

"Over the years, as Jim's attorney, I have prepared various documents for Mr. Kreider. When I was called by the hospice, I was thoroughly caught off guard. Jim requested my presence, and since it was a hospice, I felt there was some urgency. I immediately rushed to their address, which was on the other side of town. What I witnessed that day was incredibly horrific. Jim was barely sixty pounds; and if the man had not spoken, I wouldn't have recognized him. We met for an hour, and he gave me a key to a safe deposit box at the downtown savings and loan. He asked me to remove the contents and close the box, which I did. Inside the box was a notarized letter addressed to me with instructions for the people sitting in this room."

"Is this some sort of joke?" demanded Mike.

"Who plans their demise in this fashion?" asked Nate.

"I don't understand why Jim didn't think he could tell me," said Joe.

"I only wish I had called the man, but, out of respect, I didn't," said Dr. Nolan.

"Look, I went there several times and even banged on his door. How did I miss the fact that he sold his home?" bemoaned Joe.

"Miss? You? I worked with the man every day and had no idea of this crazy plan," said Nate with regret.

"Gentlemen, gentlemen, please settle down. Please. Thank you." After the room quieted down and everyone took a seat, Tony cleared his throat. "I will now read the letter Jim prepared for us."

Tony pulled a letter from his inside jacket pocket and unfolded it.

My dear friends,

If this letter is being read to you by my attorney, Tony Toncetti, then I am no longer among the living on this earth. This news will be shocking to all of you because I chose not to involve anyone during my unpleasant death.

Tony, thanks for being the caretaker of this mess I've created. No one deserves to clean up after me, but I paid you handsomely, so that should count for something.

First off, Dr. Nolan, do not feel guilty about how this came about. Obviously, you were only the messenger, and I appreciate you telling me the truth.

Joe, my buddy, I pulled another fast one on you, pal, and all because I didn't want you to own my problems. Thanks for everything you did for me. I really mean that. You've been a terrific friend.

Nate, what can I say? You're going to be very upset about all this. But please check out Dean Thompson; he's got enormous potential! I'm sorry I dropped the ball on you, but, hey, this was kind of serious.

Pastor Mike, I have felt lost in your church for some time, and I honestly appreciate all the lunches and walks you and I took together, but nobody in the church even noticed I was gone. Wow!

My dear, sweet Arleen, of all the people sitting in the room, I wish I could hold you and tell you what you mean to me. My love for you is deeper than anything I've ever experienced. You are my best friend, my true love, and the only person who actually understood me. I'm so sorry we cannot be together, but perhaps in another time and place. That is my hope. Your voice, your words, your soft kisses, and being able to hold you will be terribly missed. Please know I have gone to my grave with the knowledge that I have found my soulmate and that I count the sweet times we shared together as immense joy. With you, I've received the greatest blessings God could ever give a man. Please remember, I have not, and never will, stop loving you.

Now, the five of you have been selected to tell the story of my life at my funeral. You are the speakers chosen to represent me. Do not fail me, my friends, for you know who I am. Celebrate my short life, and remember me. I know I will dearly miss each of you.

Sincerely,

Jim Kreider

Before Tony had finished reading, Arleen quickly rose from her chair and darted from the room. She was mopping tears as fast as possible and hiding her face. No one spoke, for they were each processing Jim's words just spoken from the grave. Tony jumped from his chair and rushed to check on Arleen. He returned a few minutes later.

"I'm sorry, gentlemen, but we must adjourn until eleven o'clock tomorrow. Everyone needs to be present for us to proceed to the next step. I will see you at eleven tomorrow.

"Are you kidding me? This is the dumbest thing I have ever heard of. I've got better things to do with my time than sit around in some funeral meetings all day," Nate fumed.

In a matter of seconds, Dr. Nolan rounded the conference table. Although he was at least eighteen inches shorter, Tom pressed into Nate's personal space and pointed a finger up at the man's face.

"How dare you, Nate. This man worked for you for what? Almost forty years? And you cannot even give James a few hours of your precious time? Are you so utterly void and soulless that you cannot honor a man dedicated enough to work that long for you? Good grief, Nate, we're talking about a man's life, not some baseball score!"

Nathanial Martin was inflamed. As a retired United States Air Force colonel with combat experience, Nate had never experienced such insubordination before. He was the one who gave orders. Men jumped when he said *jump*.

Nate glared at the doctor, thinking how he could crush him with one hand.

But the doctor never backed down and stood there with his finger shaking slightly and pointing in Nate's face. Nate then realized he was acting like a jerk.

"You know, Dr. Nolan, I'm way out of line. Please accept my sincere apology. You're absolutely correct."

"Apology accepted." Dr. Nolan was shaken from the conflict but stuck out his hand.

Embarrassed and humiliated, Nate spun on his heels and dashed from the room.

"Tony, I'm afraid I have patients until eleven tomorrow. Can we adjust the time of our meeting until around noon?"

"No problem, Doctor. I'll have my secretary contact everyone. We'll meet here tomorrow afternoon. Thank you."

Tony, Pastor Mike, and Dr. Nolan left the room, leaving Joe to linger, still examining the buffet of food sitting on the credenza.

Thinking that the food would spoil just sitting there, Joe made himself a snack to go.

After looking around, Joe grabbed a fresh plate and loaded it up. It was bursting with food, so Joe grabbed another piece of china and set it on top of the pile. Holding up his treasure trove, Joe beamed with pleasure as he proudly held his "sandwich plate."

Holding the plates between his hands, Joe started for the door, but then glanced down at the stack of envelopes on the end of the conference table. Curiosity got the best of him, so he sought to investigate this mystery stack. Manipulating his trophy and balancing it with one hand and his chin, Joe attempted to reach down and move the top sheet of paper hiding the pile of envelopes. It took several attempts because he almost dropped the plate of food. On the third attempt, he was able to get his finger close enough to peek under the sheet. He saw some writing and started to lift the paper off.

"Mr. Langley!"

Joe spasmodically jumped from the intrusion and almost dumped the entire contents of his two plates. A flash-move in the last second, he managed to get a hand over the top plate, while supporting the bottom with his other.

"Whew, that was close."

Betty scooped the pile of envelopes off the conference table and, with both arms, pulled them to her bosom. Her eyes narrowed once more as she observed Joe's cache of food. Clearing her throat, Betty could not believe this brazen act, not to mention stealing two perfectly fine china plates.

"Mr. Langley, I suppose you'll require a doggy bag for your 'collection'?"

Joe looked down at the massive mound between the two plates.

"Oh, hey, that would be great." Joe flashed his best smile. "Would you mind, darlin'?"

Betty turned and stormed out of the conference room, but not before rolling her beautiful green eyes.

CHAPTER SIX

"MR. LANGLEY? PLEASE WAIT!" CRIED out Betty Thurgood, but it was too late.

Joe was on a mission and already several minutes late when he exited the elevator and blew past the receptionist's desk. Unexpectedly, the frosted glass door almost hit Betty in the face as she jumped up from her chair to stop Joe. Flustered, she turned to the folks she was helping before Joe's grand entrance and apologized.

"I am terribly sorry. Please, wait here. I'll be right back."

Betty dashed through the door and quickly ran after Joe, but her skirt prevented any fast movements. She arrived at the conference room just as Joe opened the door.

"Ah, Joe, you're here. Please come in. We've been expecting you." Tony stood to greet Joe.

Joe was dumbfounded and scanned the room, seeing that people were already seated. He was not only the last person to show up, but also the credenza was devoid of any of the previous day's goodies. A few of the men were drinking coffee, and Arleen was plucking pieces off a fresh croissant from the plate in front of her.

Joe was embarrassed. He looked at his watch.

It was only 12:17. He was just a few minutes late, so how did everyone else get there so fast?

Without Joe's knowledge, Tony had had his secretary notify everyone that the meeting was to start at twelve, but he had specifically told her to indicate to Joe a 12:15 start time.

"I'm sorry you missed the coffee service, Joe; they just took it away. Please have a seat."

Tony extended his arm toward the other end of the conference table.

Betty saw the two empty china plates under Joe's arm, and she tried to wrestle them away. Struggling with Betty, Joe quickly grasped them and shoved them forward at Tony.

"Well, here are your plates. I even washed them."

Tony received Joe's offering.

"Why, thank you, Joe." Tony then reached around the large man and handed the plates to Betty. "I'm afraid poor Betty was certain you absconded with our china, but I assured her you were just borrowing them instead."

Joe stuttered. "Ah . . . right. Sure. Just borrowing them."

Joe looked at Betty and produced his infamous smile, but Betty scowled and left immediately with the two porcelain plates treasured in her arms. Joe tried to act pleasant by greeting the other attendees.

"Afternoon, Mike. Doc. Nate."

Joe smiled again and faced Arleen as he squeezed by to reach his chair. "Miss Arleen, you look beautiful." But Joe's eyes were fixed on her unfinished croissant. He almost asked her if she was done eating the French pastry but thought better of the idea when he noticed the others watching his every move. Joe attempted to sit in his chair quietly, but the leather squeaked in protest again.

"Hey, Tony, I didn't mean to be late. Sorry."

Tony lied but was all smiles.

"No problem, Joe. We just sat down."

Looking around the table, Tony surveyed his guests. Pastor Mike was in a different suit and crisp white shirt but had forgone the tie today. Dr. Nolan was dressed as before but was wearing a white smock over his shirt and tie. A stethoscope was jammed into the pocket, and his name was embroidered above the left breast pocket.

Joe was wearing the same outfit from the previous day, and Nate was in an expensive, tailored, charcoal suit with faint pinstripes. His signature French cuffs, silk shirt, and tie were also present. The blue tie almost hurt the eyes; it was so bright. In a weak attempt to look casual, Nate had loosened the tie and unbuttoned the collar. It was uncharacteristic and a hideous aim on Nate's part to appear relaxed. Plus, everyone could tell the man looked uncomfortable in his semi-casual pose.

Arleen, radiant as ever, again looked as if she had stepped off the page of a fashion magazine. Tony was so convinced of the woman's unfaltering beauty that he suspected she could wear worn-out rags and look stunning.

"Thank you, everyone, for coming to this meeting. As we discussed yesterday, you were selected to represent Jim Kreider for his funeral services. We are expecting over a thousand attendees—"

"Which brings up something important that I need to discuss at this time," interrupted Pastor Mike.

"What is it, Mike?" Tony asked.

Pastor Mike looked at Arleen and bored holes in her head with his eyes. He was searching for the right words.

"In lieu of yesterday's disclosures concerning, well, you all know—perhaps not. I don't know how to say this without being indelicate."

"Reverend, enough with your double-speak. Come out with it." Nate was getting agitated.

"Mr. Kreider's service cannot happen in our church."

Everyone was speechless.

Finally, Dr. Nolan broke the silence. "Are you telling me that a long-time member of your church cannot have his funeral service there because of what was written in James' letter?"

"That is exactly what I'm saying. Especially, because of this . . . this woman," Mike was pointing at Arleen. "We cannot have a Jezebel participating. It would be a mockery of everything my church stands for."

"Fine pastor!" Tom looked at Tony. "James may have his memorial service in our church."

"Oh, and you've discussed this with your pastor already and received his approval, have you?" Mike interjected.

"I can assure you, Mike, and everyone else in this room that our church will welcome this opportunity. It's a simple telephone call, and the matter is settled."

"And, pray tell, what is the name of this magnanimous church you offer without approvals?"

Tom steadied himself. "Bread of Life Church."

Mike scoffed with a wordless sound. "Just brilliant. Another one of those crazy, fanatical, splinter groups. I suppose you have rock music and dancing as well?"

Tom smiled. "As a matter of fact, we do."

"Well, isn't this just fantastic? Then I'm not sure *I* can attend now."

Tony's expression became serious. "Mr. Richards, you have been selected, and you would deny Jim this one honor after attending your church for—if I remember correctly—thirty-nine years?"

"Reverend, I mean no disrespect, but it's no wonder Jim felt lost in your church. I'd feel lost, too, with your narrow-minded attitude," interjected Nate.

"None of you are members of my church, so there is no way you'll understand how I feel."

Dr. Nolan stood up, looking down at Pastor Mike. "Understand what, Pastor? That James made mistakes, and now you're passing judgment over him for what? Because he loved this beautiful woman? Evidently, King David would be excluded from your private church club, as well. I, for one, am glad that God's Son died to save us all. I'm even happier that He is the ultimate Judge in heaven, and not you."

"God has a Son?" Joe asked. "Who was His wife?"

Tony stood up. "Gentlemen, please. Doctor, please be kind enough to sit down. We'll change the venue to your church once we have your approval."

"It's done, Tony. The service will be held in our new sanctuary." Tom slowly sat down.

"I don't get it. How can God have a Son without a wife?" asked Joe.

Everyone in the room faced Joe and spoke simultaneously, "Joe!"

"Hey, I'm just asking. Wow!" Joe shrugged.

"Doctor, I have to hand it to you—you're gutsy."

"Thank you, Nate."

Mike jumped to his feet. "What do you know, Nate, anyway? Have you even set foot inside a church before?"

This was the second challenge to Nate's character in two days, so he stood up and seemed to tower over the room. He was angry now. "I'm sick to death of you two bickering about the church and whatever else you think is pertinent. I've better things to do with my time than sitting around listening to you two talk about religion. Oh, and by the way, Reverend, I'd never set foot inside your church—ever—even if you paid me!"

"Gentlemen, gentlemen." Tony held out his arms to intercede. "Perhaps we can take a small break and then regroup?"

Nate slammed his fist onto the table. "Fine with me. I need a drink." He turned to leave.

Tom stood to his feet. "I would enjoy a glass of wine as well, Nate. Mind if I join you?"

Nate stared at the doctor, but his response was monotone. "Sure."

Mike was aghast. "And you also drink, Doctor? What kind of church is yours?"

"Pastor, you need to read your Bible more and spend less time talking about it. Do you not remember that Jesus drank wine?"

Mike jumped to his feet and placed his hands on his hips. "He did not. Impossible!"

"I'm afraid you're mistaken, Pastor."

Nate interrupted. "Your church allows you to drink wine?"

Tom smiled. "Yes, Nate, and guess what? You and your family," Tom swept the room with his hand, "in fact, all of you, are welcome in our church." Tom took Arleen's hand. "This invitation is especially extended to you as well, Arleen. Anytime."

Arleen stood. "May I join you for that drink?"

Tom held out his arm. Arleen hooked hers into Tom's arm, and they walked out with Nate.

"Oh, for heaven's sake, this is the most insane thing I've ever heard of," Mike bellowed.

Tony was frustrated. The meeting had just started.

Joe stood and smiled. "So, what's for lunch?"

Tony threw his hands in the air and stormed out, heading back to his office. Joe followed the man out like a puppy dog.

Mike looked around the room in disgust. He slowly gathered his things and walked out, alone.

* * *

An hour later, Tony's phone rang.

"Hello?

"Yes, Betty, thank you. Are they situated in the conference room?

"Yes, sir," was her clipped reply.

"Excellent. Please have the stenographer join us in thirty minutes.

"Shall I postpone your other meeting?" Betty asked.

"Yes, that would be fantastic.

"Thank you again. Bye." Tony's voice was controlled frustration.

The conference room was in a pleasant mood, with the sole exception of Pastor Mike. He looked as if he had eaten sour grapes. Arleen was interacting with Nate, who appeared to have had more than one drink, as his demeanor was perfectly relaxed. Tony hoped that he was a happy drunk.

Joe still had mustard on his cheek from the four Polish dogs he had consumed from the street vendor downstairs. Dr. Nolan was now sitting with an empty chair between him and Mike.

Tony swore to himself that he would kill Jim Kreider if he weren't dead already.

He smiled. "Is everyone ready?"

Everyone at the table acknowledged him, except Mike.

"Minister, are you still on board with this group?"

After hesitating, Mike cleared his throat. "Call me insane, but, yes, I guess I am. I need to say, though, that the doctor was mildly correct. I completed my research during the break, and I believe Jesus drank grape juice, and I can see where it could be misunderstood by some to be wine."

"Hey, was Welsh's making grape juice way back then?" asked Joe.

He was ignored. Dr. Nolan faced Arleen. He then looked at Nate, and then Joe. "This will be my last statement on the subject of Jesus in this meeting, but the man handpicked fishermen who swore like sailors, a tax collector who was despised, and former prostitutes who became some of his closest followers. If Jesus loved these folks, I'm entirely sure He'll like this bunch sitting in this room. Our church welcomes all of you, and you have our approval for Jim's service, Tony."

"That's fabulous, Doctor, but can we get on with the agenda? If it makes you feel any better, in the future I'd actually like to visit your church," said Nate.

Tom smiled and nodded.

"This is wonderful, folks. Now that everyone is ready, let's get back to the meeting. Shall we?"

Mike scoffed with another wordless sound, and Tony deliberately ignored the attempt to pursue the argument further. Then the door opened, and Betty held it open for the stenographer.

"Excellent timing, Betty. Thank you."

Tony created some space, so the middle-aged woman could get situated. She looked businesslike and proceeded with purpose. As she set up her small equipment, everyone watched with intent.

Nate joked, "We'll behave from now on, Counselor. Are you taking our depositions?"

"Folks, I've invited Mary Smith to our meeting, and she will record our conversations. Rather than making copious notes or trying to remember the details of our stories, Mary will maintain a record of our discussions about Jim Kreider. I will, in turn, produce a written transcript for each of you. From the transcript, you will be able to create your speaking points for Jim's service."

Tony waited for folks to digest this information.

"Instead of the misdirected conversations of these past two days, I think this will help us stay on track. Are there any questions?" After scanning the room, he proceeded. "Jim selected each of you and the order for the speakers at the service. First will be Nate, followed by Joe, then Mike, and after him, Tom. Arleen, you will have the privilege of speaking last. I will introduce all of you at the beginning of the memorial service. Tom, perhaps your pastor will want to say something?"

"I don't think so, but I'll inquire concerning your question and get a reply back."

"Excellent. Mary, if you're ready, then we'll begin. Nate, since you're the first speaker, why don't you tell us what you know about Jim, his life, and his work. Please cover any details because we want to present a complete picture of this man's life."

"Thank you, Tony. I will have to say that Jim was an excellent employee, but I also considered Jim a friend. I remember one week before he tried to resign. He had an incident in his office. His secretary came bursting into my office, white as a ghost, and she thought Jim was dead. When I arrived, all the employees were packed into Jim's

office. When I saw him with his head on the table and his arms hanging down at his sides, I'll admit I was also frightened that the man
had had a fatal incident. Unfortunately, the first thought that passed
through my mind was, *There goes the sales figures for this quarter.*"

"Really? You were concerned about business profits at a time like
that?" Tom glared at him incredulously.

"Look, Doctor, I'm not proud of my comment. But you need to
understand that Jim was our top producer and represented over one-
quarter of our annual sales volume. This would be a monumental
loss. I'm a retired U.S. Air Force colonel and accustomed to being
detached from the people who work for me. As a physician, you of
all people should appreciate this aspect. For the bulk of my life, this
demeanor has served me well, but I was unprepared the day I saw Jim
lying face down on his desk.

"I was relieved when Jim raised his head and was still alive. He
looked awful and said he hadn't slept much the night before. Jim had
a customer meeting—which he was a little late for because of this
incident—but I ordered him to go home as soon as his meeting was
finished. When I returned an hour later, Jim's office lights were out,
and his desk was empty.

"Three weeks later, he resigned. I refused to accept his resignation
and, instead, gave Jim a leave of absence for several months. Until
two days ago, I thought Jim was home recuperating. For heaven's sake,
I didn't even know the man was sick. I told you I was Jim's friend, but
I never once thought to call Jim or visit him to see how things were
going. So, please disregard my comments about being Jim's friend
because I failed in that department."

"I think all of us can feel like we failed Jim in some ways, Nate," Joe sympathized.

"Thanks, Joe, but the Doctor is correct. I was focused on profits and business. After a few days, I never even gave Jim any further consideration." Nate dropped his head into his hands and started massaging his forehead.

Tony pulled the conversation back on target. "Why don't you start by telling us how you met Jim?"

Nate produced a thin smile. "I was a senior manager then and working with a team of twenty-some individuals, trying to beat all my sales forecasts. My personal goals were aimed for a vice president position within the company, and I was going to achieve this in record time. I needed another sales hot-shot and was interviewing several candidates. Most of the prospective applicants came with referrals by respected colleagues in the industry, but not Jim.

"When I first met the man, he looked more like a boy than a man. Jim was fresh out of college, eager, cocky, and ready to take on the world. I needed someone with experience, and Jim lacked this qualification, as well as referrals. I almost dismissed the young man and sent him down the street to a smaller firm, but then Jim changed my mind. I think he could tell by my attitude that the interview wasn't going well because he jumped from his seat and started pacing the room. He looked me straight in the eye and said, 'I can't get any experience if no one gives me a chance. Hire me, and in six months, if I don't exceed your expectations, fire me.'

"It was a gutsy move, and I respected his tenacity. When I explained that I needed someone who could hit the ground running and not stop, Jim grabbed his briefcase and started for the door. Just before opening it, he turned and said, 'Then, you'll never know my potential, but you'll feel it when I go to your competition.' Against all internal instincts, I hired the kid on the spot and never looked back."

Arleen asked, "And did James meet your expectations?"

"Whew! He catapulted my career. In less than three months, Jim met his six-month goals. By the end of the year, my department exceeded the others by a landslide. As I moved up the corporate ranks, I ensured Jim moved right along with me. I wasn't about to let the 'golden goose' go anywhere else, and Jim was loyal to me. In fact, his loyalty was only exceeded by his honesty. I always could count on Jim giving me a straight answer.

"Many of the mid-level managers were jealous, but in a healthy way. Jim seemed to draw out the competitiveness in the department, and it only made our team more successful. I remember once when Jim organized a softball tournament between the various departments. There was a lot of testosterone flowing on the ballfield, and it affected the women employees as they cheered their teams on."

"Jim played softball?" Mike interjected. "I don't get it. When we asked Jim to play for the church team, he declined, indicating a lack of interest in the game."

"What can I say, Reverend? When the final game was played, it was our group against the company's lowest-producing department. They may not have performed in sales, but they were one outstanding softball team.

"It was the top of the ninth inning, and the score was tied. Three men were on base, two outs, and Jim was ready to bat. The air was charged with electricity. One solid hit, and we could win the tournament.

"When I look back at that game, I'm not sure if Jim did it on purpose or if it was just dumb luck, but Jim struck out. The other team managed one run as they finished the inning and won the game. Oddly, the confidence of winning the game set that failing department on a new course. Within months, they were outpacing stronger departments with fantastic sales numbers. The downright strange part was how well Jim's team accepted the loss—which makes me think Jim tossed the game to help the other department. He always had a soft spot for the underdog."

Arleen smiled. "I had no idea James loved sports."

"Well, that's no surprise," Mike said snidely.

Tony slammed his palm on the table, making everyone jump. "Mike, that's enough. You keep this attitude going, and I will lose all respect for you and your title."

Mike bit his lower lip. "I'm sorry."

"Look, don't apologize to me. You owe this magnificent woman your apology."

An internal battle raged inside Mike as he debated about what to say next. Reluctantly, Mike attempted to apologize. "I regret that I spoke out loud."

Tony was furious but couldn't expect much better from the man. Having performed plenty of pro bono work in his early years as a lawyer, Tony could appreciate Mike's predicament. The man clearly played with the words to sound sincere. Nonetheless, Tony did desire a better performance, especially from a seasoned minister. "Nate, please continue with your story."

"Jim progressed through the corporate ranks, becoming a general manager about four years ago. He was smart and well-liked by most people—although we do encounter enemies in our work environment. Promoted to manager of our international team, Jim expanded his territory to cover Europe and Asia. At this point, he began to travel more and spend less time in his office.

"His secretary, Michelle, adored the man, and Jim relied on her to keep his daily schedule. They were an excellent working team."

Nate folded his hands and stared down at them for a few long seconds.

"Poor Michelle. It nearly broke the woman's heart when I disclosed the situation about Jim. In all my years, I've seen this stoic woman defend Jim in front of senior management—who could have quickly fired any other woman for such boldness. But when I told her of Jim's death, she sobbed uncontrollably.

"We've given the entire department two days off to adjust to the news, but I'm not sure they'll survive intact. It isn't until you lose someone like Jim that you realize the importance of one individual and their contribution to the organization. I'm starting to look at my employees in a different light."

"Do you feel your attitude will continue, Nate, or is this a passing moment?" Tom inquired.

"You make an excellent point, Doctor. On the one hand, I must always keep the business and profit in the forefront. Otherwise, we become yesterday's news, and in this market, we cannot afford that luxury. But, on the other hand, I think I'm starting to see that we must balance the corporate goals with a value of the individuals who help make those gains possible. Well, at least that's my desire.

"I was cleaning out Jim's desk because Michelle couldn't complete the task." Nate pulled a badly mangled picture from his pocket, along with two other photos. Laying them on the table, Nate pushed the photos toward Arleen, so everyone could see them.

"That first one is Stephanie. Jim was beside himself when Steph took off for Europe with some friends, right after high school. Jim constantly fretted over Steph's decision, but it was forgotten when she returned and started college at Stanford. She and her dad argued over her degree choice of economics, but Jim accepted her decision eventually. The young man in the picture is her fiancé, Charles. He's a medical student, and they plan on marrying after his internship.

"The second picture is Robert. After almost graduating with a four-year degree in computer science, the young man decided to attend law school."

"He's very handsome," said Arleen.

Tony smiled. "I explained to Jim that Robert would be better off as a lawyer; but being a lawyer myself, I think Jim didn't want my opinion on the subject."

"Jim protested, but I can assure everyone in this room, the man was proud of his son. Jim just hated the tuition payments," continued Nate.

Everyone chuckled. Nate then pushed a picture that was severely torn and patched together with transparent tape. One side of the photograph was still missing, and it was evident by a lone arm that the original picture was of two individuals. Using a black permanent marker, someone had tried to hide the arm of the missing person and part of their face. The woman in the picture was originally naked, but the permanent marker worked hard to disguise that fact. The woman was covered in colorful tattoos and plenty of piercings. The permanent marker attempted to make it appear as if she were wearing a shirt, but it looked cartoonish.

"This is Staci, Jim's youngest. She's rather rebellious, and Jim wouldn't discuss the picture when I pointed to it in his office one day. Jim said she was in art school in south Texas and dating a high school dropout. He refused to mention the boy's name. Jim didn't volunteer how the picture arrived in this condition, and I didn't ask either. I suspect Jim damaged it in a fit of anger but had second thoughts afterward. It was proudly displayed alongside the other two. Jim loved all three of his children. I need to ask—has someone contacted them yet?"

"I'm afraid I've been assigned that task, Nate. I'm waiting until we're through with our discussions here before I initiate contact," replied Tony.

"Tony, if any of the children need airfare or accommodations, the company will cover the expenses."

"You're quite generous, Nate. I'll let them know. Did you have anything else you'd like to add about Jim, or were you finished?"

Nate nodded.

"When Jim's wife, Samantha, passed away nearly a year ago, I thought for sure the man would take some time to grieve, but, instead, Jim took off for a month-long business trip to Asia. He left the day after the funeral. Most employees felt that Jim's resignation was tied to his delayed grief over Samantha. I felt that granting the man a few months leave of absence would take care of the situation, but I was mistaken.

"In retrospect, I feel inadequate to be Jim's friend, but I also feel Jim wasn't quite honest with me either. I guess it goes to show that we don't know people very well—even though we work with them nearly every day. We only get to see one facet of the individual. I guess we all have our secrets."

After a lengthy pause, Tony stood. "Okay, I think we all could use a break. Let's meet back here in ten minutes." Tony pointed to the side of his cheek. "Joe, take some time and look in the mirror."

"What? Is something wrong with my face?"

As they filed out of the conference room, everyone smiled at Joe.

CHAPTER SEVEN

"HEY EVERYBODY. I'M JOE LANGLEY, but you knew that already."

Being a grade school teacher, Joe still practiced the same techniques in any group setting. His voice projected loudly across any room, and, despite his girth, he made himself seem friendly, open, and accepting. Also, as a former teacher, Joe was prone to explaining too many details.

"I'm a retired sixth-grade teacher and taught for over forty years. I run into my students as adults all the time." Joe's expression became serious. "It makes a person feel old." Joe looked up at Dr. Nolan and smiled. "Of course, I mean no disrespect, Doc, because you certainly have far more experience."

"None was taken, Joe."

"I purchased the only two-bedroom home in our neighborhood, and, a few months later, Jim and Samantha moved in next door. Sam was pregnant with Robert and had Stephanie in her arms the first time we met. They purchased a charming two-story, four-bedroom home, and not too long afterward, they added another daughter, Staci. Man, that little girl was constantly sick."

Joe's thoughts trailed off as he stared at the table. Tony waited a few long seconds, then helped bring the conversation back.

"Joe? I'm sure you have much more to share with us about Jim. Are you okay?"

Joe looked up and gave Tony a thin smile. "I need to apologize, folks. When I was asking my questions about God's Son and Jesus, I wasn't trying to be a smart aleck. I just don't know anything about the subjects. I grew up Jewish and—"

Pastor Mike interrupted. "But Langley isn't a Jewish name, is it?"

"No. I'm adopted. And, Doc, I stretched the truth when I told you I came from a family with big bones. My adopted parents met each other when they were young teenagers in a German concentration camp. Somehow, they survived, despite losing their entire families. I think that's what drew them together—surviving their ordeal and knowing what they knew about the horrors they witnessed on a daily basis. I can only imagine what that would do to a person.

"Anyway, when they immigrated to the United States, they decided to change their last name. Pop said when they were at Ellis Island, he and mom spoke no English but learned a little by making friends with others there. As they were being processed, they were asked by the clerk what their names were. Pop had met someone named Langley the day before, so that's the name he gave them."

Nate said, "So if Langley isn't their real name, do you know what it should be?"

"Oh sure. Abraham and Golda Ben-Hatzkel became Ben and Golda Langley. Pop said they were lucky to be alive and wanted a fresh start. Mom was barren and incapable of having children. It had something to do with their experience in the death camps. They had been married almost five years when they adopted me. Mom and Pop choose me from a line of kids waiting in an orphanage."

"Do you know who your birth parents are, Joe?" asked Arleen.

"No, I don't, and I can't find any records either. I was only a month old when they adopted me, so for all intents and purposes, these are my real parents. Mom and Pop loved me."

"Are your parents still alive?" asked Tom.

"Pop died when he was eighty, and Mom—she lasted less than a month afterward."

Joe started to tear up, so Nate reached for the tissues in the middle of the conference table and slid the box toward Joe.

"Sorry, folks. My parents were my best friends and treated me with absolute kindness. When I was a kid, the other students picked on me for being a Jew; but if they had known I was adopted, I felt it would have only made things worse. Mom loved to cook these sumptuous meals, and it made her smile when I would ask for seconds all the time. As I got bigger, I noticed the other kids left me alone, so I started eating more. Pretty soon, I was this gigantic, fat kid, and nobody was bothering me. I could make people laugh, so I was this enormous, laughable, big guy.

"When I started teaching, the students thought I was Santa Claus without a beard because of my belly laugh. My students loved me. I became a teacher because I hated the fact that none of my teachers stood up for me when I was a kid. So, when I became a teacher, I defended the kids being picked on and the ones everybody shunned. Those actions just made me more popular with the kids.

"Mom and Pop weren't religious at all. Pop said God had abandoned the Jews, and it's why they suffered at the hands of the Nazis, so Pop wanted nothing to do with God. I never attended anything religious. I've never read the Bible, and the only time I mention the names God or Jesus is when I swear, which is kind of rare. So, when all of you started talking about that God stuff, I wasn't trying to be funny, I just know so little."

A small wave of guilt washed over the group, who sat stunned by Joe's disclosures.

Finally, Pastor Mike shocked the group when he made his next statement. "Joe, I want to apologize for being brash. If you want, I have a spare Bible in my car, which I will give you to read."

"Joe, your lack of knowledge concerning the Bible is nothing to be ashamed of, and it's never too late to learn either," said Tom.

"I'm with you, Joe. I have never attended church and, for the most part, never understood the need either," Nate said "What's fascinating is listening to your story and hearing about the Doctor's faith, which I assume is quite reliable, I'm suddenly interested in knowing more. It's something I can't explain. I'm a self-made and wealthy man who never saw the need for anything religious, but these last two days have got me thinking about things I would never have considered before."

Joe just nodded in agreement with Nate's comments. Tony didn't want to be insensitive, but he needed to get the group back on track again. When there was a break, he shifted the conversation and slipped a note to Mary, the stenographer, indicating she should disregard the personal information Joe had disclosed. Mary curtly nodded and tucked the note into her purse.

"It appears you've made some new friends here, Joe. I suggest you take advantage of their offers, but that's the lawyer in me speaking."

Everyone laughed.

"So, if you're ready, Joe, let's get back to your story about Jim."

"I forgot where I left off. Oops."

Mary pulled the folded paper from the tray and read Joe's last paragraph of substance. "Jim and Samantha moved in next door. Sam was pregnant with Robert and had Stephanie in her arms the first time we met. They purchased a charming two-story, four-bedroom home, and not too long afterward, added another daughter, Staci."

"Wow, that's great. Thanks. Now I remember. Jim and I became good buds, and he would come to my house often. I think Jim used my place as an escape from the turmoil at home. He and Samantha would get into these shouting matches, and I swear, it was 'he who yells the loudest wins.' It reminded me of my sixth graders sometimes.

"Jim loved coming over and watching a ballgame on TV and drinking beer. He wouldn't stay long—just long enough for things to subside at home. One Saturday, he overstayed and drank a little too much. Things spilled out of Jim's mouth that would be best unspoken.

"Sam came banging on the door after about two or three hours. When I opened the door, she was obviously very upset. She had Staci in her arms, and the kid was screaming her head off. Poor Stephanie and Robert stood on each side of their mom, looking shell-shocked and bug-eyed. Samantha wanted Jim to drive her to the hospital that instant; but when Jim tried to get up from the floor, he fell over the coffee table, drunk as a skunk. It was stupid at the time, but I couldn't help but laugh.

"Sam went nuclear. She yelled at Jim, shoved Stephanie and Robert into my house, and told them to stay with their dad. She then grabbed me by the shirt collar and buried her face into mine. Meanwhile, Staci was screaming in my right ear. 'You're driving, Neighbor. This is your fault,' she yelled at me. After that incident, Jim wasn't allowed to visit for a few months."

Joe looked at Arleen, who was stifling her laughter.

"Beginning that day, I became Stephanie and Robert's babysitter anytime they needed to rush Staci to the doctor. It gave me time to teach the kids stuff they'd eventually learn in school. They, in turn, learned to trust me and were soon telling me things I didn't need to know. Robert told me at some point that Jim moved into the downstairs study, converting it into his bedroom."

"When was this, Joe?"

"I think about ten years into their marriage, Mike. Why?"

"That's odd because that's when Jim started spending time with me. We'd have lunches and go for walks."

"Jim liked his time with you too, Mike. He said you and he would talk about things he couldn't discuss with anyone else. I hoped he was talking to you about the issues between him and Sam."

Pastor Mike frowned and shook his head slowly.

"Anyway, things seemed to get better because I heard less yelling after Jim moved downstairs. Plus, the kids didn't share any more secrets, so I assumed they were getting along better. Not too long after that, Jim was promoted at work and started spending less time at home."

Mike couldn't contain his thoughts any longer. "If what you're saying is true, Joe, then what I know about this family doesn't make sense. Almost every Sunday, Jim, Samantha, and the children would be sitting in the third pew from the back. They attended regularly and tithed to the church."

"What's tithed mean?"

"They gave money to the church. That's what the word *tithe* means."

"Really? They give money to your church?"

Mike began to pursue the conversation further, but Tony patted the back of Mike's hand and smiled at the man.

"I'm sorry. Tony is correct. It's your turn, Joe. You may continue."

"No problem, Mike. Let's see—at some point, Jim started liking port wine and cigars."

"Excuse me, Joe, you said James smoked cigars?" Tom interrupted.

"That's correct, Doc. Not often either—because Jim didn't like just any port or cigar. He seemed to like expensive port and Cuban Crooks. I know the Cuban cigars are banned in the United States, but Jim was buying them in Asia someplace. When Jim was in Europe, he started bringing back bottles of port from Portugal."

Arleen let out a short burst of laughter.

"Something funny, Arleen?" asked Tony.

"The port wine were gifts from me," said Arleen, smiling.

"Oh, I see. Anyway, Samantha didn't like Jim stinking up the house with the cigars, so he brought them to my house. One night, we sat on the back patio, drinking and smoking for hours. We must have had too many of both because the next day Jim complained that it felt like a dog dumped his business in our mouths."

"Serves you right," said Mike.

Everyone started laughing.

"The cigars lived a short life, but now and then Jim continued to enjoy the port wine. Years went by, and the kids slowly headed off in different directions. Not too long after, I heard Jim and Sam going at it again. It lasted a few years and, eventually, it stopped. Right after that, Jim was on one of his extended business trips. I was working in the kitchen and spotted Samantha kissing a young man in their backyard. Several times, I saw the man drop by and visit; sometimes he'd be leaving early in the morning."

"Had you ever seen or met this man before, Joe?" Mike inquired.

"No, Mike, and he never showed up whenever Jim was around either. This went on for almost a year, and it was way too quiet over at Jim's house all the time, so I popped the question one evening. Jim said it was Sam's boyfriend and that the young man was from her workplace."

"And Jim didn't get upset or do something about it?" Nate asked.

"Not to my knowledge, Nate. He seemed to accept the situation as fact. I've never married, but it somehow bothered me more than it did Jim."

"Did Samantha spend nights away with the man?" Now Arleen was curious.

"Not to my knowledge, Arleen. I only saw them together whenever Jim was gone. If they worked together, who knows what happened after she went to work. It wasn't any of my business, anyway."

"As just a neighbor, you seem to know a lot about their personal life."

"That's true, Nate, but then Jim and I were buds. Did any of you know Jim was a painter?"

This statement captured everyone's attention. Tony straightened up.

"Do you mean a painter—as in painting walls and a house?"

"No. A painter—like an artist!"

"Incredible." Tony was surprised.

"Jim was great. He and I were sitting around one day just talking. The subject eventually got around to things we always wanted to do but hadn't gotten the chance—like a bucket list. I expressed a desire to become a writer, and Jim surprised me with a gift of several writing workshops. I enjoyed the seminars, and I'm now dating a woman I met there.

"Jim expressed his desire to become an artist. So, without his knowledge, I purchased some canvases, paints, brushes, and an easel and surprised him one afternoon. The man started crying like a baby; he was so happy. If I had known something as simple as this would make Jim happy, I would have done it years ago. I cleaned out my study and set it up as Jim's studio."

Nate looked around the table. "Did any of you know about this?"

Everyone shook their heads.

"Jim didn't paint all the time, and, at first, the paintings were crude and similar to some of my students. I lavished praise, but Jim saw through my flattery. He'd set them on fire in the barbecue pit on the back patio, toasting a beer over their demise. Then, one day, I was watching TV and saw this infomercial. The next time Jim stopped by, I presented several instructional DVDs.

"Well, in no time, Jim's work started improving. In fact, his paintings were looking better than that guy with the big, fuzzy hairdo on the DVD. I was actually impressed. Shortly after that, Jim started getting creative, and the paintings improved even further. He still burned the ones he disliked, despite me trying to rescue them.

"I never bothered Jim whenever he was in his studio and never entered the room when he wasn't in there."

Tony's voice was excited. "Are you telling us that Jim's paintings are still in the studio? How many do you think, Joe?"

"I don't know. Of the one's that have survived—thirty, maybe forty. They're excellent, too. Gallery quality, if you ask me. I showed some to a friend who manages the downtown museum, and she loved them."

"This is absolutely incredible, Joe. Does anyone in this room object to having the paintings on display during the service?" Tony observed each face and received overwhelming approvals. "Joe, I'll swing by tomorrow and check on the paintings if that's okay with you."

"What are you planning to do with the paintings, Tony?" Tom asked.

"To display them at the service, of course, Doctor, but after that, it will be up to the family."

"Well, I'd like to buy one," said Dr. Nolan.

"Me, too," stated Joe.

"So would I," added Pastor Mike.

"It would be terrific to have one in our office as well," mentioned Nate.

"If I may, I'd be honored to own one of the paintings," said Arleen.

Tony was overwhelmed. "Folks, let me take an inventory tomorrow. I'll speak with Jim's children and see what they want to do, but I will express your feelings to Jim's children. Joe, were you finished?"

"Not really."

"Well, by all means, please proceed and excuse this interruption."

"Jim seemed to be in good spirits after his trips. I asked him about this, and I inquired if he had met a woman, but Jim just smiled and kept quiet. Now that I've met you, Arleen, I can see why Jim was so excited."

Arleen blushed, giving Joe a small nod.

"The weekend Samantha and her boyfriend were killed in a car crash, something strange happened to Jim. He was neither happy about it nor sad. I went with Jim to Samantha's service, but none of the kids showed up. I think that bothered Jim. Most of the people at the service were Sam's work associates."

"I actually conducted the service. You don't remember me, Joe?" Mike asked.

"Sorry, Mike, but no. It was a sad day, and I was focused on being Jim's friend. Did any members of your church show up?"

"I don't think so."

Joe threw his hands in the air and rolled his eyes. "Why is that, Mike? You said Jim went to your church every Sunday. Then Jim says in his letter that no one from the church visited him when he was sick. Why?"

Mike started getting defensive. "How should I know, Joe? Did you ever visit Jim at the hospice?"

"Look, Mike, Tony just told us that nobody knew where Jim was until two days before he died. Did you ever visit his house? I did— several times. At least, I tried."

This sudden change in attitude caught Tony off guard. Mary quit typing on her machine and sat with her mouth open.

"Gentlemen, gentlemen, please. This isn't going anywhere."

"If James were a member of our church, we would certainly make sure we were available to be supportive," inserted Tom.

"You know, Doctor, don't start in with your high and mighty, know-it-all attitude again," said Mike.

"Reverend, everyone has a point here," Nate began. "Perhaps you should—"

"Oh, shut up, Nate." Mike folded his arms and stared at the table.

"Reverend, I mean no disrespect to you," said Nate. "But Joe is angry, and he feels disappointed in your church's interest in Jim's situation. Granted, most of us were not aware of Jim's circumstances, except Dr. Nolan."

"And James made me swear I wouldn't contact anyone regarding his condition," said Tom in defense.

"See, Reverend? Even I admitted to being a poor friend to Jim by not checking on the man. Can't you even accept your failure?" implored Nate.

Tony could not believe what had just occurred. He had thought everything was fine just a minute ago, but now things seemed to have gotten off-track somehow.

Tony looked at Mike, who was breathing hard, arms folded, and ignoring everyone. Joe had his arms crossed over his large belly and was sulking like a child.

Arleen stood and walked over to Joe. "You're upset because you lost your dear friend. You feel helpless that you couldn't change anything. Do you think by blaming the Reverend that it will make things better? We must all accept the fact that James is no longer here. Perhaps we could have done something different. Perhaps James could have shared his pain with us, but no, he was selfish. We all have reasons to be mad at James, yet we all have reasons to blame ourselves."

Arleen turned and put her face in front of Pastor Mike, but he shifted his eyes away from Arleen.

"Reverend? I'm talking to you, sir. Please look at me."

Tony was shocked. This otherwise quiet and reserved woman was now in control of the room. Mike slowly looked up but refused to cast his eyes directly on Arleen.

"I said look at me. I know you hate me, but you know nothing about me. Do you?"

"I know *what* you are."

"Yes, you know that Jim and I were lovers. You know I am not his wife. But beyond this, you know nothing, Reverend. I am willing to admit my adultery with Jim. Are you ready to admit you failed to care about the man beyond the money he gave to your church?"

Mike jumped to his feet and slammed his Bible on the table. "Enough!" Mike screamed. He finally locked eyes with Arleen and pursed his lips, breathing hard through his nose.

Joe stood up. "Look, everybody, I overreacted. Please sit down and let me finish my story."

Arleen and Mike said simultaneously, "NO!"

Joe slammed his palm on the table, making everything on the conference table jump in the air. The room was shocked by Joe's reaction and his outburst. Joe was even surprised by the force he used.

"You listen to me—all of you." Joe's sixth-grade teacher skills kicked in, and he was now addressing unruly students. His voice was loud, deep, and demanding immediate attention. "I want every one of you in your chairs this instant. Now! This is my turn to talk, and you're going to sit there and listen. You'll get your turn, but right now it's my turn to talk." Joe made his point by using hand movements.

Joe continued. "You're right, Arleen. I'm upset about Jim, but Nate is also correct. We all failed Jim. The question is—can we move past the pain and honor the Jim we knew before he got sick?"

Mary was starting to gather her things and getting nervous. Tony was speechless. After a lengthy silence, Mike sat down. Nate sat back in his chair and relaxed. Arleen returned to her seat. As easily as one shifts gears in a car, Joe changed his demeanor to the smiling, pleasant person from earlier in the day.

"Mary, I'm sorry, but I forgot where I was a minute ago. Would you be kind enough to read back the last thing I said?"

Tony motioned to Mary. Her eyes were wide in fright. With some hesitation, the woman sat back down and read the lines from her stenographer machine.

"I went with Jim to Samantha's service, but none of the kids showed up. I think that bothered Jim. Most of the people at the service were Sam's work associates."

"Now I remember. Thank you, Mary. I tried to be a friend to Jim, but he became a recluse. Jim changed from that day forward. He rarely was home, and he quit painting, except on rare occasions. Jim seemed to be absorbed in his work. He and I didn't talk so much either. A few of his paintings took on this dark, ominous appearance.

"A few months back, Jim came home in the middle of the day. His car was parked in the driveway and never moved. I called his house several times, but no one answered. I rang the doorbell twice and peered into the windows, but Jim never responded. After dark, there were no lights on. Just before midnight, I banged on the door and called out his name, but still no answer.

"The next morning, I saw Jim, dressed for work, jumping into his car. I tried calling his cell phone, but he never picked up. That was the last time I saw Jim. I feel ashamed I didn't know he sold his house and moved out. No movers ever showed up. Another couple started visiting the house, and I figured Jim was on one of his long trips, and the people were house sitters. I wish I had inquired more, but I thought Jim was upset with me."

Joe sat back down and looked around the room.

"Look, folks, my blood sugar is running a little low, and I think it affected my emotions. I'm sorry about my outburst. I'm done, Tony."

Tony stood up. "Well, it's been a long day. Can we meet tomorrow? Doctor, what time works best for you?"

Mary hurriedly packed her things and darted out the door.

"My schedule is open tomorrow, and I don't usually see patients."

"Okay, does anyone have any objections to meeting at ten in the morning?"

Nate asked, "May we end sometime in the early afternoon? That way I can get some work completed in the morning, and then I can return later in the day to wrap things up at the office."

"Does anyone have any objections to Nate's proposal?" Tony scanned the faces and saw people who were emotionally drained. Rubbing his palms together, Tony dismissed the group.

"Excellent. Since we're all in agreement, we'll meet at ten tomorrow and end sometime early afternoon. Have a good evening, and I'll see you in the morning."

Nate immediately headed for his office. Slowly, the room emptied as the individuals filed out of the conference room in silence.

CHAPTER EIGHT

"MR. MARTIN?"

Nate looked up from his desk. His administrative assistant was standing in the doorway of Nate's spacious office. Against one wall were rows of flat-screen monitors displaying various moving images, including the major cable news channels. Pressing the large remote control on his desk, Nate silenced the sound emitting from the wall of information.

"Yes, Katherine?"

The woman was tall and around thirty-five years old. Long, auburn hair accentuated the features of Katherine's face, and she could easily be mistaken for a TV news personality. Extremely professional, Nate had also been impressed with her education and intelligence when he had hired her many years ago.

"A Mr. Toncetti is waiting for you on line six."

"Thank you, Katherine. Did he indicate his purpose for this call?"

"No sir. He only said the matter was urgent."

Nate became concerned and frowned. "Thanks, Katherine. Would you be kind enough to close my office door on your way out?"

"Yes, Mr. Martin."

Katherine closed the door very gently and watched Nate through the narrowing opening as her boss got up and walked toward the large, glass windows looking outside. His arms were crossed with one hand resting against his lips.

Nate loved his office sanctuary because the views of the city below were unobstructed. A brave construction firm once attempted to erect another building alongside Nate's office, which would have blocked this grand view, but a lawsuit ensued. After extensive political manipulation, the errant firm was forced to halt construction two floors below Nate's window. Nate's office occupied the floor just below the CEO and the boardroom. Whenever Nate looked down on the stub below, he'd smile to himself. His motto was *one victory at a time.*

Before answering any calls—especially ones prefaced with the word *urgency*—Nate preferred thinking about the situation first. He mentally examined all possible scenarios in his mind and felt prepared to receive Tony's call. Pressing line six on the telephone console, Nate took a deep breath and picked up the receiver.

"Tony! To what pleasure do I owe this call at such an early hour?"

"I'm afraid I have some sad news, Nate. Last night, about an hour after we split up from our meeting, Minister Michael Richards suffered cardiac arrest. He was rushed to Mercy Hospital."

Of all of the scenarios Nate had run through his mind, this was one possibility he had not considered. Nate lowered himself into his large leather chair.

"A heart attack? How old is the man, Tony?"

"I believe his wife told me he was fifty-nine."

"Good gracious! Have you a prognosis yet?"

"So far, it does not look good for the minister, but I'm waiting for an update from his wife any moment. I'm contacting each of the team members and will keep you apprised as the situation progresses. In the meantime, we're postponing any further meetings."

Nate was speechless. He stared at the wall of monitors, watching the moving pictures flash over the screens.

"Nate? Are you still there?"

"Yes, Tony, excuse me, my thoughts gained the upper hand. Did you say Mercy Hospital?"

"That's correct."

"Have you contacted Joe?"

"Not yet—he's my next call."

"Good gracious, Tony, go easy on the man. He is going to feel responsible."

"I will, Nate. Trust me. I've already considered his possible reaction to the news."

"All right then. Good luck. Thank you for the call. Goodbye."

Nate momentarily cradled the telephone receiver and lifted it again. He then pressed one of the side buttons.

"Yes, Mr. Martin?"

"Katherine, would you step into my office, please?"

"Yes sir, I'll be there immediately."

When Katherine walked into Nate's office, she was holding a notepad and pencil.

"Yes, Mr. Martin?"

"Katherine, please order a set of flowers for Reverend Michael Richards and have them delivered downtown to Mercy Hospital. The man will probably be in ICU, but please ensure they reach Mr. Richards and not get lost on someone's desk."

"I will take care of this personally. Did you wish to add a note or card?"

"Oh, yes, thanks. Please place the Reverend's name on the card, and you'll need to call Mr. Toncetti to get the name of his wife. Now, the message.

"'Dear Reverend and wife's name.'" Katherine started quickly writing. "'Please accept our heartfelt sympathy for you and your family during this difficult time. Our thoughts are with you, and we look forward to Mike's speedy recovery.'

"Katherine, please sign my name and add our company name as well."

"Anything further, Mr. Martin?"

"I can't think of anything else. Do you have any suggestions?"

"With your permission, I'd like to take your notes and draft a slightly longer version?"

"Oh, by all means. Please."

An hour later, Katherine returned with a beautiful card, including a handwritten note inside. Nate leaned back in his chair and read the card. When he finished, he signed it and handed the card back to Katherine. Standing, Nate resumed his earlier thoughtful stance and stared out his window. After a long pause, he turned toward Katherine.

"Excellent work, Katherine. You did a superb job. It has depth and meaning. You're a peach, and I cannot thank you enough."

Katherine smiled, gave her boss a small nod, and disappeared from the room. Nate returned to watching the city below and shook his head as he thought about how young fifty-nine was to have a heart attack.

* * *

"Hello?"

"Good morning, Joe. This is Tony Toncetti."

"Hey, Tony, what's happening?"

"I'm afraid I have some sad news, Joe. Last night, the minister, Michael Richards, suffered a heart attack. He was rushed to Mercy Hospital."

Joe's expression became serious. "Really, a heart attack? He isn't dead, is he?"

"Oh no, but he's in ICU at the moment. I'm waiting for a call from his wife for an update. In the meantime, we're postponing any further meetings."

"That's just great. Wasn't it Mike's turn to speak this morning?"

"That is correct."

"You know, some people will do anything to avoid their responsibilities."

Tony wasn't sure if Joe was serious or being humorous. "I don't think the man planned this out, Joe. You sound upset."

"You're right; I'm upset. He could have at least given his little speech first. Now we may never find out what he was going to say about Jim. This may turn out to be two funerals in the end. I suppose everyone thinks this is my fault?"

"Joe, absolutely not! No one in their right mind would think that."

"Well, nonetheless, I shouldn't have pushed the man like I did. Plus, my little outburst probably didn't help either."

"These events aren't planned out in advance. It's just unfortunate timing, that's all."

"Okay, what's next?"

"We wait. As soon as I know anything further, I'll contact you immediately."

"Thanks, Tony."

Joe looked at the cordless telephone receiver in his hand and deliberately punched the off button with his other hand. Taking a pitcher's swing, Joe threw the phone at the adjacent wall, smashing the plastic device to pieces. The bright display dangled from the shattered case by an electrical umbilical wire and flashed several times before fading to nothing. The electrons released into the air as a slight wheezing sound emitted from the speaker.

Joe walked over to his kitchen cabinet and pulled a large tumbler out. Grasping his favorite bottle of Scotch Whiskey, Joe hastily filled the glass until it nearly overflowed. He stared at the forty-year-old scotch and shrugged.

Taking a big sip, Joe retreated to his recliner and plopped his full weight into the easy chair. Switching on the TV with the remote, Joe searched the various channels until he found an active sports game being played. He hoped that this would take his mind off the current situation.

The distraction had the desired effect, but then the telephone started ringing again. Joe fought his way out of the recliner and walked to the cordless phone base, then glanced at the receiver in pieces by the wall. The phone continued to ring, so Joe dashed for the kitchen wall phone. On the seventh ring, Joe grabbed the receiver and was out of breath.

"Hello?"

"Hello, Joe, this is Tom—Dr. Nolan."

"Hey, Doc, what's happening?"

"Are you okay, Joe?"

"Sure, why?"

"Well, I just finished my call with Tony and wanted to check on you."

"Doc, I told you, I'm fine."

"You're not to feel responsible for what happened to Pastor Mike."

Joe didn't have a response. His tumbler was empty, so he snatched the whiskey and refilled his glass again as Tom continued to talk.

"Joe, I'm not seeing patients today and thought I would stop by the hospital and check on Pastor Mike. Why don't you meet me there in about thirty minutes? We could go somewhere and grab some lunch."

Joe looked at the tumbler, which was now half empty. "You know, Doc. I don't think I should be driving right now. Could you call me later and give me an update?"

"If you want, I'll come by your house when I'm finished at the hospital."

Joe sat the empty tumbler on the counter. "No, Doc, that won't be necessary. I'm not in the mood for company. Perhaps another time."

"Okay, Joe, then I'll call you later. Goodbye."

Joe grabbed the whiskey bottle and started to refill his glass. He stopped when the tumbler was three-quarters full. Shuffling back to the recliner, Joe finished his whiskey and then leaned the recliner back. In no time, Joe was snoring loudly.

* * *

When Dr. Nolan walked into Pastor Mike's hospital room, he noted several older couples standing and conversing with Mike. He was glad to see the man was awake; that was a good sign.

The pastor's room was private, with no other patients. Several potted plants and flower arrangements were spread around various surfaces, along with multiple cards. Conversations were in hushed tones, so Tom waited by the door. An attractive and heavyset woman noticed Tom and walked over.

"I'm Cyndi Richards. Mike is my husband. Are you one of the attending doctors?"

Earlier, Tom had slipped on his white smock when he entered the hospital. He always kept one handy in his car for an occasion such as this. In addition, it gave him the freedom to move about the hospital and ask pertinent questions. He gave the woman one of his grimacing smiles.

"No, Mrs. Richards, I have a private practice and was just checking in on Pastor Mike. My name is Dr. Tomas Nolan." He extended his hand.

The woman displayed a perplexing frown but returned the handshake.

"Your husband and I are members of a funer—I mean, we're meeting regarding the services for James Kreider. Perhaps Mike has discussed this with you?"

"Oh, yes. I see. Mike mentioned the theological discussions you and he had, but you must know," Cyndi leaned in close and almost whispered, "Mike can be rather stubborn at times." Cyndi gave Tom a motherly, all-knowing smile.

"To me, Mike has been true to his calling so far."

Cyndi raised her eyebrows and smiled even more.

"I see Mike is alert and talking. Did his doctor mention anything concerning Mike's prognosis?"

"I haven't met his doctor yet; that's who I thought you were."

"There are lovely flowers throughout Mike's room."

"Yes, the peach-colored bunch is from the church members. The yellow and white grouping is from Mike's brother. Various visitors have dropped off the plants. And that rather large bouquet is from a Mr. Nathanial Martin of Tynedex Corporation, but I'm afraid I don't recognize the name."

"That would be another team member concerning Jim Kreider's services."

"Oh, I see. The arrangement does seem a bit over the top, but it's beautiful."

"If you'll excuse me, I'll slip out and see if I can contact Mike's attending physician. I'll be back in a moment."

"Sure thing, Doctor. And thank you for visiting."

*　*　*

When Tom reappeared thirty minutes later, he was following another man in a white doctor's coat and advancing quickly.

"Nurse! Nurse! Why wasn't I informed my patient is alert? And why didn't someone notify me that he had been moved from ICU? I've been down there wasting my time."

A woman in scrubs sprung from her chair at the nurses' station and quickly followed the two doctors, trying to explain.

"We're shorthanded, Doctor, and I was told by ICU they needed his bed for more critical patients."

The doctor stopped and stared at the woman. "Well, thanks for your timely information." He narrowed his eyes and examined her hospital badge. "Nurse Jenkins. Now go back to watching your soap opera on TV. I can handle it from here." The doctor started flapping his downturned hand in dismissal.

The woman retreated in a huff but snarled, "Yes sir, Dr. Williams."

When the two doctors entered the room, Tom noticed that two more visitors had joined the group. The room was getting congested.

Dr. William let out a heavy sigh. "Okay, folks, I'm going to have everyone leave this room while I examine the patient." The doctor held the door open and motioned with his arm for the people to leave immediately. "You may return when I'm finished. Thank you. Dr. Nolan, would you care to join me?"

Tom watched Mrs. Richards attempt to speak to Dr. Williams, but the man ignored the woman. Tom took Cyndi's hand and patted it gently.

"We'll be only a few minutes, Mrs. Richards. Thank you for your patience."

Dr. Williams pushed the door closed.

Approximately ten minutes later, Dr. Williams opened the door. "Mrs. Richards, could you step inside, please?"

When she stepped into the room, Dr. Williams offered her a chair to sit in; but with the shake of her head, Cyndi refused.

"Your husband has suffered a myocardial infarction. Although this was a minor event, we are going to keep him here in the hospital for about a week. We need to monitor his progress. He is going to experience some discomfort, but the medication I prescribed should be helping." He turned and faced Pastor Mike. "Is the medicine helping you regarding the pain, Mr. Richards?"

Pastor Mike nodded. The whisper noise from the oxygen tube under Mike's nose made him fidget with the device.

"Please leave the oxygen tube alone. If you're still doing well tomorrow, I'll ask the nurse to remove it. In the meantime, you need your rest and to keep your stress levels low." Dr. Williams looked up. "We'll run a stress test, echocardiogram, and blood work before releasing your husband, Mrs. Richards. If he has any complications, this could extend his stay further, but we'll cross that bridge when we get to it. For now, please limit the number of visitors to no more than three at a time. You're welcome to stay with your husband and ignore the visiting hours, but this doesn't apply to anyone else. Understand?"

Cyndi nodded and produced a weak smile.

"I'll be back later to check on your husband. Good day."

Tom and Cyndi stood in silence after Dr. Williams left.

"Mrs. Richards, if you'd like, I'll speak to the folks waiting outside, so you may remain with your husband."

Cyndi smiled. "I'd appreciate that, Dr. Nolan. Thank you. Unlike the other doctor—" Cyndi stopped herself from disclosing her thoughts aloud. "Well, what I'm saying is thank you again for your kindness."

After shaking hands again, Tom met with the visitors and explained the situation. He then left the hospital and went home.

* * *

Grasping the phone receiver, Nate pressed a button and waited.

"Hello, this is Michelle."

"Michelle, this is Nate."

"Oh, Mr. Martin, how may I help you?

"I've been thinking about Jim Kreider's accounts and how we should redistribute his customers."

"Yes, Mr. Martin, I thought you might be thinking about Mr. Kreider's clients, so I started gathering his files together."

"Michelle, you're an excellent secretary. I see why Jim loved you so much."

Michelle stuttered, "Why thank you, Mr. Martin. I, well I, ah, I was wondering—"

Nate sat up straight and could sense something was wrong. "What is it, Michelle? Is there something on your mind?"

Michelle was immediately embarrassed. "I'm sorry, Mr. Martin. It's nothing, really. Now, what were you saying about the files?"

Nate paused. He had been a successful leader too long to let subtle nuances slip by so easily. Besides, if he were to make good on his proclamation about caring as much about the people who worked for him as he did about profits, well, this was a good time to start.

"Michelle, I know you're afraid to say something, and my experience with you indicates you're bold enough to speak your peace when you want to. I've witnessed this firsthand when you defended Jim to the higher-ups. Now, why don't you just speak the truth and tell me what's bothering you at the moment?"

This time, Michelle paused to gather her thoughts. "Mr. Martin, I wanted you to know that I've enjoyed my time working for Tynedex Corporation, and—"

"Hold on a sec, Michelle." Nate heard Michelle's use of the past tense in her words. "You're not thinking of quitting, are you?"

Michelle was caught off guard. "Why, why no, Mr. Martin."

"Well bravo, Michelle. I don't want to hear of our company losing someone of your qualifications to our competition. You're an excellent employee. Tynedex Corporation needs folks like you."

"Well, thank you, Mr. Martin. Thank you very much. The truth of the matter is this—after Mr. Kreider's untimely death, I was concerned the company may not need me further. I thought your call was to prepare me for a decision to let me go."

"Absolutely not, Michelle. I'm sorry you perceived this call that way. No, we need to distribute Jim's workload, and I was hoping you would assist me, since you're familiar with his clients. Are you okay doing this, or do you need more time?"

Michelle was relieved and let out a sigh to indicate so. "Thank you, Mr. Martin. You've lightened my burden, and I feel much better. I'd be delighted to assist you with Mr. Kreider's customers."

"Terrific, Michelle. Can we schedule a time for this Thursday, say around 4 p.m.?"

"I'll be ready, Mr. Martin. Shall I come to you, or would you like to meet in the conference room?"

"Let's meet in my office. It will be a long evening; so, if you don't mind, I'll have Katherine order some food, so we can work late."

"Excellent, Mr. Martin. I look forward to Thursday evening."

"Thank you, Michelle. Goodbye."

Nate hung up the phone but then picked it up again and pressed another button.

"Hi, Katherine. On Thursday afternoon at four, I'll be meeting with Michelle, Jim Kreider's assistant, to go over his client list. I'll need you to order dinner for us as we will be working late. I'll also need you to join us and keep notes. Could you ensure you're available? Call Michelle and see what she'd like for dinner, too."

"No problem, Mr. Martin. And what shall I order for you, sir?"

"Oh, surprise me, Katherine. I'll be okay with anything. You know this will be a tough meeting because I don't think Michelle will get through it without a good cry. I really need you there for support—if you catch my meaning."

"You can count on me, Mr. Martin, but I believe Michelle is tougher than you think."

"Perhaps, but I'd appreciate you being there nonetheless."

"Yes, Mr. Martin. Is there anything else?"

"No, Katherine, not for now. Thank you. You're a peach."

After hanging up the phone, Nate rose from his chair and walked over to the large windows facing the city. He assumed his usual contemplative posture.

* * *

Tony picked up his phone and pressed a button, waiting for his secretary to answer.

"Yes, Mr. Toncetti?"

"Shelly, please look in Jim Kreider's file and bring me the contact numbers for his three children—Stephanie, Robert, and Staci."

"I'll have them to you in a few minutes, sir."

"Thanks."

Tony looked at his watch. He noted that there was a three-hour different to the West Coast and two hours difference to Texas. It was already five p.m., so he'd have to call them when he got home that night.

After a soft knock on the door, a young woman in her mid-twenties walked in and smiled. She handed a note to Tony and waited. Tony quickly scanned the page.

"Excellent. Thanks, Shelly."

Tony was dreading the calls to Jim's children. He may have been a hardened lawyer, whose skills were honed in trial courts, but he had children of his own and knew the messenger always ends up being the bad guy.

Later that evening, after dinner with his family, Tony excused himself from the dinner table and retreated to his study. Pouring a glass of treasured cognac, Tony sat behind his desk and studied the note his secretary had given him earlier. Sighing, Tony punched in the number for Stephanie into his cell phone. On the third ring, she answered.

"Hello?"

"Good evening, Stephanie. This is Tony Toncetti, and I'm your father's lawyer. Is this a good time to talk?"

After a lengthy pause, Stephanie responded but was trying to identify the voice. "Tony who? Do I know you?"

"Tony Toncetti. You and I met some years ago. You were quite young then, and your father brought you to my office. I let you sit behind my desk and play with the telephone while your dad and I spoke."

Suddenly remembering, Stephanie responded, "Oh yes, I do remember. Wow, that was eons ago. You say you're my father's lawyer? Is he in trouble?"

"I'm afraid I have some rather sad news, Stephanie. I'm sorry to tell you, but your father recently passed away."

There was an extended period of silence. "What? Is this some sort of a joke? How?"

"I assure you, Stephanie, this is not a prank call. Your father summoned me to his dying bedside, and I had no idea the man was even sick."

"He can't be dead, Tony. I just received a voice message not more than a week ago. I know I've been busy and should have called him back, but school has been brutal."

"Your father, Jim Kreider, unfortunately, has passed away. I'm so sorry for your loss."

Tony could hear Stephanie softly crying.

"Perhaps I should call at a later time to discuss this matter further. Shall I call you back in a few hours?"

Between tears, Tony heard her say, "Yeah, sure. That would be nice. Bye."

There was a click, and the line went dead. Tony muttered under his breath, "Good grief Jim. This is nearly impossible."

Tony picked up his glass and drained its contents and then poured another. After taking a sip, Tony checked his watch, noting that it was 6:30 p.m. in California. He hoped Robert was available.

Reading the note, Tony punched in the next number and waited. Before Tony heard the first ring in the receiver, a severely hushed voice whispered a response.

"Yes? Who is this?"

"This is Tony Toncetti, and I'm your father's lawyer. Is this a good time to talk?"

"I'm in class!" Then the line went dead.

Exasperated, Tony stared at the cell phone in his hand. He immediately jumped when the cell phone buzzed. The display indicated he had received a text message.

"How do they do that so fast?" Tony said to himself.

The text message contained abbreviated language—"Cal L8r 2hr"

He shook his head. He was batting a zero.

He got up and headed to the dining room. He then showed the text message to his twelve-year-old son.

"Seriously, Dad?"

"Just give me the translation, please."

"It says, 'Call me later in two hours.'"

Tony stared at his cell phone. "Really?"

His son shook his head. "Dad, you've got to work on your texting skills. Wow."

Tony leaned over and kissed his son's forehead. "Thanks, I will."

As Tony walked back to the study, he voiced his thoughts out loud, muttering, "Third time is the charm."

After entering Staci's number into his cell phone, Tony paused with his finger above the send button. Snatching his glass, Tony added more cognac, but drained the contents in a big gulp and then pressed the button, initiating the phone call. After six rings, Tony was about to hang up when he heard Staci's voice.

"Hi. It's Staci and Marcus, and we're too busy to answer your call. You know the routine. Later."

A few seconds later, Tony heard the distinctive beep.

"Good evening, Staci. This is Tony Toncetti, and I'm your father's lawyer. I have an important matter to discuss with you. Please call me at your earliest convenience." Tony then gave his cell phone number and repeated his name and the number again. He then hung up.

Tony picked up the bottle of cognac and started to pour another glass but realized he was about to pour his third glass of an expensive liqueur. Quickly changing his mind, Tony recorked the cognac and retrieved a bottle of less expensive sherry. He selected a twelve-ounce tumbler, dropped a handful of ice cubes in from the small ice machine sitting on the bar, and filled the glass full. Before capping the sherry bottle, Tony guzzled the glass empty and then refilled it to the top.

"Good grief, Jim, no amount of money covers this kind of nasty work."

Tony sat at his desk, sipping his sherry when the cell phone rang out. Tony recognized the number.

"Hello, Stephanie. Thank you for calling me back."

Her voice was shaky. "I'm sorry, but the shock of your call was a bit much to digest, Mr. Toncetti."

"Please, call me Tony."

"Okay, Tony. Please explain to me the details concerning my father's death. I cannot remember a day when my father was ever ill!"

Despite the steely response, Tony could hear the raw emotions in the young woman's voice.

Tony lied about the timing.

"About a week ago, I was summoned by a hospice because your father wanted to speak with me. I must say, I saw your dad about three months earlier in my office to arrange for details in his will, but I hardly recognized Jim when I saw him at the hospice. I don't think he weighed more than sixty pounds."

Stephanie gasped. "Oh my. What on earth was happening? And why didn't he reach out to his family?"

"According to Dr. Tom Nolan, your father was battling several rapidly growing cancers that devastated his body in short order. He passed away two days after my visit. Stephanie, please accept my deepest condolences."

There was a long silence, and Tony checked the cell phone screen to ensure he was still connected. The call was still active.

"Dr. Tom is still alive? He must be close to a hundred by now."

"Mid-eighties, I believe."

"Has someone contacted my brother and sister?"

"I've initiated contact with all of you, but you're the first person I've spoken with."

"Well, good luck with any response from Staci. Robert will not know what to do. You want me to call them?"

"No, please don't. I have instructions from your father; and if you're okay, I'd like to handle the calls."

Stephanie was a little hurt, being she was the oldest and felt responsible. "Are you sure, Tony?"

"If I need help, you'll be the first person I call."

After a lengthy pause, she said, "What, if any, are the arrangements for Father's funeral?"

"Your dad took care of many details ahead of time."

"That figures, and it would be just like him! So, what's next, Tony?" Stephanie's voice was obtaining an icy edge.

"I'm following your father's instructions, and I suspect we should have everything arranged within the next few weeks or so."

"Three weeks for closure?" Stephanie was exhausted by this point and losing patience. "Fine, Tony. Just let me know when the three of us will meet. We can stay at the house."

"Well, that isn't going to be possible. Your father sold the home a couple of months ago."

This bit of information exceeded Stephanie's limits. She was being overwhelmed with all the news, and it was too much to comprehend. Tony could hear her voice quickly fading away as Stephanie abruptly ended the call.

"I look forward to your next call, Tony." The line went dead with a loud click.

Tony was not amused. And this was just the first call!

Not enough time had elapsed to call Robert back, so Tony tried calling Staci again. As before, the phone rang six times, and then he received her voice message. Tony repeated his message after hearing a beep on the phone.

"Good evening, Staci. This is Tony Toncetti again. It's important that I speak with you soon regarding your father. Please call me at your earliest convenience." Tony then gave his cell phone number and repeated his name and the number again. He then hung up.

The alcohol was having the desired effect, and Tony was starting to feel less tense. He looked at his watch and realized he had just enough time to catch the last innings of the game.

Tony grabbed his sherry glass and headed to the family room. A muted commercial was scrolling across the TV, and Tony's young son rapidly filled in the necessary details of the game up to this point.

Grateful for some semblance of normal life, Tony smiled and eased onto the sofa, alongside his son.

Less than thirty minutes later, Tony's cell phone buzzed again. When he looked at the phone, he saw another text message from Robert. The message was another cryptic jumble of letters. Again, his son interpreted the message, indicating it was okay to call now, but after hours studies would begin shortly. Standing, Tony started walking back to his study.

"Ah, Dad, where you going now? The game isn't over yet."

Tony leaned over and kissed his son's forehead again, running his fingers through his hair.

"Work beckons me, son. I'll be back shortly."

"Yeah right, like never!"

Guilt stabbed at Tony's heart. "I'll want the details on the game when I get back. Okay?"

His son stared at the TV and ignored Tony. Frustrated, Tony exchanged looks with his wife, who produced a thin smile and shrugged. Tony turned and went to the study. The sherry bottle was still sitting on the bar, so Tony poured a half a glass and sat behind his desk. Pressing the numbers, he took a deep breath and touched the send button. One ring later, Robert answered.

"Mr. Toncetti, to what do I owe the honor of this call?"

"Robert, please call me Tony."

"Okay, Counselor, first name basis means bad news."

"Are you doing okay in college? Oh, and I'm sorry for interrupting you in class earlier."

"Cut to the chase, Tony. Is dad cutting off my funding?"

"Robert, I have some unfortunate news. I'm sorry to tell you, but your father recently passed away. Please accept my condolences."

Tony could hear background noises, and Robert breathing hard. He let the silence hold space.

"How am I going to get through my studies? I haven't got the kind of money required for a school like Santa Clara. Besides, I still have two and a half more years! Your timing couldn't be worse, Tony."

Thoughts flashed through Tony's mind. This kid was thinking about the money first. He would be a killer attorney.

"Robert, you have nothing to worry about. Your father has provided for all three of his children in advance."

"Well, he better have. It costs a fortune to be here. Also, wasn't it you who talked me into being a lawyer in the first place? I hope you let my control-freak sister know about all this!"

"I contacted Stephanie first. You're my second call."

"Well, good luck on reaching Staci and her teeny-bopper squeeze."

"Your sister said the same, and I have made two attempts so far."

"So, is her circus-freak boyfriend invited to the services? Dad was pretty clear about not liking him, not one bit."

"Nothing has been determined, Robert. I'm initiating the calls now and following through on your father's arrangements."

"I suppose Stephanie said we'll gather like a loving family at Mom and Dad's house?"

"I'm afraid that won't be possible. Your father sold the home a couple of months ago."

"Why? He didn't need the money."

"I suspect he was preparing for his untimely demise and didn't want to burden his children."

"Well, I'm just glad Mom isn't around to deal with this mess. She'd be a basket case or screaming or both!"

Tony didn't know how to respond to Robert's comment.

"Robert, I'm following your father's instructions, and I suspect everything should be arranged within the next few weeks. I'll contact you with the details. When does your semester end? I'd like to coordinate the timing of the service so that you don't miss any classes."

"We're off for two weeks during Thanksgiving."

Tony scanned his calendar. "That's next month and about four weeks away. I think that will be perfect."

"Tony, I need, to be honest with you. I'm not sure I can swing the travel costs."

"Not to worry, Robert. Your father's company is picking up the tab for all the family travel and lodging."

"Wow."

"I agree, Robert, very generous indeed."

"Well, I know you're probably charging my dad's account for every minute we're on the phone, so I'll sign off and wait for your next call. Thanks, Tony."

"Good night, Robert."

When Tony checked the time, he realized it was too late to call Staci. He'd have to try again at work tomorrow. Besides, he was tired.

Tony finished his sherry glass and hurried to the family room. He could hear his son cheering on their team. Tony was all smiles when he entered the family room.

CHAPTER NINE

"SHELLY, DO ME A FAVOR. Please take my cell phone and try calling Jim Kreider's daughter, Staci. I've not been able to reach her and left two messages, so no more voice messages. It takes six rings before the voicemail kicks in, so keep trying throughout the day." Tony had stopped at his secretary's desk to hand over his personal cell phone.

"What shall I tell her, Mr. Toncetti, when I reach her?" Shelly asked somewhat bewildered.

"Tell her to hold and then find me. Whatever you do, don't discuss her father or his death. Please."

"No problem, Mr. Toncetti. Consider it done."

"Thank you, Shelly. It's important I reach Staci within the next day or two."

* * *

On Thursday, when Nate returned from his sales meeting with the department heads, he was startled by the rearrangement of his office. Generally, there were two leather sofas facing each other on the other side of the room, opposite his desk, with a large, square coffee table in the middle. These were missing and replaced by a large conference table and three comfortable, rolling side chairs. For a moment, Nate could swear the funeral meetings at Tony Toncetti's firm had been moved to Nate's office. A cart loaded with file boxes sat at one end of the table, and Katherine was sorting the files and arranging them on the long conference table.

"Hello, Mr. Martin."

"Katherine, what's all this?"

While holding a stack of folders in one arm, Katherine swept her other arm across the table. "These, sir, are Mr. Kreider's clients."

Nate was surprised. "I knew the man was a go-getter and provided a huge income base for this company, but I had no idea he was covering so many clients. There must be over one hundred folders here."

"Counting the ones still on the cart, 258, to be exact."

"Oh my, this will be a long night. I'm afraid we may have to complete this project over a couple of evenings."

"You're probably correct, Mr. Martin, but at least Mr. Kreider was well-organized, and it's going to make our job much easier."

"What do you mean?"

"Mr. Kreider used different colored folders, which represented divisions of his clients." Katherine pointed to the far end of the table. "The blue folders on that end are his European clients. The dark blue folders are high volume accounts; the light blue are smaller accounts—ones under 10,000 a month in revenue."

"Wow, I had no idea he went to the trouble."

"Michelle said he started this process last year and was making slow progress, but about three weeks before he took his leave of absence, he pulled some all-night shifts and finished this in just over one week. Michelle was surprised by the effort; but in retrospect, we all know why now."

Standing in his contemplative posture, Nate surveyed the table. "I swear Jim was a man of mystery. I'm still learning things about the man, even though he is gone from us. May he rest in peace."

"Michelle is still going through the archive folders to make sure we didn't miss anything. Over there—the pile of colored folders that have the wide, black stripe—those are accounts that were closed or moved to another company. He maintained the color designations even in his closed accounts."

Nate looked down. "And these with the gold star on the cover represent what?"

"Those, Mr. Martin, are the clients that needed immediate attention during Mr. Kreider's absence, and Michelle, along with help from his employees, handled them herself."

"You mean to tell me, Michelle was handling Jim's clients?"

"She's a great assistant, Mr. Martin," said Katherine analytically.

Nate walked over to the windows and stood contemplating this current situation. Katherine immediately continued sorting the folders. After another twenty minutes of silence, Nate turned and faced the conference table.

"Tell me, Katherine, have I underestimated Michelle?"

Katherine smiled. "Perhaps, Mr. Martin, but it's never too late to start afresh."

When four o'clock rolled around, Katherine had finished sorting the folders into their respective piles. Michelle came into the room and set a stack of white, folded tent cards on the table. Names of various sales managers were printed on the cards.

Nate immediately sorted through the tent cards and was impressed by the quality of employees working for him. "This is excellent work, Katherine and Michelle. Excellent work indeed."

Both women smiled and nodded in appreciation. They were interrupted by a knock at the door. Everyone looked up as Katherine walked over and opened Nate's office door.

"Oh goodness, you're early?"

"Yes, ma'am," came the voice outside the door.

"Just set the food on the credenza over there." Katherine extended her hand to the far wall.

The caterer moved toward the credenza while Nate cleared the top off. He then reached for his wallet and pulled some cash out.

"Thank you very much." Nate placed the money into the hand of the young man.

As the man briskly gathered his totes and headed for the door, he paused briefly. "You're welcome, sir. Please enjoy your dinner." With those words, he disappeared.

During the following four hours, the three individuals sorted and categorized each of Jim's clients, dividing them into various piles. The working group paused for dinner toward the end of their session. While the two women ate, Nate examined the European accounts with interest. Both Katherine and Michelle noted Nate's keen attention over those particular folders.

"Are you looking for something specific, Mr. Martin?" Katherine asked.

Nate tried to act nonchalant, but it was clear to the two women that Nate was evasive.

"I think we could easily have others handle Jim's accounts, except the European ones. Those will need special handling."

Michelle thought otherwise but kept her opinions to herself and just nodded in response. Uncharacteristically, Nate abruptly called an end to their meeting.

"Let's call it a night, shall we? Again, we'll start tomorrow afternoon at four o'clock. Terrific work, and I appreciate what you two have done here."

Nate had not touched his food and seemed anxious to clear the room, so the two women gathered their things and excused themselves from Nate's office.

"Have a good evening, Mr. Martin."

"Yes, good night, sir."

While Nate sat at his desk, pouring over the European account folders, the two women slipped out. Both were puzzled by the abrupt dismissal.

Between single bites of his dinner, which was getting cold, Nate poured over the European folders with voracity. Suddenly, he stopped his fork midway to his mouth.

"I'll be a son-of-a-gun." But no one was around to hear Nate's exclamation.

Nate looked at the clock and saw it was after 10:00 p.m.

"Rats, Finance will be closed now."

Nate grabbed a pen and started making copious notes. It was late, so he reread his notes to ensure he had everything correct. He then jumped on his computer and typed a quick email to the manager of Finance, requesting certain documents. Satisfied with the contents of his message, Nate clicked the send button and smiled.

"What have you been up to Jim, my boy? Nothing nefarious, I hope?"

Nate stood. He then grabbed his suit jacket from the coat hanger by the office door. Pausing, Nate scanned the conference table and then shook his head in disbelief. Turning off the lights, Nate headed home for the evening.

*　*　*

Shelly made multiple attempts to reach Staci during the day. When she was ready to head home, she returned the cell phone to Tony and apologized.

"I'm so sorry, Mr. Toncetti. I tried maybe twenty times but wasn't able to get through."

"Thanks anyway, Shelly. Have a good evening."

"Good night, Mr. Toncetti."

Tony was frustrated but put the matter aside. As he was gathering his coat and heading home, his cell phone buzzed. The text message was in all capital letters, indicating the sender was not pleased.

"STOP CONTACTING ME. I'M CALLING THE COPS IF YOU DON'T STOP BUGGING ME!!!!!!!!!!!!"

Tony typed his response. He was slow, and he had to read it several times to make sure everything was spelled correctly. Tony hated text messaging because it was impersonal and open to interpretation by the reader. "This is Tony Toncetti, and I'm your father's lawyer. I have an important matter to discuss with you. Please call me at your earliest convenience."

The text response was instantaneous: "he ok?"

Tony typed quickly. "No! Call me please."

An eternity of time slipped by, and Tony was not sure she understood his response. He was about to type another text message when the cell phone rang. Tony recognized Staci's number.

"Hello, this is Tony Toncetti. Is this Staci?"

"No, this is Marcus. Staci is in lab class all day. Who are you, and how do you know my father?"

"Marcus, I'm sorry, but this call isn't for you; it's for Staci."

"What's wrong with her father?"

"Please, Marcus. It is important I speak with Staci as soon as possible."

"She gets home late. If I see her, I'll give her the message." His voice was indignant.

"Tell me. Is this Staci's cell phone or yours?"

"Look, old man, you're awfully nosy."

Tony took a deep breath. "I'm sorry. I'm an attorney, representing Staci's father. He cannot contact Staci, and he has instructed me to call his daughter in an emergency. This is really important, and I need you to get a message to Staci as soon as possible. Can you do that for me?"

Marcus hesitated. "What's the big emergency, Mr. Lawyer?"

Tony saw no other way to do this. He was getting nowhere fast with this kid and had reached an impasse. "Marcus, please do not share the following information with Staci, but her father has passed away. I need to explain things directly to her, and so I need you to have her call me immediately. Can you help me?"

"No way! Her old man is dead? She's gonna freak out!"

Tony immediately regretted his comments. "Marcus, listen to me. Do not share this information with her. Have her call me, and I will break the news to her. I only told you so that you would understand the urgency of my call."

"Okay. I'll tell her."

Instantly, the phone line went dead. Tony looked at the screen and saw the call was disconnected. Holding his cell phone in both hands, Tony shook the phone and screamed a long, wordless cry of anguish.

A security guard rounded the corner and stopped in front of Tony.

"Are you all right, Mr. Toncetti?"

Tony quickly regained his composure, shoving the cell phone into his pants pocket. "I'm fine, Bill. Thanks."

As Tony walked to the elevator, he chanced a brief look over his shoulder at the security guard. Bill was still standing with feet apart, one hand resting on his nightstick, and a look of concern on his face. The elevator door opened, and Tony stepped in. He then feebly waved to the guard.

"Good night, Bill."

Once the elevator door closed, Tony let out an exasperated sigh. "Good grief, Tony," he said, chastising himself.

* * *

When the cell phone rang, Tony was fast asleep. His wife was shaking her husband.

"Tony, it's your cell phone. It's two in the morning. Who calls at 2:00 a.m.?"

Struggling to gain consciousness, Tony fumbled for the phone on the nightstand. The numbers were blurry, so Tony clicked on the light. It was Staci's phone number. Tony jumped to his feet and headed to the bathroom, closing the door.

He whispered, "Hello, Staci?"

The voice on the other end was sobbing. "My daddy is dead?"

Tony gave out a wordless groan. He should have known Marcus wouldn't be able to keep his mouth shut. It was his own fault for trusting him.

"Staci, please accept my deepest condolences. I'm so sorry for your loss. I asked Marcus to have you call me. He wasn't supposed to tell you. Again, I'm so sorry."

Staci continued to sob, trying to talk, but everything she said was garbled. Tony just waited for a break. In the meantime, his wife came into the bathroom and pointed at the toilet. Tony moved aside, allowing her to use the facilities. Staci was finally able to speak, but her sentence was punctuated with sobs between each word.

"How . . . did . . . Daddy . . . die?"

Tony realized the conversation would be impossible at this pace, so he switched strategies in hopes of getting her calmed down.

"Staci, are you alone?"

"Yes."

"Is Marcus nearby?"

"No."

"Are you sitting down?"

"Yes. I am now."

Tony instantly sensed a shift in Staci's mood.

"What did Marcus explain to you, Staci?"

"Just that Daddy died, and you wanted to talk with me."

She started to softly cry again, so Tony waited. When the timing was right, Tony continued.

"It's unfortunate that Marcus chose to tell you because he agreed to let me explain the situation. Are you doing better?"

"A little. How did it happen?"

"Your dad started getting sick about three months ago, but I was unaware of his illness. A hospice called me a few weeks ago, telling me your dad wanted to talk. Two days after my visit, he passed away."

"What happens now?"

"Your father left me instructions, and I'm making arrangements for a service. Will you have a school break for Thanksgiving during November?"

"Yeah, I think so. Hold on a sec."

Tony could hear Staci rummaging through things.

"Got it. We have a week off for Thanksgiving."

"That's great. Your father's employer is covering the expenses for travel and lodging, so—"

"What about his house? Can't we stay there?"

"I'm afraid he sold it about three months ago."

"Oh."

"It's the middle of the night. Can I contact you tomorrow with more details?"

"Yeah, sure. Send me a text first, so I know it's you."

"Okay, Staci. Try and get some sleep. Again, I'm so sorry."

"Thanks. What did you say your name was?"

"Tony Toncetti, but please call me Tony."

"Thanks, Tony."

"Good night, Staci."

Tony's wife finished, so she jumped up and wrapped her arms around him and lovingly kissed his neck. Tony smiled and spun around, facing his wife. She felt wonderful.

"You know, we're both awake, and the kids are asleep."

Tony's smile reminded his wife of the day they got married.

"Mr. Toncetti, we are not teenagers, and we both have jobs in the morning."

"It is morning already, my love."

Tony's wife pushed her husband away while he tried to kiss her face.

* * *

When Tony appeared for work the next morning, Betty noticed he was in a very good mood.

"Mr. Toncetti, you're in rare form this morning."

Suddenly, Tony became aware of the image he must be portraying. Tony leaned over and whispered, "I got plenty of rest and slept well."

Betty smiled.

"Have a beautiful day, Mr. Toncetti."

"Yes, it is, Betty, yes indeed."

Amused, Betty watched Tony walk down the hall to his office.

Tony stopped by his secretary's desk to give her new instructions.

"Good morning, Shelly."

"Good morning, Mr. Toncetti. You're in a good mood."

Tony ignored her comment. "Do me a favor. Call each of Jim Kreider's children and please obtain their mailing addresses. They'll be expecting your phone call. Also, you'll need to take my cell phone again and contact Staci, but send her a text first, so she knows who is calling. Bring the list to my office when you're finished. Thanks."

Shelly quickly wrote some notes but replied to Tony's instructions at the same time. "No problem, Mr. Toncetti."

CHAPTER TEN

"GOOD AFTERNOON, MR. MARTIN. DID you enjoy your lunch?"

Nate abruptly halted and flashed a huge smile at Katherine, hoping that it wasn't too obvious how *much* he had enjoyed it.

"It was okay, Katherine, thank you. It's been a long time since I've hung out with the boys at Charlie's."

Katherine could smell alcohol on Nate's breath. She deftly reached into her desk and pulled out a box of strong breath mints, then offered them to her boss. Nate leaned over and nonchalantly received the mints, giving Katherine a sheepish grin. Katherine leaned forward, whispering her next statement.

"CFO Jonathan Pendergrass is waiting in your office, sir."

Nate stiffened. "How long?"

"He arrived about thirty minutes ago. I tried calling your cell, but you didn't answer."

"It's sitting on my desk." Nate adjusted his tie and smoothed his hair with flat palms.

Katherine stood and pointed to the men's room. "Go. I'll check on Mr. Pendergrass and let him know you're here. Take some time to gather yourself together."

"Rats! Bad timing," Nate grumbled.

He turned toward the men's room, annoyed that the CFO would show up today of all days. When he returned, Katherine handed Nate two aspirins and a steaming cup of hot coffee.

"Is it that obvious?"

"You know, Mr. Martin, you're not thirty years old anymore. Those guys will drink you under the table and then head to the gym after work to sweat it out of their systems."

"Thanks for reminding me, Katherine. Shall I remember this conversation at the end of the year—when we write out bonus checks?" Nate was attempting to create humor in a tense situation.

Katherine never flinched. "I just hope it was worth it, Mr. Martin."

Gulping hot coffee, Nate swallowed the aspirins and winced because they were starting to dissolve before he could get them down. Nate made a face and coughed, like a cat ejecting a hairball.

Katherine smiled and shook her head slightly. "Are you okay?"

Nate lied. "Never better."

Katherine shoved two more mints into Nate's hand, which he immediately tossed into his open mouth. "Thanks again. You're a peach."

With her arms folded, Katherine's response was an all-knowing, motherly grin.

When Nate entered his office, Mr. Pendergrass was sitting at Nate's desk and reading over the European files. Nate swallowed the mints to push the remaining aspirin taste out of his throat.

"Jonathan, what brings you down here?" he inquired too cheerfully.

Mr. Pendergrass was a slight man, unattractive, and gloomy. His reading glasses sat perched on the end of a long, pointed nose. Without any expression, he closed the folder he was reading and sat it purposefully on the desk. While remaining seated in Nate's chair, he then held up a piece of paper with a printed copy of Nate's email message. "Perhaps you could explain the meaning of this message and why it wasn't routed to me directly."

Nate deliberately moved into Jonathan's personal space, reached behind the man, and grabbed a crystal, unmarked carafe of scotch and two glasses. After pouring a half glass for himself in one, he offered the empty glass to Jonathan. Mr. Pendergrass held up his fist, forming a narrow band about a finger's width between his thumb and first finger. Nate splashed a small amount into the glass and handed it to the CFO. Jonathan only allowed the liquid to touch his lips and then sat the glass down. He hated the stupid ritual of sharing a drink with colleagues, as if this act provided a smooth path for confidential disclosure, never to be shared outside the confines of one's office.

After draining his glass, Nate set it on the edge of the desk. He then downplayed his reason for the memo. "It's just an investigation. I'm trying to divide up Jim Kreider's accounts, and I ran into some questions concerning the ones in Europe. I didn't want to bother you with tedious information-gathering."

"You're referring to Jim Kreider, the man who recently passed away from cancer?"

The fact that the Chief Financial Officer was sitting in Nate's office was worrisome enough, but Nate wasn't ready to spend time chatting about details of his department with an outsider, especially a bean-counter type like Pendergrass. Jonathan bore holes into Nate's head, never blinking. It was a technique he had perfected over many years. It made others feel uncomfortable and gave the CFO the upper hand.

As far as Jonathan was concerned, departmental feuds between the finance and sales/marketing departments were well-founded.

Finance was certain Sales and Marketing operated over-inflated budgets consisting of useless travel around the world, luxurious meals, and hidden expenses to cover visits with prostitutes. Sales and Marketing detested the insidious scrutiny, haggling over a penny here and there, by bean-counters, only to require fudging of one's expense report numbers so that it would include expenses a boss approved, but Finance rejected.

Nate stood in his contemplative position, staring out the office window, and watched the movement of people and cars below. The game of chess was in full play, and Nate's military experience gave the man nerves of steel. He would stand firm until Jonathan admitted defeat and retreated from Nate's domain. Nate kept his back to the unwelcomed visitor.

"What is wrong with you people?" fumed Pendergrass. The CFO was getting frustrated with the communication impasse.

In the reflection of the window, Nate watched Jonathan snatch up his glass and drain its contents. Nate smiled. He knew he had Jonathan. He remained fixed, staring out the window.

"Do me a favor, Mr. Martin. Keep me in the loop. I don't trust you or your testosterone-filled jocks, which you place far too much loyalty in. I only need the smallest excuse to cut your expense budget."

Nate knew he was reaching and thought to himself that he had nothing. Like a statue, Nate stood his ground until Jonathan felt uncomfortable. It was time for Pendergrass to leave.

Jonathan cleared his throat, slowly tapping a finger on the stack of European folders as if he was making one more attempt to create influence over a department vice president. He failed miserably and finally walked toward the office door. Pausing briefly, he lobbed his last volley. "I'm sure we'll discuss this matter at a later time." Jonathan then slipped out the door.

Unmoved, Nate grinned, never casting his eyes upon Pendergrass. "One battle at a time, Jonathan, and one victory at a time."

Walking back to his desk, Nate looked down and saw that Jonathan had also deposited the requested answers to last night's email. Smiling again, Nate sat down and quickly read through the material. Nothing alarming showed up, which troubled Nate. His instincts were honed, and he knew something didn't add up, but the report didn't shed any further light. Nate dismissed his thoughts on the subject for the moment. Walking across the room, Nate continued sorting the folders covering the conference table.

* * *

A soft knock on Tony's office door interrupted his thoughts.

"Yes, come in."

"Here is the list you wanted, Mr. Toncetti."

"Did you have any difficulties, Shelly?"

"Robert was short and gruff; Stephanie was the ice-queen and asked me too many questions I couldn't answer; and Staci was the nicest of the bunch. I could hear her softly crying."

"That about sums it up. Thank you. I assure you, Shelly, when you meet these three kids, the visual won't match their responses."

She gave Tony a sideways glance.

"You'll see. Thanks again, Shelly. This is excellent work."

Tony scanned the calendar dates on his computer screen and jotted some notes on paper. He then picked up the phone and dialed a number.

A woman answered, "Good afternoon. Tynedex Corporation. Mr. Martin's office. How may I help you?"

"Hello, Katherine. Tony Toncetti for Nate, please."

"Well, hello Mr. Toncetti. I'm surprised you remembered my name. We only spoke one time."

"A voice as sweet as yours, I could never forget."

He could imagine Katherine blushing on the other end of the line. "Why, thank you, Mr. Toncetti. And what shall I tell Mr. Martin is the purpose of your call?"

"This is regarding the travel arrangements for Jim Kreider's children."

"I see. Mr. Martin is busy at the moment. Perhaps I could handle this matter for you?"

"That would be terrific, Katherine. Nate indicated your company would cover the travel and hotel costs for Jim Kreider's children. All three of the kids are in college, so we're planning Mr. Kreider's services during their Thanksgiving break. I figure if we have them here for the week, we could meet with them before the funeral service and give them some time to decompress afterward."

"That sounds fantastic. I know a lot of employees have been asking about Mr. Kreider's service. I'm ready for the information, whenever you are."

"Excellent. I'll have my secretary send over their contact information and the dates for their travel. Do you have a private fax number we could use?"

"Yes, one moment." Katherine located the number and supplied it to Tony.

Tony scribbled the number down. "Thank you, Katherine. We'll send the fax in just a few minutes. Goodbye."

"Good afternoon, Mr. Toncetti."

* * *

When Michelle and Katherine joined Nate later that afternoon, he had already sorted through nearly all the folders. Both women were impressed. Neatly stacked folders of even height had the name card of the various sales staff resting on top.

"You've accomplished a tremendous amount, Mr. Martin."

"Thanks, Katherine, but the recognition goes to Michelle. Her efforts to manage Jim's clients made my job much easier." Nate made eye contact with Michelle and smiled.

Michelle actually blushed over the attention and praise.

"I'm serious, Michelle. Losing Jim Kreider was devastating to my department, but your ability to step up has opened my eyes to your talents. I'd like you to consider joining my team as a sales manager."

Michelle was speechless. "I, ah, well . . . I'm not sure, Mr. Martin."

"Just think about it, Michelle. You have in-depth knowledge of the department and Jim's clients. I'd like to bring you onboard as a team player by first briefing the other sales staff concerning Jim's customers, and then I'm giving you a share of his workload to manage."

Nate placed his hand on top of a stack of folders, which did not contain a name card.

"In fact, Michelle, this is yours, if you want it."

Nate was beaming and pulled a name card out from under the folder stack and placed it on top of the folders. Michelle's name was boldly written across the card. Michelle faced Katherine.

"Did you know about this?"

Katherine shrugged.

Nate grabbed Michelle by the shoulders and seriously looked into her eyes.

"This is an opportunity of a lifetime, Michelle. Make me and this department proud."

"What about the other men in this department? I'm older, and a woman."

Nate grinned. "I know. That's one of the reasons why this is going to work. It's called competition, and I'm hoping they'll go crazy trying to out-perform you. But I also think you're going to teach them a thing or two."

Michelle was surprised. "Mr. Martin, I don't know what to say."

Katherine gave her colleague a hug. "Congratulations, Michelle."

"But I haven't said yes!"

Nate handed the name card to Michelle. "You will. If you two could arrange a departmental meeting on Monday evening, we'll make the announcements and divvy up Jim's accounts. It will be your last secretarial function, Michelle."

"Mr. Martin, if I'm no longer assisting a sales manager, who—" Michelle's voice trailed off.

Nate's expression was serious. "Oh, take Bob Hendricks and make him your assistant. He's underperformed from day one."

Both women exclaimed in unison. "Seriously?"

Nate smiled. "No, I'm just kidding. We'll cross that bridge later. But I take it, by your question, that you have accepted my offer?"

Michelle beamed. "Absolutely, Mr. Martin."

"Well, for starters, you can start by calling me *Nate*. If you're one of my team, I go by first names, except in company meetings."

"You got it, sir. And thank you."

Katherine handed Nate a manila folder.

"What's this?"

"Mr. Toncetti called and forwarded the contact information for Mr. Kreider's children. He provided dates for the service. He also indicated our company would be covering these expenses. Based on his information, I took the liberty of ordering airline tickets and rooms at the Grand Marquis for his children. A limo will collect them at the airport. The tickets and their itinerary will be mailed with your approval."

Nate handed the folder back. "I approve, and I'm sure you've done an excellent job. Thank you, Katherine. You're a peach. Oh, make sure I get copies of their itinerary to take with me for our next meeting."

"Mr. Toncetti said he would handle the distribution. I'll put the dates on your calendar and have a copy ready for you."

"Thank you again, Katherine. You two have a good evening."

Nate watched the two women walk out of his office, noting that Michelle had a certain lightness in her step. Once outside the confines of Nate's office, Katherine and Michelle discussed the current situation.

"Katherine, tell me the truth. Did you know about this?"

"I was as surprised as you. But did you glance at the folders?"

"Yes. The colors made sense for the sales team and how they were broken down."

"No, I'm referencing the European folders."

"Okay, that all looked normal, too. Did you see something out of the ordinary?"

Katherine pursed her lips. "The Chanel S.A. folder was absent from the conference table."

Michelle looked back at Nate's closed office door. "Are you certain?"

"I am. It was very thick and impossible to miss. I didn't see it anywhere near the other folders. Do you know anything special about that account?"

"Not really, but then Jim guarded his European accounts and rarely shared specifics."

"Do you remember the name of Jim's contact?"

"A woman, I think—give me a minute. I'm sure I'll remember. Wait! Chin something—that's it. Chenair. Now I remember, Arleen Chenair. Jim was rather fond of this client."

"What makes you say that?"

"Jim's face always lit up whenever he discussed this individual. I knew the man was married, but there was a twinkle in his eye when discussing Chanel S.A."

The two women mulled over their discussion in silence. They also experienced a natural instinct moment, indicating they knew there would be more to this story.

* * *

Nate re-read the response from Finance and compared this information with the Chanel S.A. folder. Jim Kreider's expenses weren't out of the ordinary, but something about how they were being reported bothered Nate. Having extensive experience in sales and marketing, Nate was familiar with doctoring one's expense report to hide certain items.

Nate remembered being sent to Boston one summer to assist with a new client. When he arrived, it was pouring down rain, and Nate forgot to bring any rain protection. A gift shop in the airport sold mediocre, collapsible umbrellas that cost ten dollars each. By the end of the visit, between the wind and constant use over the four-day trip, the umbrella was a disaster. One rib was severely bent, preventing complete closure, and the thin fabric had ripped on an overhanging tree branch. At the airport for the return trip, Nate tossed the defective umbrella into the nearest trash receptacle.

Upon returning to work, a battle ensued between Finance and Nate over claiming the temporary purchase as an expense. His report, although approved by his manager, was tersely rejected with a discordant note attached by someone in Finance: "We do not pay for umbrellas!" Nate spent unnecessary, precious hours writing a lengthy memo, explaining the reasons behind the umbrella purchase and the fate of the item once his client visit was over. This was to no avail, and again the report was rejected with the same nasty note attached from Finance.

Upon a third attempt to submit his expense report, Nate attached his own note to the submission, which stated: "The umbrella is in here—find it!" By fudging the numbers for meals, tips, mileage, and phone calls, Nate had managed to disguise the ten-dollar purchase without directly disclosing it. Oddly, the expense report was approved, and a reimbursement check arrived the next week. Whereupon, Nate's infamous quote developed—"one victory at a time."

Frustrated, Nate scooped up the reports, his notes, and all the material for Chanel S.A. and shoved them into his desk drawer. He knew he would have to wait until the funeral group met again before he would be able to ask Arleen Chenair about it.

* * *

Joe was half-asleep in his easy chair when he heard the front doorbell. He glanced at the clock and noted it was just before seven. Struggling to extract his hefty frame from the over-stuffed chair, Joe shuffled to the door and glanced in the peephole. It was an unfamiliar face. Joe yanked the door open.

"Can I help you?"

A pleasant young man with a suit and tie smiled and handed Joe his business card. Joe read the printing.

"Sorry to drop by so late, Mr. Langley, but my name is Frederick Wells. I work for Mr. Toncetti, and he has asked me to stop by."

Joe scrutinized the lad. He looked to be about twenty-five and was professionally dressed.

"Come on in."

Joe stepped back and ushered the man in. He then walked to the living room and indicated the young man could sit on the sofa. Joe stood with his arms folded.

"What's this about?"

"Mr. Toncetti has asked me to—"

They were interrupted by the telephone.

"Hold on a sec. I'll be right back."

Joe dashed for the kitchen phone and kept an eye on his guest. At the same time, Mr. Wells spotted the smashed cordless receiver by the wall and raised his eyebrows.

"Hello?"

"Good evening Joe, this is Tony Toncetti. Are you busy?"

"Well, Tony, yes and no. Your man Fred just arrived, and we were about to have a discussion. He said you sent him."

"Excellent. I was hoping to call you before Frederick arrived, but, apparently, he was faster than I thought."

"Why is he here, Tony?"

"Do you remember our earlier discussions about Jim Kreider's paintings?"

"I do."

"Well, I've been busy and couldn't come myself, but I've asked Frederick to swing by and collect Jim's paintings for me."

"I see." Joe's voice sounded cautious.

"With your permission, of course, Joe, I've asked Frederick to inventory the paintings and bring them to our office. Is that okay with you?"

"Sure, Tony. And those of us who asked for Jim's paintings—will we be able to get one?"

"Joe, if you remember, I said it would be up to Jim's children. When I meet with them, I will mention your desire to own a painting. Can you assist Frederick?"

Joe was feeling a twinge of jealousy and regretted his disclosure about Jim's artwork in the first place. It felt as if the last vestige of Jim's memory was about to be taken away, and Joe hated to see that happen.

"Are you still with me, Joe?"

Processing his feelings, Joe quickly realized he was acting foolish, and he couldn't keep Jim's paintings. "Yeah sure, Tony. I'll help him out."

"Excellent. Thank you, Joe. We'll see you next week."

After hanging up the phone, Joe slowly walked back to the living room where Frederick Wells sat patiently waiting. He looked up at Joe with expectation.

Pointing his thumb over a shoulder toward the kitchen, Joe said, "It was your boss on the phone." Joe struggled with his words and felt at odds with the decision to let the paintings go somewhere else. "Follow me. Jim's artwork is in here."

Inside the private studio Joe made for his friend and neighbor, Frederick Wells snapped copies of each painting with a digital camera he carried inside his jacket pocket. The camera was rather small, so Joe commented on that fact.

"It looks like a toy. Do the images actually come out okay?"

Frederick stopped and showed Joe the back display. Pressing a button, he flashed the painting images, which indicated he had captured exact copies.

"Wow, they look even better in the camera."

"Yes, sir. We'll print them out for Mr. Toncetti once I get back to the office."

Joe's thoughts faded away as he watched Frederick methodically set up each painting and painstakingly capture the image. Each picture represented a particular time and moment when he and Jim Kreider were together as friends. The memories flashed by as Frederick snapped pictures, and Joe's emotions tugged at his throat. Joe walked to the kitchen and poured a glass of Scotch Whiskey. He was about to drain the contents but suddenly remembered Frederick. Grabbing another tumbler, Joe filled it half-full with scotch and walked back to the art studio.

"Fred, would you care to join me?" Joe held the glass out.

Mr. Wells stared at the glass with discernment.

"It's just one glass, and I won't tell Tony."

Frederick took the glass. "Thanks. What's the occasion?"

Joe held his glass with two hands and stared into the amber liquid. "This is hard, what you're doing here. Harder than I imagined."

"Mr. Kreider was your friend, wasn't he?"

"I purchased all the painting supplies, so Jim could experience the art medium. I even converted my study into an art studio for him. Yeah, he was like a brother to me."

Frederick touched his glass to Joe's. "Well, then, let's toast Mr. Kreider. May your fond memories of him help you get through your period of grief. I do mean that, Mr. Langley."

Still looking down into his glass, Joe paused, and then muttered, "Thanks, and please call me Joe." After a few long seconds of silence, Joe lifted the glass to his lips and emptied its contents.

Once all the paintings were loaded into Frederick's vehicle, he shook hands with Joe.

"Thanks for your assistance, Joe. I will treat these paintings with deep respect and ensure their safety. Have a good evening."

Joe was devoid of any emotions by this point, so he slowly nodded to the young man and then unhurriedly walked back to his house. Just before closing the door, Joe watched Frederick drive away, making Joe feel anxious. His emotions were mixed—the same as a parent sending their child off to college or the military. The uncomfortable sensation in the pit of his stomach left Joe with the thought that he would never capture these moments with Jim Kreider again. As Frederick's vehicle disappeared, Joe knew the memories of his friend were fading as well.

CHAPTER ELEVEN

"EVERYONE EXCEPT THE MINISTER IS now in the conference room waiting, Mr. Toncetti."

"Thank you, Betty. Please have Mary, the stenographer, join us immediately." Tony rubbed his flat palms together and said to no one in particular, "Well, Jim, I hope you're smiling down on us, my friend, because this is turning into a train wreck."

A little over two weeks had elapsed, and now the team was gathered to continue their discussions for Jim's service. Arleen had been away on business in Asia. Nate appreciated the break, for it allowed him time to hire Jim's replacement and get his sales team back on their goals.

Dr. Nolan had also hired a very sweet young doctor, finishing her residency, and a physician's assistant to help in his office. If things worked well, Dr. Nolan was hoping he could sell his practice to the young doctor and finally retire. Besides, his wife had been pestering Tom about taking the time to enjoy some world travel.

Joe was frustrated over several aspects of the meetings, including the length of time it was taking to honor his friend Jim Kreider. He was also upset over the issues Pastor Mike had created.

Tony was ambivalent about the delays. He did want to hear the stories from all the team members and was concerned about the duration of the project, but at the same time, he was charging Jim's account by the minute and making a sizeable profit. Nonetheless, there was a nagging element of guilt because Jim was a terrific client for Tony, and he considered Jim a friend.

As Tony entered the conference room, he saw Dr. Nolan wasn't wearing a tie and but had on a sports shirt and dress slacks, like he may have just come from the country club. Joe was dressed in a different Hawaiian-printed shirt, but, otherwise, he looked the same. Nate was in his usual business attire, and Arleen was radiant and gorgeous as ever.

The room was noisy with idle chatter until the conference room door opened. When everyone looked up and saw who was entering, the silence was broken by a collective gasp in choreographed unison. Pastor Mike looked ghastly. The man had lost nearly thirty pounds. He was pale, almost ashen gray in color, and moved like he was one hundred years old. Arleen jumped from her chair and offered it to Mike, since she was closest to the door. She walked around the table and sat next to Dr. Nolan.

"Thank you, but you didn't need to move. I'm not on my last leg. Although, it does feel like a semi-truck ran over me."

The people in the room chuckled with forced laughter. Tony and everyone else watched Mike's movements with intensity and sympathy for the man. Once he was situated in his chair, the conference door opened again, and Mary, the stenographer, walked in with her machine. She set up her equipment but continually stared at Mike as if she didn't recognize the man.

"Okay, folks, I'm glad to see the team is back together this morning. We will continue where we left off a few weeks ago. Mary is now ready, and our next speaker will be Reverend Mike Richards, followed by Dr. Nolan, and then Arleen. Around noon today, the caterers are bringing in a light snack, and at that time, we'll break for thirty minutes. When you're ready, Mike, you may begin."

"Thank you, Tony. I want to first apologize to those in this room for my outburst during our last meeting."

"Pastor Mike, your apology isn't necessary," Tom replied.

"The doctor is correct, Reverend. We were all venting our frustrations. No need to apologize," said Nate.

"Nonetheless, I've spent time thinking about our last meeting and want to apologize for my conduct. Doctor, I especially want to say thank you for your visit, and I'm sorry you and I started out on the wrong foot."

"Mike, it's my fault, because I was pushing your buttons pretty hard during our last meeting. I think I owe you an apology," Joe spoke up.

"Joe, your openness and candor are refreshing. I'm not upset with you. I'm asking everyone in this room to allow me to start afresh. I will make an effort to keep an open mind."

Mike looked at Arleen but couldn't bring himself to admit he was wrong. Arleen took note of Mike's passive-aggressive attitude as well, which only angered her further. This was the extent of Mike's apologetic non-apology to Arleen. Being a lawyer, Tony recognized Mike's maneuver but was hoping no one else was aware. He knew Nate had probably figured out Mike's tactics but was hoping he was smart enough to keep quiet about it.

"Thirty-eight years ago, I came to the pulpit of the downtown First Baptist Church. It was my first ministerial position, and I had just graduated from seminary. I started out as an associate pastor; and because of the senior pastor's untimely demise, I was advanced to his position ten years later."

"What happened to the senior pastor, Reverend?" Nate queried.

"He had, well, what I'm saying, Nate, is he had health issues and complications with his heart."

"Oh, is this an occupational hazard then, Reverend?"

Mike tried to see the humor in Nate's comment, but in lieu of the recent heart attack, it was hard to laugh at Nate's joke.

"Let's hope not, Nate."

Mike folded his hands on the table, and he studied them awhile. He was trying to find a starting point to discuss his relationship with Jim Kreider. Looking up, he tried to smile.

"Jim was a regular attendee of our church, gave a sizeable tithe each year; but to be honest, I didn't get to know Jim until the last decade." Looking down the table and staring at Joe, Mike continued. "Of course, I had no idea Jim was an artist either," Mike paused and glanced up at Arleen. "So, I question whether I really knew the man."

Tony clenched his pen so tightly, his knuckle went white, and a tiny gasp emitted from the stenographer in anticipation of another breakdown. After an uncomfortable pause, the angst passed as Mike continued with his story.

"I watched Jim and his wife, Samantha, add children every other year to their family—two girls and a boy. They sat in roughly the same place each Sunday. Jim wasn't very active in church, beyond Sunday attendance, until his children started in Sunday school. When Stephanie and Robert were about eight or nine, Jim became interested in helping out at church. Suddenly, Jim began assisting in their Sunday school classes."

"Jim taught Sunday school, Reverend?" Nate could hardly believe what he was hearing.

"Yes, Nate—for several years in a row I might add. I suspect he wanted to be in his children's classes, so he could have more time with his kids. We've seen this happen before. Dad gets busy at work, toiling for days and hours at a time. They want more time with the kids, so the fathers volunteer to help out. As soon as the kids grow up, the dads disappear."

"Was Jim any good at teaching? Did the other kids like him?" Joe wondered out loud.

"As a matter of fact, Joe, the kids did like him. Jim was nervous and awkward at first, but in no time, he had a group of children that followed him around the church like puppies, looking up to the man. Robert, his son, was jealous of the attention, but Jim made sure his son knew where Jim's loyalties rested.

"Other than his time in Sunday School, Jim didn't participate in many other church activities. The family would occasionally show up for potluck dinners and special functions, but they usually didn't socialize much. Once their children went off to college, Jim and Samantha attended sporadically. Most Sundays, Jim would be alone in the church.

"Right after their children started college, Jim came to me, indicating he wanted to discuss personal matters. You know, I'm never sure what that phrase means to a person until we actually talk. Jim was interested in talking about various religious subjects. Unfortunately, I had no idea he and Samantha were having problems."

Mike's mind trailed off as he stared at his open palms. His eyebrows were furrowed. Then he realized he had people waiting. He looked up.

"Sorry, folks. You know, you think you know someone pretty well, and then something like this happens. It's disconcerting, but I'm hearing a lot of new information concerning Jim. Information I never knew, and some I'm not sure I want to hear. In fact, I'm certain I didn't want to know some of the details."

"Pastor Mike, all of us are discovering new things about Jim," inserted Tom. "Each of us has seen one perspective of the man's life, yet it wasn't a complete picture. I think it's important we don't judge the man."

Mike snickered. "That's easy for you to say, Doctor."

Some imaginary button was suddenly pushed for Nate. "Excuse me, Reverend? Who died and made you God? Have you led a perfect life?"

Mike's hands began to tremble, then his whole body. Tony looked at Nate and shook his head. The minister was fighting urges to let his emotions flare. He reached into his shirt pocket and fumbled with a small vial of pills. Struggling to get the lid off the container, the pills instantly spilled onto the conference table. Tony stood to assist, but Mike harshly waved him off. Mike snatched two tiny pills and, with shaky hands, placed them under his tongue. Mike deliberately slowed his breathing and rolled his eyes back. The room sat in silence. Tony poured a glass of water and set it in front of Mike. He then softly spoke to the minister.

"Do you need to take a break?"

Mike shook his head but kept his eyes shut, trying to concentrate on his breathing. Nate started to feel guilty.

"Look, Reverend, I didn't mean to upset you, but you're awfully judgmental of Jim. He was a good man with a great heart."

Mike opened his eyes and stared at Nate.

"Being *good* won't send the man to heaven, Nate."

This time Dr. Nolan interjected his opinion. "Nate's correct, Pastor. We're not supposed to judge people. I think you might want to reconsider your position."

"Gentlemen, please." Tony stood. "Shall we stay focused? Mike, are you doing okay? Do you need a break?"

Mike shook his head and then stared at Nate first and then the doctor. "I'm fine." Mike's eyes were filled with anger.

Waiting, Tony observed the room was again calm. He then leaned over and spoke to Mary, the stenographer. "Would you please read back Mike's last comments?"

Mary nodded and pulled the paper from the tray. "Jim was interested in talking about various religious subjects. Unfortunately, I had no idea he and Samantha were having problems."

Mike frowned, knowing he spoke more than Mary had recorded, but he didn't want another incident to occur. He dismissed the omission.

"Jim and I would sometimes go for a walk. When it comes to disclosures, I find it helps individuals to be outdoors and in open spaces. Jim asked me about my relationship with my wife and what I saw in other couples. Our meetings weren't on a regular schedule, so sometimes we'd go weeks between our visits."

"Did Jim ever talk to you about being a Christian?" asked the doctor.

"Not that I recall, Doctor. I assumed because he attended church and tithed regularly, that his faith was solid."

Dr. Nolan hung his head and slowly shook it back and forth.

Mike's voice elevated in pitch and volume, "What's wrong now, Doctor?"

Tom stared into Mike's eyes and replied with a flat, monotone voice. "I don't think this is the time or place to discuss this matter, Pastor."

Tony was grateful the doctor exercised prudence. "I'm afraid the doctor is correct, Minister. Would you please continue?"

Mike nodded but was getting irritated. "A few months ago, I received a call from Jim regarding Samantha's untimely death. I knew nothing of the issues between Jim and Samantha, nor did I know she was seeing another man. Hearing about this information in this very room . . . well, it's quite unsettling. It makes me think I don't know or understand the people attending my church."

"Stay with that thought, Reverend, and explore it further," said Nate. "You'll be a better man and leader for it."

Tony's body went rigid, and he stopped breathing.

Mike didn't want to respond to Nate because it further irritated him beyond words, but he acknowledged him anyway.

"Perhaps." Mike had a clipped edge to his voice.

Tony slowly relaxed.

"As I was saying, Jim was distraught over Samantha's death. He didn't utter one word to me during the funeral service. I also noticed he didn't cry, and for a man to do that at his wife's funeral is very strange. I gave an eloquent service and received comments to that effect from several of the attendees."

Up to this point, Joe had been relatively quiet. "Tell me, Mike— we've listened to you blathering on for maybe an hour, and in all that time, you've told us more about you than Jim. Why is that?"

Before Mike could respond, Arleen jumped into the conversation. "Joe is correct, Reverend. His point is well-taken."

Suddenly, everyone sat forward in their chairs, staring at the minister. Tony knew it was happening again.

Mike sat upright and puffed out his chest. "I don't believe you!"

The lawyer jumped to his feet. "Okay, folks—let's take a five-minute break."

Mike sat upright, finding the strength to assert himself. "Hold on a minute, Tony. I feel like this whole room is against me. I'm rather uncomfortable with all these accusations, and they need to hear my response."

Dr. Nolan came around the conference table and stood next to Mike. "Pastor, we're all tired, and no one is specifically attacking you. We want answers about Jim Kreider's life."

"I disagree. I feel like everyone is attacking me!"

"Tony, please have everyone leave the room, except the stenographer. I want to speak with Mike privately," Tom requested.

Without another word, the room emptied. When the conference door closed, Tom motioned for Mike to sit. Hesitantly, Mike agreed.

"Pastor, Mary is going to read your words back, so we can hear them in another voice. Please listen carefully to your words—the same way you'd listen to people in your office seeking counsel."

Mike was upset, but he agreed. "Okay, I'll listen."

"Thank you, Pastor. Now, Mary, please read Mike's story from the beginning."

The stenographer was nervous, but she pulled the paper from the tray and started reading Mike's words. Her voice was flat and had almost no inflection. When she finished, Mike's face was red, and tears were falling. The stenographer got up to leave but paused to push the box of tissues in front of the minister before respectfully leaving the two men alone.

"Pastor, did you hear something in your words that touched you?"

"I'm embarrassed. I initially didn't believe what everyone was say-ing about me, but . . . How could I be so stupid? I can't argue with what I just heard." Mike placed his palms on his face and sobbed.

Dr. Nolan reached out and wrapped an arm around the man's shoulder, holding Mike tight.

"Pastor, please listen to me very carefully. You have years of training and have carried enormous responsibilities, but the burdens and the worries that accompany that are breaking your heart. God never demands something this unreasonable.

"Jesus said, 'Take My yoke upon you and learn from Me, for I am gentle and humble in heart, and you will find rest for your souls.'[1]

"When we set ourselves above others, pretending to be better than everyone else, we're no better than the Pharisees, whom Jesus condemned. We are human. Even you are human and make mistakes. It's okay for people to see humility in their pastor."

Mike looked up at Tom. "I didn't intend for this to happen. In fact, my heart attack has opened my eyes to many of my personal faults. You must know, I am trying—"

"We all make mistakes, Mike. After nearly fifty years of doctoring people, I recently realized I've not taken care of my wife the way she expected. I placed my patients ahead of her. I, too, am learning these same, painful lessons."

"What shall I do now? I can't have this room filled with people who won't respect me. It's too embarrassing."

"Mike, you'll learn to earn their respect because you'll humble yourself and ask for their forgiveness."

"But what if they won't forgive me?"

---

1   Matthew 11:29

"I forgive you—because if I didn't, then how could I seek forgiveness from God?"

"These people aren't Christians, Doctor. Why would they show me mercy?"

"Because we are all humans and make mistakes. However, you should be careful with your labels. You have no way of knowing if they are Christians or not—you cannot make a decision of that magnitude."

Mike looked down and shook his head. "I don't know. My situation seems impossible."

"And just like the Bible says, '... with God, all things are possible.'"[2]

"I'll try, Doctor, I really will; but if they start attacking me, I'm finished here."

"I have faith this will work."

"I hope you're right."

"Sit here, Pastor. I'll return with the others in a few minutes."

Mike looked worried, but Dr. Nolan gave the minister one of his grimacing smiles and patted Mike on the shoulder. Tom then walked out of the room. Looking around, Tom saw the team clustered near Tony's office door.

"Could I ask all of you to step inside the room and close the door?"

The room filled quickly, with some individuals standing. Tom took a few minutes to gather his thoughts while everyone watched with intensity.

"Pastor Mike and I sat and listened to Mary read his statements. After taking time to reflect on this information, Mike has reached a humbling decision. He realizes that when we shared our criticisms, we were correct—not an easy pill for him to swallow. He's concerned we'll

---

2   Matthew 19:26

judge his character harshly. I assured Mike that we are human and make mistakes. At first, Mike's attempts may seem awkward, but I'm willing to give the man a chance to redeem himself. Anyone care to join me?"

Momentarily, a long silence filled the room.

"You can count on me, Doctor," assured Nate.

"Me too, Doc," added Joe.

"Absolutely," said Tony.

"Of course, Monsieur," pledged Arleen

Dr. Nolan made eye contact with Arleen. "Thank you. We must endeavor to remain positive, moving forward. Mike warned, though, that if he feels attacked again, he may end his participation."

Tony stood up. "We're intelligent adults, Doctor. I expect everyone in this room to be professional." Tony observed the room to ensure everyone was in agreement. "Shall we head back to the conference room, Doctor?"

Tom nodded, and the room filed out quietly. When they entered the conference room, Mike had his head down and hands folded on the table like he was praying. Interrupted, Mike looked up and feebly smiled. Standing, he nervously shoved his hands into his pants pockets and glanced at the floor. Tom patted Mike's shoulder.

"Are you prepared to move forward?"

Mike looked up, sighed heavily, and lightly nodded. "I'm okay."

Everyone returned to their respective chairs.

Mike remained standing and took a deep breath. "Folks, please accept my sincere apology. I believe my attitude was perceived as arrogance—something I sincerely regret. I humbly ask for your forgiveness."

No one spoke or moved for a long while, making the room feel uncomfortable. Dr. Nolan clenched his teeth, silently praying his speech had not fallen on deaf ears. Finally, Nate stood and reached out with his hand.

"Reverend, with your words, you've earned my respect."

They firmly shook hands.

"We're good here, Mike," Joe agreed.

"Thank you, Joe."

"Minister, it takes a man with character to admit he is wrong. When he does it publicly, and in front of a room such as this, you demonstrate courage," Tony said.

"Thank you, Tony."

"Reverend, I will reflect in kind the courtesy and respect shown," said Arleen.

"Fair enough, Arleen." Mike bowed his head toward Ms. Chenair. "Madam, please accept my humble apology."

"But, of course."

Tony stood up and rubbed his flat palms together. "Excellent work, people—this is probably a good time for lunch." Tony picked up the telephone receiver and dialed a number. "Hello, Betty, I believe we're ready for lunch.

"Yes, that would be excellent. Thank you."

"Great, I'm starved!" Joe proclaimed as the room filled with light laughter.

CHAPTER TWELVE

"AFTER WE'RE FINISHED TODAY, ARLEEN, would you have time to meet concerning a business matter?" whispered Nate while sitting next to Ms. Chenair.

Arleen smiled. "Of course, Nate. Our meeting has been expected."

With lunch consumed, Tony felt the room was in a pleasant mood. When the catering crew entered the conference room to clean up, Joe was still eating. He hurriedly refilled his plate before the food was whisked away. The room watched Joe with fascination, but clearly, he was unaware of the attention.

Tony rubbed his flat palms together. "Okay, folks, is everyone ready to begin?"

The members in unison stared at Joe, who was still shoveling food into an open mouth. He looked up in silence.

"Perhaps we may continue while Joe is finishing his lunch?" Tony didn't wait for a response to his rhetorical question. "Mary, please read the last statement made by the minister for us."

Mary hesitantly reached into the tray but cast her eyes toward Mike, silently seeking his permission. With the slightest perception, Mike nodded his approval, completing their non-verbal communication.

"As I was saying, Jim was distraught over Samantha's death. He didn't utter one word to me during the funeral service. I also noticed

Jim didn't cry—which is quite strange. I gave an eloquent service and received comments to that effect from several of the attendees."

"Could we strike the last sentence?"

"Don't worry, Mike. Outside this room, you are the only person who will view these written words. Do you have enough information to continue your story, or shall I have Mary read more?"

"No, I'm fine. Thanks. I must admit, I was also surprised by the lack of our church members who attended Samantha's service. Until you mentioned it, Joe, I hadn't paid attention to that detail. It is an error I wish hadn't happened."

"Hopefully, we learn from our past mistakes and move forward, Mike," encouraged Nate.

"Yes, thank you, Nate. Efforts to have Jim talk about Samantha's death was fraught with obstacles. Every time I brought the subject up, he dismissed it immediately. Jim would then talk about the weather, sports scores, or his children. In situations such as this, training teaches us not to confront the individual but to let them arrive to the discussion on their own and in their own timing. Grief takes time and affects everyone differently.

"As Nate mentioned earlier, Jim was proud of all three of his children. Granted, he didn't like some of their individual choices, but for the most part, he loved them completely."

"I'm curious—what gave you the impression he loved his children?" Joe asked.

"Well, Joe, on occasion, Jim would break down and get emotional when describing the frustrating circumstances surrounding one child or another. To me, this says the man cared deeply and had compassion. He was passionate concerning their individual situations. He was also wise enough to recognize that he could not force or control their lives."

"I'm all too familiar with that scenario," said Tony.

Mike nodded.

"When Jim and I were together, I struggled to provide an open space for his confessions, but Jim guarded his innermost feelings. I got the impression he wanted to say more but didn't for reasons I couldn't understand at the time. In retrospect, I'm beginning to understand his situation better.

"I need to ask, Tony, have Jim's children been contacted?"

"They have, Minister. I have some information to share regarding the subject, but it will wait until you're finished."

"I'm almost finished, Tony. During the last six months, Jim's presence in the church was infrequent. It didn't concern me because I've watched others who have experienced similar family loss. They rarely attend or quit altogether, only to return later. When Jim stopped attending, I have to admit that I didn't notice because we have a large church. That's not an excuse, but the reality of my situation."

"Reverend, I mean no disrespect," interrupted Arleen. "And I'm basing this on your information, but it seems your relationship with James was mostly superficial?"

Mike looked down and softly spoke. "I'm sorry to admit this, but you are correct, Arleen. I wish I had done things differently. When I look back, I wish I had been aware of Jim's illness, but when I look around this room, I see everyone else had the same idea. Jim was too young, and it seems his last couple of years had been beset with troubles."

Dr. Nolan noted the pastor's melancholy mood. "I think I can speak for everyone in this room, but we could have done a better job."

After a lengthy pause, Mike looked up at Tony.

"I think that's everything, but I'd like permission to add further comments should the occasion arise."

"Oh, absolutely. In fact, and this applies to everyone, if you find you forgot something, please feel free to speak up. Mary, should this scenario occur, please ensure the additional comments are delegated to the individual reports."

Mary curtly nodded. "Yes, sir."

"Thank you, Reverend. This seems like a good breaking point, so I'd like to bring everyone up to date regarding Jim's children. First off, we owe an enormous thanks to Nate, Jim's employer, for providing traveling arrangements and lodging."

The people in the room nodded approvingly.

"I was successful in reaching all three of Jim's children and provided them with the details concerning their father's untimely passing. Since all three are in college at the moment, I felt having the service during their Thanksgiving break would minimize the impact on their studies.

"All three children had the impression they would stay in Jim's house, but the property had been sold earlier. They're grateful, Nate, that your company is handling this aspect of the service. I'll be meeting with them here in my office a few days prior to the service to share Jim's prepared will. If everyone agrees, may we schedule the service for the Saturday before Thanksgiving?"

Again, the folks around the table nodded in agreement.

Dr. Nolan raised his hand slightly. "With the prior tentative agreement to use our church, I'd like to confirm with our pastor regarding the actual date."

"That would be terrific, Tom. Now, before we turn the room over to the good doctor, does anyone else have any further comments?"

Tom raised his hand again.

"Go ahead, Doctor."

"When James became ill, he asked me to not contact his family, and I honored his request. However, this may be the time to bring up the subject. You see, James has two living brothers—one older and one younger. They had an older brother who passed away while serving in the Army in Vietnam. I believe I may have the contact information for each sibling and would like the opportunity to communicate with them myself."

"Oh, by all means, please. Jim left me a contact page as well, and I can share this with you later." Tony was instantly relieved after the disastrous attempts with Jim's children.

Nate began shifting in his chair and checking his watch.

Tony smiled. "You look like you need to say something, Nate."

"I'm afraid I need to request a break for the rest of the day. I regret having to interrupt the flow, but work demands my attention. I should have mentioned it sooner, but—"

Tony hid his disappointment. "We understand, Nate." Tony looked at the faces sitting around the table and saw relief. "Shall we begin afresh tomorrow at ten in the morning?"

"Thank you, Tony."

The lawyer just smiled. Slowly, the room began to empty. Nate stepped closer to Arleen and spoke in hushed tones.

"May I have my secretary call you later and set up a time when we can meet this evening?"

"But, of course, Nate." Arleen reached into her purse and produced a business card. She wrote down her cell number on the card and handed it to Nate. "Shall I know the approximate hour for this meeting?"

Nate smiled. "I can assure you, madam, this is strictly business-related, but would you care to join me for dinner?"

Arleen was cautious. "Perhaps."

Joe slapped the shoulder of Mike, startling the minister. "Great job, Mike. Thanks for being honest, finally."

Mike just frowned. "Thank you, Joe. I'm trying to do my best."

"Pastor, I have to agree with Joe," said the doctor.

"Thank you, Doctor."

As Tony watched everyone leave the room, he could see the individuals were slowly changing into a cohesive group. Maybe this would work after all.

* * *

Nate reached into his desk drawer and pulled out the Chanel S.A. folder and arranged it for reviewing. He re-read the report from Finance regarding the account activity and made some notes. Just as before, Nate couldn't see the reasons behind the red flags going off inside his head concerning Jim's handling of the account. In his gut, Nate knew something was amiss, but, somehow, he was not finding it. He stood and walked over to his window, taking his usual stance.

As Nate closed his eyes, he reviewed the documents again, looking for something, and then it hit him. He opened his eyes wide and darted for his desk, snatching the folder up. He smiled.

"Jim, you scoundrel. Very clever—in fact, brilliant."

Grabbing his pen, Nate furiously jotted down notes while scanning the folder and the financial report. He couldn't believe he had almost missed it.

Nate chuckled to himself. Picking up his phone, he dialed a number.

"Hello, Michelle. Did Jim Kreider keep copies of his expense reports at his desk?"

"No, Mr. Martin, but he did ask if I would hold them for him. I have all his expense reports here with me at my desk."

"It's Nate, Michelle, please."

"Okay, Nate. What shall I do with Mr. Kreider's files?"

"Michelle, do me a favor and have one of the interoffice couriers bring the files up to my office."

"If it's okay with you, I'm on my way to see Katherine, and I could drop them off with her."

"That would be terrific, Michelle, but only if it's not inconvenient."

"No problem, sir. I'll be there in fifteen minutes."

"Thanks."

After hanging up the phone, Nate walked over to the window and looked down into the street. Several floors below his office, cars and people were moving in silence, like ants marching off to unknown responsibilities. Massaging his newfound information, Nate contemplated his next move, wondering if Arleen was involved in Jim's scheme.

With his arms crossed, Nate could feel something in his shirt pocket. He reached into the pocket and pulled out Arleen's business card. Walking back to the desk, Nate punched another button.

"Hello, Katherine. Michelle is on her way up and bringing me a set of files from Jim Kreider's office. Please bring them to my office immediately. Also, I need to arrange a dinner meeting. I'll provide the details when you deliver the files."

"Yes, Mr. Martin. Anything else?"

"No, that will do for now. Thanks, Katherine, you're a—"

"Yes sir, I know, I'm a peach."

Nate smiled. "Yes, you are." He then hung up the phone. Closing the Chanel S.A. folder, Nate dropped it into his drawer and laid the financial report and his notes on top. A few moments later, there was a soft knock on his office door. Katherine poked her head in.

"Is this an ideal time, Mr. Martin?

"Terrific, Katherine, come on in."

Katherine carried a large stack of folders about twelve inches thick. "Here are the files you requested." She set them on the corner of Nate's desk. She had a small pad and pen in her hand. "You wanted a dinner date, Mr. Martin?"

"You know that expensive place on the corner of Fourteenth and Broadway?"

"You mean Le Cardon?"

"Yes, that's it." Nate looked at his watch. "Please make reservations for two at six-thirty tonight. Tell them I'd like a private, quiet area, where we may discuss business."

Katherine jotted down some notes and looked up, waiting.

"Thank you, Katherine. That will be all for now. By the way, you may leave early tonight. I'm nearly finished here."

"Thank you, Mr. Martin. Have a good evening, and enjoy your dinner."

Katherine didn't hesitate but turned and left Nate alone. Once his office door closed, Nate took out Arleen's card and dialed her number. The call rang four times, and Nate was about to hang up.

"Bonjour, Monsieur Nate."

Nate was taken back. "How did you know, Arleen?"

"I recognized the number."

Then it dawned on Nate. All company outbound calls are routed through the main switch, so the caller identification was always the company's primary phone number. "Would dinner at six-thirty work with your schedule?"

"Where would you like to meet?"

"Are you familiar with Le Cordon at the corner of Fourteenth and Broadway?"

"Of course, it is famously French."

"Terrific, shall I arrange for transportation?"

"No problem. Until we meet at six-thirty."

"I look forward to the opportunity. Goodbye."

"Adieu, Monsieur."

Again, Nate pulled the Chanel S.A. folder out and placed it on the desk. Then reaching for the folder stack delivered by Katherine, Nate searched through the individual folders, looking at the dates. The folders were grouped by year, so Nate pulled only the expense folders which matched his search criteria. The rest he restacked on the corner of his desk.

Sitting down, Nate began a systemized search of each expense report, comparing the information found in the financial reports. Slowly, Nate spotted a pattern, and it matched his hunch. Grabbing a pen and his note sheet, Nate scribbled down his findings. Nate shook his head in disbelief. Speaking out loud, Nate exclaimed, "My goodness, Jim, what were you doing with all this money?"

When Nate finished, he glanced at his watch, shocked to see that it was already six o'clock.

Nate grabbed his jacket from the chair back, dropped the Chanel S.A. folder into a drawer, and tucked the financial report and his notes inside the jacket pocket. Nate then smoothed his hair back with flat palms and adjusted his tie. Walking to his office door, Nate paused, looked back at his desk and smiled. Turning out the light, Nate dashed for the elevator.

* * *

At six-thirty-five, the taxi dropped Nate off in front of the restaurant. After paying the cab fare, Nate took several quick strides, leaping up two steps at a time, and arrived slightly winded to the maitre d' station. Again, Nate smoothed his hair back with flat palms.

"Good evening, Mr. Martin. Your guest is waiting. Please follow me."

Nate tugged on the gentleman's sleeve, stopping their journey.

"Please have a double martini, neat, made with Reyka vodka and no vermouth brought to my table immediately." Nate shoved a fifty-dollar bill into the gentleman's hand.

The man glanced down at the bill and quickly placed his hand into his pants pocket. Smiling, he replied, "Immediately, sir."

As they neared the table, Nate spotted Arleen waiting at a quiet table in the corner of the room. Despite her reddish-blonde hair, she proudly wore a bright red dress and a wide brim, white hat with a red band. Nate gave out a subtle whistle of exclamation.

Taking her right hand, Nate leaned over and lightly kissed the back of Arleen's hand. "Thank you for agreeing to meet, Arleen. You look absolutely stunning."

Arleen smiled and coyly glanced downward, turning her head and indicating her delighted embarrassment over Nate's comment. Nate took his seat, and, incredibly, his martini appeared on the table, with the waiter instantly dissolving into the room. Nate deftly swooped the glass off the table and took a sip. Pausing to savor the liquid trickling down his throat, Nate then drained the martini glass. He smiled at Arleen, amazed that this lovely woman would have been attracted to Jim.

As soon as Nate placed his empty drink on the table, the glass was replaced by a fresh martini. In one swift, soundless transfer, the waiter exchanged the two glasses and then vaporized into thin air. Arleen sat quietly, waiting and watching Nate's movements. She was accustomed to having men act foolishly around her because of her attractive looks. Nate took a sip and set the glass down. The warming consequences of the vodka soothed Nate's apparent nervousness.

Folding his hands, he propped his elbows on the table while tapping his clasped hands to his lips. He was looking for the right words to start their conversation. Their private dinner was suddenly interrupted.

"Bonsoir, Mademoiselle Chenair."

A well-dressed gentleman stopped beside the table. He took Arleen's hand and kissed it; then the two began a lively conversation in French. Nate could swear he heard Jim Kreider's name mentioned, especially noting Arleen also reflected an instant sadness. Nate suspected the gentleman was an acquaintance or colleague. The man then turned, facing Nate.

"Monsieur, I am Paien and the owner of this restaurant." He held out his hand.

Nate stood and noticed he was a good six inches taller than Paien. As is customary in the military, Nate introduced himself by his formal name and title.

"Nathanial Martin, vice president of sales and marketing for Tynedex Corporation." Nate extended his arm and firmly shook hands, ensuring he produced a firm grip as a sign of authority.

Paien smiled. "It is a pleasure, Mr. Martin. Please enjoy your dinner. And may I recommend the lobster? They were flown in this morning and appear excellent."

"Thank you. It's a pleasure meeting you as well and thanks for the recommendation."

"Magnificent. A bottle of Chardonnay will be delivered with your meal, compliments of the house. Bon appétit."

"Thank you again."

The gentleman turned to Arleen, and the two exchanged pleasantries in French before he walked away.

"I'll assume you've been here previously?"

Arleen smiled. "It is our favorite restaurant. James and I dined here many times."

Nate slowly nodded. "I'm not seeking to ruin your testimony during our meeting at the lawyer's office because, quite frankly, I'm anxious to hear about your relationship with Jim. Our discussion tonight concerns Jim, but purely from a business perspective. Are you comfortable speaking about this matter?"

"But, of course. James and I were close, but we were also business associates. I have no problem separating the two."

Nate thought differently, given Arleen's earlier reactions in Tony's office. Nonetheless, Nate decided to navigate tonight's conversation with caution. Nate selected a non-threatening approach.

"How familiar are you with Jim's business activities when he was working in Europe?"

Arleen took her time to respond. "Are you interested in whether or not James was a trustworthy employee?"

Nate was surprised by her straightforwardness. He reassured Arleen, "I trusted Jim implicitly. What I'm asking is if Jim discussed company business with you and to what degree?"

Again, Arleen took her time to respond.

"I suspect you have a motive for these questions, Monsieur?"

This time, Nate delayed his response, looking for the correct language. It was evident Arleen loved Jim by her defense of his honor. Nate decided to cut to the chase and alleviate her concerns. "Arleen, I liked Jim Kreider and had absolute trust in his business demeanor, but it has come to my attention that Jim's expense reports were not matching his expense receipts. Fortunately, the numbers were resolved by the end of each quarter, and it raised no suspicions in our finance department."

Arleen frowned. "Exactly what are you asking, Nate?"

Waiters suddenly appeared with dinner, interrupting their conversation. The two guests sat quietly as four service staff hovered near their small table. As quickly as they had appeared, the staff evaporated and was gone. Nate smiled, and Arleen politely responded in kind. As Nate began to pick up their conversation, another figure loomed over their table.

"Ah, magnificent, I see your bottle of Chardonnay arrived. The lobster is flash-broiled in distilled water and Moroccan spices, bathed in butter, and served over a bed of crisp chard. The green beans are fresh from an organic farm and picked daily. The petite potatoes au gratin are smothered in a buttery hollandaise sauce, created years ago by my family, and topped with fresh cilantro and lemon. Bon appétit."

Before Nate could thank Paien, the owner vanished from their sight. For the next forty-five minutes, Nate and Arleen enjoyed their dinner with idle chatter. Nate picked up the bottle of Chardonnay, attempting to read the label.

"The wine is from the Alsace-Lorraine region, near my parent's home. It is a limited selection with availability to certain respected clients."

"It's excellent and complements the lobster quite nicely. I taste a hint of butter, peach, and citrus. The finish is amazingly smooth."

Arleen smiled, casting her eyes downward. "The winery has served royalty since King Louis the seventh in the early 1200s."

"Are you serious? That's amazing. Nothing in America comes close to the kind of history you're describing."

Again, she smiled. "Nate, earlier you mentioned some issues with James' accounting." Arleen frowned as if trying to understand the meaning of Nate's comments.

The service staff arrived and whisked the finished dinner plates away, clearing the table. Nate was impressed—not only by their efficiency, but also by the quiet speed at which they accomplished their goals. In less than a minute, their table was spotless. Two glasses of aperitif appeared.

"Compliments of Monsieur Paien. Please enjoy." Then the waiter faded away.

Nate sat up and folded his hands on the table, searching for the correct words, which he suspected would be sensitive ones. "Nothing indicates Jim is in any trouble because all accounting records are free of errors. Please understand. I am not questioning Jim's loyalty to our firm, or his honesty either."

"But, there is more?"

Nate nodded, regarding her observations. "But he withdrew large sums of money from the company for traveling expenses."

Arleen frowned again. "I don't understand. This seems perfectly reasonable, and I do the same for my expenses."

"Ah yes, but do you use your personal credit card for your daily expenses or a company credit card?"

"I use both. It depends on the circumstances. Still, I feel there is more to your story, Nate."

"There is. Jim used the company business card, and he obtained the cash advances. At the end of his travel, he submitted expense reports, indicating he carried the cash advances forward to the next reporting period. Again, perfectly normal, except at the end of each quarter, he would write a personal check back to the company, covering the remaining advance monies. When I compared the receipts, I noted Jim used his own credit card on some occasions and the company card on nearly all the rest. No issues were raised because he submitted expense reports reconciling the monies by the end of each quarter."

"I'm sorry, Nate, but I don't understand. What was the problem?"

Nate took a deep breath, realizing his next comment would be difficult. "Jim was in possession of large sums of cash during his travel to Europe. All his other travel was business as usual, except the trips to Europe." Nate allowed this information to sink in before he proceeded further. "I have no answer to my question, but I'm asking myself why anyone would need large sums of cash for travel to Europe, but not for other places."

It was evident Arleen was processing Nate's accusations. "How much money are you talking about, Nate?"

Nate was slightly uncomfortable with the disclosure. "This is a rough estimate, but all total? Between eighty and ninety thousand dollars."

Nate watched Arleen carefully, observing her eye movements and facial expressions. The blood in Arleen's face slowly drained away, and her pupils widened. She maintained her composure, but it was apparent to Nate that she knew something. Nate waited patiently.

Arleen's nostrils flared as she took a deep breath. "I see."

For a long, uncomfortable time, the two people studied each other in silence. No one moved a muscle. It was apparent that Arleen would not readily disclose what she knew. Acting unconcerned, she opened her purse and pulled out a makeup mirror, applying a fresh coating of lipstick to her pouty lips. Arleen picked up her aperitif glass and sipped.

Nate remained calm and tried to keep his facial expression in a neutral, non-judgmental state. He knew she would be saying something, but he could see she was searching for the exact words to start. Nate sat very still.

"In our village, where I grew up, was a boy a few years older than me. For as long as I can remember, he and I were great friends, but I held a secret crush on Robert."

Arleen took another sip of her aperitif.

"On the day of my sixteenth birthday, he and I spent the afternoon walking and talking. When we stopped, our path brought us to a small creek that emptied into a lake within the forest. Without a thought, we undressed and played like children in the cool water. It was fun, and I was enjoying my time with Robert.

"We laid in the sun, warming our bodies, when suddenly our passions took charge. It was my first time with a man, and I experienced emotions and feelings, unlike anything I had ever known. I was only sixteen, but Robert was twenty-five." Arleen blushed as she said, "You can imagine what happened next.

"One week later, I was devastated when I saw him with a woman from his college, and they were kissing passionately. When I caught his eye, he smiled and then whispered something into the woman's ear. They both started laughing. I was humiliated and embarrassed. It broke my heart.

"Over the rest of the summer and into the fall, I noticed my body changing, and I was slowly gaining weight. Assuming it was a natural progression of my age, I dieted and was able to slow the progress. In reality, I had no idea why my body was undergoing these changes. About six months after our time in the forest, I could no longer keep my tummy flat, so I started wearing loose clothing to hide the changes.

"One day, I was standing in front of my mirror in the bedroom, admiring my body and the roundness of my tummy. I was fascinated with how I was changing, and I was unaware that my mother was watching me through a crack in the door. Suddenly, she burst into my room, filled with rage.

"Walking straight over, she slapped me so hard, it left a bright red imprint of her hand on my face. She then called me the worst names she could think of. I was speechless because my parents had never struck me before. I was ashamed and cried. She locked me in my room until my father came home.

"For the next several weeks, I was kept a prisoner in the house and not allowed to leave. About the eighth month, I experienced stabbing pains in my belly and cried out for my mother. My parents loaded me into their car, and we drove for several hours to a place I had never visited. I spent most of the time in the back seat, moaning and writhing in pain.

"It was dark when we arrived, and it was an old building. A man appeared at my side and injected me with a needle; and from that point forward, I could not remember anything. When I awoke the next day, my body was in tremendous pain, and I found fourteen stitches running down my belly."

Arleen was trembling slightly as she took another sip of her aperitif. Nate reached across the small table and held Arleen's hands, waiting patiently.

"I never saw the child. I didn't know if it was a girl or a boy. I was so confused. For weeks, whenever I heard a baby cry, I would soak the front of my blouse with milk, which only increased my embarrassment. Later, my parents sent me to a boarding school, where I spent the next several years. I was able to visit my parents during Christmas and occasional weekends in the summer.

"When I turned twenty, I was sent to college. My parents never discussed my situation again and acted as if nothing ever happened. Years later, I approached my parents, seeking any information concerning the incident, but they refused to even acknowledge I gave birth to a child. For them, it never existed, and no one I considered a friend in the village would discuss the situation either."

"What happened to Robert?"

Arleen pursed her lips. "He was killed in a tragic auto accident the year after our encounter. I never told him about the child."

"I'm truly sorry, Arleen."

Beyond these four words, Nate was at a loss. To look at this beautiful woman, one would never guess she had experienced such devastation. Then, suddenly, like the fog lifting from a bay, Nate grasped the situation with Arleen and Jim. Nate's expression became serious.

"Was Jim using the money to help you locate your child?"

Arleen jumped to her feet. "If you'll excuse me, I need to visit the lady's room."

Astonished, Nate stood and watched Arleen strut across the room. Moments later, Mr. Paien appeared, and two cups of café au lait were set down on the table.

"Is everything alright, Monsieur?

Nate sat down and smiled. "Of course, thank you. Excellent meal, Mr. Paien, and thank you again for the lovely bottle of Chardonnay."

"My pleasure, Monsieur."

The next fifteen minutes dragged by slowly, while Nate kept scanning the room. He was certain Arleen would not be return-ing and decided it was best to settle his bill and go home. When he looked around for his waiter, a silver tray instantly appeared under Nate's arm.

"I'll take care of your bill whenever you're ready, Monsieur."

Nate reached into his jacket pocket and pulled out the papers from his office, laying them on the table. He then took out his wallet, retrieving the corporate credit card, and set it on the tray. The waiter disappeared. When Nate looked up, he was shocked to see Arleen seated across the table.

"Is it time for us to leave?"

"Well, to be honest, I wasn't sure you'd be returning."

"Oh, Nate, you must not be so sensitive. I needed some time alone, so I could think. Now, what were we talking about?"

"I asked if you knew Jim was using the money to help you find your child." Nate's response was a bit chilly.

"I thought James was using his personal money to assist me. I had no idea he was using corporate funds, and I certainly didn't know how much money was involved. Are you absolutely confident about the amounts?"

The waiter reappeared with the silver tray, requesting Nate's signature. Nate hurriedly signed the receipt and handed it back.

"Pardon, Monsieur, would you have my café cup warmed for me? I'm afraid it's become cold during my absence."

"No problem, Madam." The waiter snatched the cup from the table and again disappeared.

Arleen's innuendo did not escape Nate. He picked up the papers off the table and held them out for Arleen. She began perusing the papers. Stopping, Arleen looked up, amazed.

"Au sérieux? Nate, this is a lot of money!"

"And you had no idea?"

"None."

"I believe you. Do you know where the money was being spent?"

"Not specifically, but I believe James hired a private investigator to help me find my child. The French government would not assist in locating the child, even when I showed them the box of letters I had written over the years to this unknown child."

"I hope for your sake that you were successful."

Arleen's face brightened. "Not at first, but yes, eventually."

"I see."

Nate didn't really understand and only spoke those words because they seemed appropriate. Even though Nate was divorced and remarried, he could not relate to Arleen's situation. Nate and his first wife had grown distant as they added two children. Unfortunately, Nate's career was more important than family, and he had allowed his work to take priority over everything else.

On one occasion, Nate was traveling on business for two weeks and returned home to find a moving van parked in the driveway. After supporting her husband through a well-connected military career, Nate's wife was tired of playing second fiddle. She had loaded the vehicle, grabbed the two children, and headed for the car just as Nate walked to the front door. She stopped momentarily and handed an envelope to Nate.

She kissed him on the cheek and said, "Goodbye, darling. I left your favorite in the fridge."

Nate watched the car drive down the street and turn the corner, followed by the moving van. In a fit of anger, Nate had crumpled her unopened envelope and tossed it into the rose bushes. Proceeding into his now-empty house, Nate found two cold six-packs of beer in the fridge and began drinking the bottles until they were all empty. After passing out, Nate awoke the next morning in a panic, vaguely remembering the events of the day earlier. Dashing for the front door, Nate shred his arms trying to fish the crumpled envelope out of the rose thorns.

Unfortunately, the sprinklers had started early in the morning, so now the envelope was soggy. Nate carefully opened four pages of handwritten notes filled with anger and hurts dating back twenty-seven years.

Despite their differences, Nate and his ex-wife eventually became good friends. In fact, Nate and his ex's new husband became even closer friends. Nate had remarried, and the two couples spent many holidays and occasional summer vacations together. Nate had maintained a healthy relationship with his son and daughter, and everyone treated each other with open respect. Nate's second wife was a career-driven executive, who seemed to enrich their relationship. Nate could not relate to Arleen's situation, and to confess he understood her struggles made him feel guilty. It was a lie.

"Arleen, I owe you an apology."

She looked puzzled. "Why?"

"I'm divorced and remarried and have children from my first marriage. My ex, her new husband, my new wife, the kids—we all get along fine. I have a terrific relationship with my ex and the kids. So, you see, I have no frame of reference for your unique situation."

"I appreciate your candid honesty, Nate. Thanks for listening to my story with such attentive kindness."

"You're an accomplished woman, terrific-looking; and you seem like someone who has control of their life. Your story contradicts all outside appearances."

"Ah, I guess I should thank the Catholic sisters from the boarding school for your compliment."

"To look at you, one would never assume you had experienced such tragedies."

"Thank you. I suppose I hide it well."

"Please tell me about the private investigator. Whose idea was it to pursue your quest in this manner?"

"James and I had many discussions about my situation. One day, he indicated he had found someone who could help me. James was so sweet. When I inquired about the cost, he dismissed my concerns, suggesting he would take care of it for me."

"Did you have any knowledge concerning how much it would cost?"

"Not at all."

"How long did it take to locate your child?"

"The investigator found my daughter in about seven months, but we spent the next ten months with government bureaucratic paperwork in an attempt to initiate contact."

"And Jim covered all the investigative expenses?"

"I believe so, yes. There were government papers and fees, and we needed an attorney as well."

"Well, lawyers aren't cheap. So, you have a daughter. How old is she now?"

Arleen's voice became animated. "I discovered I have a daughter, a son-in-law, and two grandchildren."

"That's good news."

"When we initially met, we were awkward at first, but not too long afterward, we became terrific friends."

"Did you ever see Jim pay the investigator?"

"Never, but then James wouldn't discuss the subject either." Arleen could see Nate processing her words. "Is there something I said that troubles you?"

"No, not at all. I'm concerned that Jim took so many risks with the monies he was borrowing from the company. He used Tynedex as if it were a bank."

"Now that I know the truth, I'm concerned for the same reasons."

"I suspect Jim had enough money for the investigator, but not in liquid assets. By using the company's money, it gave Jim time to arrange for the monies through his personal accounts. I'm making some assumptions because I don't really know. And now, we'll never find out. As I said earlier, I'm just glad it worked out for you."

"I cannot thank James enough for his contribution. It's sad he isn't here to enjoy my new family."

"Did Jim ever meet your daughter or her family?"

Arleen's face displayed deep sadness. "I'm afraid James only saw her pictures from the investigator. Had I known then what I know now, I would have found a way for them to meet."

"Arleen, I want to thank you for meeting me this evening. I know our discussions have been difficult, but I appreciate you sharing sensitive details. Please note I will treat your private information with my utmost respect."

"Merci beaucoup."

Arleen's eyes began to tear up, so Nate pulled his silk handkerchief out and handed it to Arleen. She politely nodded in acknowledgment.

"Arleen, may I ask you a personal question?"

"Of course."

"Have you ever been married? Perhaps I should ask it another way. Did you and Jim ever get married?"

"The answer is no to both your questions."

Nate sat back and folded his arms. "How is it possible that no man has ever asked for your hand in marriage? I would think that you have a trail of men lined up to ask you."

"Nate, like most men, you see the pretty package and assume the contents inside are perfect. I have plenty of males who fawn over and charm me. While in my presence, I watch grown men act like complete fools. In fact, I use my beauty to an advantage in my line of work. Many men have asked to marry me, but I rejected them all because they see the outside, not my real heart."

"But, not Jim Kreider?"

Arleen's face brightened. "No. James was very different from any man I've ever known. He was sweet, kind, attentive, and sensitive. James saw my heart and loved me for who I am, not for what I look like."

"And you can tell the difference?"

Arleen's expression dramatically changed. "But, of course. When the right love appears, it is like a fire burning within your soul. It elevates you to unimaginable heights."

Again, Nate was at a loss for words. He loved his wife and children and even believed he loved his ex-wife, but he would never describe his love in such passionate terms. Nate was mildly jealous.

"You make me wish Jim were still alive."

Arleen exhibited diametrically converse emotions by crying and laughing at the same time. "Oh, Nate, I miss James terribly."

CHAPTER THIRTEEN

"MARGARET SAYS DINNER WILL BE ready in thirty minutes." There was no response. "Did you hear me, Thomas?"

Dr. Nolan slowly pulled his eyes away from the lake behind their property and casually turned his head. "I beg your pardon."

His wife, Susan, moved closer, wrapping her arms around her husband's chest. She rested a flat palm over Tom's heart. "What is it, dear? You seem far away."

Tom turned his head, staring across the lake. He pursed his lips and lightly shook his head. Susan became concerned but forced her usual, everything-is-okay smile. Her husband was a perceptive man, and she loved that he was both equally strong and sensitive.

"Now, Thomas, I know you cannot discuss your patients because of some government hippo laws, but perhaps you could tell me something."

Producing his grimace-smile, Tom looked into his wife's eyes. "It's called HIPAA, not hippo, and it protects confidential patient information."

Slightly irritated, Susan again attempted to have her husband share his troubles. "HIPAA or hippo, that's not the point, and personally, I like hippo myself. Thomas Nolan, I know when something is troubling you. Since arriving home, you've held that glass of wine in your hand and stood on this deck, staring across the lake."

Looking down at his glass, Tom initially tried to refute her statement, but he quickly realized she was correct. Tom had not touched his wine.

"It's James Kreider's service arrangements."

Susan took Tom's glass, sipped his wine, and handed the glass back. "This is delicious, Thomas. Come sit with me."

She took his hand and pulled him toward a table and chairs. Tom reluctantly dragged his feet. Susan sat still and watched her husband twist the stem of his wine glass back and forth. Rainbow colors from the glass and burgundy shadows danced on the white linen tablecloth. Susan reached over and placed her hand on his, stopping his actions.

"Thomas?"

Taking a deep breath, Tom took a sip of the wine. "You're right, this is delicious."

"Of course, it's been allowed to breathe for quite some time now."

Tom grimace-smiled again. "I love you."

Susan leaned over, took Tom's face into her hands, and gave him a kiss. His breath was sweet with the aroma of the wine.

"Tomorrow, it's my turn to talk about James Kreider, and I don't know what to say."

"Oh my, that poor family. Far too much tragedy. It does make one wonder why these things happen. I know God has plans for each of us, but I do question the rationale for allocating so much pain to one family. His children must be heartbroken. First their mother, and now, just months later, their father has perished."

Tom silently nodded in agreement. "Unfortunately, we—our team meeting at the lawyer's office—are discovering things about James that none of us knew. It's getting rather complicated."

"I suppose you'll do an excellent job of sharing from your heart."

"I hope."

The sliding door from the house opened, and a woman stuck her head out. "Are you two ready for dinner?"

"I'll be there momentarily, Margaret."

Susan stood, walking toward the house, but Tom grabbed her wrist. "May we eat outside?"

Susan made a wordless, groaning sound. "The bugs are terrible this time of year."

"Please?"

"Oh, Thomas . . . okay."

Moments later, Margaret and Susan rolled a service cart out of the house and onto the deck. In a quiet and efficient manner, the two women set the table with fine china and two candles. Margaret lit them.

"Thank you, Margaret. We'll take it from here," Susan dismissed her.

"Are you sure?" Margaret was slightly disappointed. Even though she was their cook and maid, oftentimes she was treated like a family member and invited to join the couple.

"Everything looks beautiful, Margaret," Susan said firmly. "Have a lovely evening."

"Thank you. Tom, Susan. Enjoy your meal." Her voice was curt and precise.

After Margaret entered the house, Tom reached over and held his wife's hands. They bowed their heads, and Tom said grace over their meal.

"Our gracious Father, we ask Your blessings on the food we are about to eat and bless the hands that prepared our meal. Fill our hearts with thankfulness that Your grace may abound. Amen."

Tom looked up at his wife. "It's possible you may have hurt her feelings."

"I know. I'll speak with her tomorrow. I think it is important we have dinner alone this evening."

"Thank you."

Throughout their meal time, Susan kept the conversation light. They enjoyed a wonderful dinner of pecan-encrusted salmon, wild rice, and steamed vegetables. Tom ate only about half his meal.

"You're not hungry?"

"Margaret is a fantastic cook. Give her my highest compliments. I'm full."

Tom enjoyed his wine, and Susan finished eating, but she kept a watchful eye on her husband.

"Red wine with fish? I'm sure you're breaking a Martha Stewart rule."

"Perhaps, but I enjoy reds much more than whites. Besides, red wine is better for you."

Susan set her plate aside and moved her chair closer to Tom. "May I?" she asked as she pointed to his glass.

"I'll pour you a glass if you'd like."

Susan smiled. "No, I like sharing this one with you."

"You're a terrific wife, a superb mother, and I love you more and more each day."

"So, Thomas, tell me, what's eating at you?"

Frustrated, Tom looked around. Tears began to well in his eyes. "Do you realize that I delivered James Kreider and held him as he took his first breath? This is painful. I feel old today. This isn't the natural order of things."

Tom toyed with his wine glass, which was almost empty, so Susan poured more wine into his glass.

"You were always closer to James than the other boys. Trust God for wisdom. He will guide your feelings and words regarding this matter."

Tom slowly shook his head. "James was like a son to me. I cannot believe he is gone."

"Honor the memories of James that give you joy and share those."

Tom stared intently at Susan. "Do you ever regret only having one child?"

"Oh, of course not. Like the story in the Old Testament with Abraham's wife, Sarah, I was delighted to have one child. I know you wanted a son, but, apparently, this body of mine wasn't designed for more than one child."

The two sat in silence, pondering these words for some time.

"Oh, Thomas, speaking of children, I received a telephone call from our daughter today."

"And how are things in Italy?"

"They've decided to come for a visit during Thanksgiving."

"Just Charlotte alone, or the whole family?"

Susan smiled. "Charlotte, Gino, and the twins—Robyn and Bobby."

Tom smiled. "Excellent. It will be fun to see them again. It's been years since we saw them last. How old are the twins now?"

"They're turning twenty this year. They also want to visit some colleges while they are here."

"Hopefully, the children will speak English while they're visiting. I always have trouble understanding them over the phone."

"Then I suggest you start by learning some Italian."

"Oh, Susan, don't be silly. I'm much too old to learn a new language." Tom broadly smiled. "I'm looking forward to their visit, and I'll have more time for them this go-around."

"Which reminds me. I have been meaning to tell you how much I appreciate you making the changes at your practice. You and I have grown closer these past few months."

"I was worried about bringing in the help and not sure I could afford it—what with all the changes in medical insurance these days—but I'm starting to like the arrangements. Even though Dr. Prentiss is so young, she knows more medicine just out of residency than I've acquired in all my years of practice. I learn something new from her every day."

"Thomas Nolan, I thought you were too old to learn a new language!"

Tom chuckled. "Okay, okay, you're right. I'll start learning Italian."

"I'm just happy to see more of my husband these days. You seem less worried, too."

"During our meetings at the lawyer's office, I've come to realize that I was focused on my medical practice more than caring about you. I hope I'm not too late."

Susan hugged her husband tight and kissed his face. "No, you're perfect, and I love you, Thomas."

They stood and walked over to the railing of the deck, watching a family of ducks swim by. The parents worked to keep the small babies in a line as they floated across the water's edge. Tom loved this place because it was quiet and peaceful.

Their home was formerly owned by Tom's aunt, whom he visited frequently and spent his summers with as a child. His aunt was childless; and when she had passed on, she granted the home and the five acres of wooded, lakefront property to Tom. He and Susan spent a fortune upgrading the home to more modern standards with new bathrooms and a fantastic chef's kitchen. Tom's thoughts drifted off as he swept in the views of the lake.

"While Charlotte is visiting, I hope you don't mind, but we're going to have a girls' day and go shopping. You, Gino, and Bobby can have some male bonding time."

Tom pursed his lips and grimaced.

"You'll be fine, Thomas. Gino is a doctor, and you two will share things in common."

"My love, Gino is a cosmetic plastic surgeon. I doubt he and I have much in common. Nonetheless, we'll be okay. Maybe we'll go play a round of golf."

"Thank you, Thomas. I knew you would understand."

"And, since we're on the subject—"

"Which one?" Susan asked.

"Plastic surgery."

Susan was hesitant. "Okay?"

"I didn't say anything when they sent us family photos from their vacation on the Rivera, but did Gino do anything to Charlotte's body?"

Susan smiled and pretended to not understand. "Why, what are you referring to, Thomas?"

"I may be a busy doctor, and not pay close attention to family details, but if I didn't know better, I'd say our daughter modified certain parts of her body."

"Thomas, she's married to a plastic surgeon."

"Susan, has she altered anything else I should know about?"

"She's a grown woman and can make her own choices."

"What's wrong with what God gave her in the first place?"

"I think you're asking, what's wrong with what we gave her?" Susan was defensive.

Tom was frustrated. "What is the fascination with kids these days wanting to have perfect bodies? Look at us. We love each other just how God created us. Don't we?"

Susan chuckled. "I think I understand your point, but you should know, what you just said could easily be misinterpreted."

Sounding just slightly exasperated, "Susan, you know what I mean, and you're perfect. I like you, just the way you are, unmodified."

"Thomas, you must know that when Charlotte was younger, many of her friends teased her horribly. It was embarrassing for her. We spent many hours in mother-daughter discussions on how beautiful she is and how unimportant one's body is shaped."

"I truly didn't know. She could have talked to me."

Susan wrapped her arms around his waist and placed her head on his chest. "You were busy saving lives, delivering babies, and providing a living for your family. We all have our roles to play. Charlotte is still your daughter, modified or not. Please respect her personal choices."

Tom set his glass on the railing and hugged his wife. "I guess you're correct. You're an amazing woman, and I'm lucky to have you as my wife."

* * *

When Tony's cell phone rang, he was just sitting down to have dinner with his family. He recognized the number and sheepishly looked at his wife, Rachel.

"This won't take long. I'll be right back. I promise."

"Famous last words, Tony. In five minutes, we start eating."

He smiled. "Five minutes, Rachel. Got it." As he walked away, he muttered under his breath, "What a guilt trip, Rachel."

As Tony rushed away from the dinner table, he pressed the phone button. "Hello?"

Staci sounded upset. "Mr. Toncetti, Robert told me I couldn't bring Marcus to the service for Daddy. Is that true?"

"No, Staci, that is not true." Although Tony instantly thought he agreed with Robert's declaration, based on Tony's previous experience with Marcus.

"He also said I look like a freak and will embarrass everyone."

"Good grief, Robert, grow up," Tony mumbled.

"Excuse me?" asked Staci.

"Staci, you are important, and I look forward to you being here for your father's service. If you want Marcus to join you, that's your choice. I'm sure the company will cover the expenses."

"And will I embarrass you, too?"

The photo Nate showed during their meetings flashed into Tony's mind. He hated to admit it, but it was difficult to look at Staci's picture and not feel slightly repulsed. He lied.

"Staci, Robert was way out of line with his comments, and I will tell him so to his face when I see him. As I stated before, you're important, and we want you here, along with the whole family. We're in the process of contacting your uncles as well."

Staci started cheering up. "I read on Facebook that Uncle Jake just had both hips replaced, so I'm not sure he can make it. It will be good to see Uncle John and Aunt Mary, though."

Tony felt relieved that Staci was positive. "Excellent, Staci. We'll see each other in a week or so. I want to meet with you and your siblings in my office and go over the details of your father's will."

For a short period, there was nothing but silence on the phone. Tony checked the screen to ensure there was still a connection.

"Okay, Mr. Toncetti. Thank you."

"You're welcome, Staci, and please, call me Tony."

"Goodbye, Tony."

After checking his watch, Tony dashed back to the dining room. He made it back to the table in just under five minutes. "I'm back, Rachel."

Her smile indicated he was still in her good graces.

* * *

Sitting on the edge of their bed, Dr. Nolan lovingly kissed his wife and gave her a big hug.

"Thomas, please don't stay up too late."

"I won't. I just need to take down some notes before our meeting tomorrow. I love you, Susan."

"I love you too, sweetie. If I fall asleep, please wake me when you come to bed. I want to snuggle next to you."

Tom smiled. "I will."

He walked to his study and grabbed his tape recorder. He loved this device because he could free-form process his thoughts and later have his receptionists transcribe the recording into notes. His glass of wine was still nearly full, so he sipped the burgundy liquid and savored its distinctive flavors. Then, with his usual clinical method, he pressed the record button and began to speak. He listed the facts as he knew them.

"The family names of each of the Kreiders were as follows: James' parents were Paul and Jane. Their sons are Joseph, Jake, James, and John."

Trying to remember the dates, Tom spoke, "Write the word *deceased* next to Paul, Jane, and Joseph. Next to Paul, also write *suicide* and *after the Korean War*, which I believe would be 1958. Jane gave birth to John that same year, and it was this child who kept Jane from falling apart when Paul killed himself."

Working backward, Tom calculated the birth years for the boys. "James was born in 1955, Jake in 1949, and Joseph in 1946. Please look in the Kreider family patient folders to verify these dates."

Tom's thoughts drifted off to Paul. "Poor man suffered too much death in two wars. Depression consumed Paul. Jane thought adding children to their family would help. After Paul had died, I decided to help be a role model for the boys. Joseph was killed in Vietnam— I think, 1965. He was too young."

Tom shook his head in disbelief. "After Joseph died, I stepped in to help. Susan and I would stop by every Sunday and collect Jane and the boys and take them to church. Jane was a resilient woman who remained positive, despite her circumstances, and worked three part-time jobs so that her sons could attend college. I was particularly close to James and treated him like he was my son."

Dr. Nolan sipped his wine as he processed further thoughts. "Jane raised her sons alone and did a fantastic job. All the boys are successful.

"In 1980, Jane was diagnosed with ovarian cancer. She survived five years." Tom shuddered. "Oh my, I feel old— wait, please ignore my last comment." He turned the recorder off and sipped the last of his wine. He began to reminisce about the past. He quickly jotted down some quick notes. Suddenly, Tom felt drained. Turning out the lights, Tom trudged off to bed.

When he climbed into his bed, Susan was lightly snoring but aroused the instant Tom touched the sheets.

"What time is it, dear?" Susan asked with a sleepy voice.

"It's late, my love."

Susan rolled over and wrapped her body around Tom, snuggling her head into his chest. Tom smiled in the darkness, thanking God for his beautiful wife whom he loved so much.

* * *

Early the next morning, Tom woke with a broad smile. He slowly slipped out of bed and looked down at Susan, who was still sleeping. He leaned over and carefully pulled the bed clothes over Susan. He kissed her shoulder, and she moaned softly.

Tom slipped into his bathrobe and saw Susan's nightgown tossed to the floor. Tom smiled again.

Tom tiptoed from the room and shut the door quietly.

After exchanging the empty wine glass for a freshly brewed cup of coffee, Tom returned to his study. Staring at the recorder, the doctor sipped his coffee, knowing he was just postponing the inevitable.

Holding the recorder in his hand, Tom stared out the window overlooking the deck and lake. The table where he and Susan had dinner just the evening before sat in solitude as the morning gray light vaporized into warm sunshine. Tom pressed the recorder button.

"Jane was a God-fearing woman, who deserved to see her sons grow old. Surrounded by one tragic event after another, one has to wonder what God had in mind when He looked at the Kreider family. Jane's ability to stay positive, despite her circumstances, was a personal inspiration. James was a middle child and the peacemaker. He was a jokester, too. Jake taught James how to fish. I taught James how to play golf. Their brother, John, was much younger.

"When Jane died, Jake brought John to stay with his new family and provided John with a stable home environment. The household income was modest, but Jake managed to see John attend college. Thankfully, none of the other Kreider boys ever served in the military."

Tom stopped the recorder and sipped more coffee. He suddenly became aware of someone's presence. He swung his chair around and saw his wife leaning against the doorway. She smiled at her husband, like a young woman. Despite the span of time, Susan still captured Tom's attention.

* * *

Showered and dressed in classy, comfortable attire, Susan sat at the breakfast table with Margaret. Susan's feet were propped on an adjacent chair as she slowly ate her meal. Tom entered the room, leaned over, and kissed his wife on the head. He looked across the table.

"Good morning, Margaret."

Surprised, both women stared at the doctor.

"I thought you had a meeting this morning."

"You look like you're dressed for golf."

Tom was wearing a colorful, pale green golfing shirt with a light print; tan, comfortable slacks; and loafers. His favorite panama straw fedora was perched atop his head.

"You look delicious, sweetie."

Instantly, Margaret jumped from the table and gathered her dishes. Looking down at the floor, she dashed for the kitchen.

"If you don't mind, I'm going to play a round at the country club afterward. Care to join me there this evening for dinner?"

"What time shall I meet you?" Susan said smiling.

"Six o'clock would be excellent. Oh, and before I forget, I love you so much, Susan."

"You're not going to sit down for breakfast with me?" Susan asked, almost pouting.

"I'm afraid I'm running late, dear."

"I understand, but I'm disappointed you can't join me."

Tom passionately kissed his wife. "Me too, but I look forward to seeing you this evening."

Susan deliberately pulled Tom into a heartfelt hug.

Tom quickly scanned the room, ensuring Margaret was not present. Tom kissed his wife goodbye and headed out the door.

CHAPTER FOURTEEN

"GOOD MORNING, BETTY. THESE ARE for you."

Betty Thurgood looked up from her computer monitor and spotted a large bouquet of flowers. But her beaming smile was instantly wiped from her face the moment she saw the person presenting the flowers.

"Why, Mr. Langley?"

Joe was dressed in black slacks, a pale blue button-down oxford shirt, and a simple dark tie that stopped six inches above his beltline. Betty was shocked to see Joe's shirttail tucked into his trousers. He actually looked quite presentable.

"We started off on the wrong foot my first day here. I want to apologize."

Betty forced a smile. "Why, thank you, Mr. Langley. These are lovely." Betty set the flowers on the desk. "Please, follow me—a few of the others have arrived."

Betty escorted Joe to the conference room. When they opened the door, Dr. Nolan, Nate, and Arleen were waiting. The credenza was filled with an assortment of drinks and snacks. Joe frowned.

"What's wrong, Joe? You look like you swallowed sour grapes!" noted Nate.

Joe looked down and mumbled, "I'm on a new diet and lost twenty pounds so far.

Tom darted around the table and stuck out his arm. "Congratulations, Joe! That's fantastic!"

"Thanks, Doc."

"Come, let's see if there is anything here that you can eat that will benefit your diet."

Joe turned and walked to the opposite end of the conference table. He sat down in his usual chair and stared straight forward, avoiding any eye contact with the credenza.

"Thanks anyway, Doc, but I'll pass."

Betty actually gave Joe an approving smile. "Thank you again for the flowers, Mr. Langley. They're gorgeous."

Both Nate and Tom looked at Joe with an expression of surprise but, being polite, said nothing.

Joe was shocked to see the doctor dressed so casually. Tom's fedora was sitting on the table, alongside a glass of red wine. Nate was also casually dressed in cotton chino slacks, a tartan plaid short-sleeved shirt, and loafers. He was sipping on a glass of red wine.

Arleen was wearing red high heels and dressy slacks that cropped close to her ankles. She also had on a wispy, chiffon blouse with see-through sleeves. Despite her attempt to look casual, her ensemble was again picture-perfect and straight out of a fashion magazine.

Then the conference door opened, and Tony walked in.

"Ah, good morning, everyone. Thank you for coming here on a Saturday." Tony's cheerful greeting was met with various responses.

Noticing Joe at the other end of the room, the lawyer looked stunned. "Joe, you look classy today. Since today is Saturday, I've asked everyone to dress casually and comfortably."

Dr. Nolan added, "Joe has been on a diet and has lost twenty pounds."

Joe nodded and smiled.

"That's great, Joe. I think you do look thinner."

"You really think so, Tony?"

Oh, absolutely."

"Congratulations, Joe. You look terrific," agreed Arleen.

"Thanks, Arleen."

As folks were going to their respective chairs, the conference door opened again, and Pastor Mike entered, followed by Betty and the stenographer. Mary quietly set her equipment up and sat waiting.

"Mr. Toncetti, shall you need anything further?"

"Thanks, Betty, but I think we're good. I apologize for having you work the weekend."

Betty smiled. "No problem, sir. You're paying me double time today." She closed the conference room door and returned to her desk.

"If any of you would like something to eat or drink, please help yourself."

Joe sat with his arms folded while the others gathered something from the credenza. Finally, Joe got up and surveyed the goodies begging for him to indulge, but, instead, Joe plucked a couple of water bottles from the icy bowl holding various sodas and drinks.

Pastor Mike glared at Tom, Nate, Tony, and Arleen as they each poured a glass of wine. Mary accepted water from Dr. Nolan. Once everyone was situated in their seats, Tony handed out a piece of paper.

"I had the opportunity to speak with Jim Kreider's children. Stephanie, Robert, and Staci will be attending, along with Stephanie's fiancé, Charles, and Staci's boyfriend, Marcus. Without your permission, Nate, I said yes to their guests. I hope this meets with your approval?"

"There shouldn't be any problems, Tony."

"Thanks. Doctor, were you able to reach Jim's brothers?"

Tom cleared his throat and opened a manila folder, glancing down at his notes. "I was able to make contact with both of James Kreider's brothers. His older brother, Jake, just recently underwent replacement surgery on both hips. Because Jake is undergoing rehabilitation therapy, he feels that he cannot travel at this time. He sends his regrets. Their youngest brother, John, will be attending, along with his wife, Mary, and their two youngest children.

"When I spoke with John, he also indicated that he would send out emails to the distant family members regarding the services. Looking at your handout, I see a date and time has been determined for the services, so I will ensure this information is given to John."

"Excellent, Doctor. And now, please pass this down to Joe." Tony pulled a thin, black, three-ring binder out and slid it across the table. Mike pushed it to Tom, who then stood and handed it to Joe.

"What's this, Tony?"

The lawyer just smiled while Joe examined the binder. The pages were brightly colored with sleeved photographs of the paintings collected earlier by Frederick. Joe's serious, business-like expression turned joyful as he flipped the pages. Suddenly, he became animated, and, opening the rings, he pulled pages from the binder. Standing, Joe pushed a photograph toward Nate.

"This painting was the first one that Jim considered worthy of keeping."

"What happened to his earlier paintings?"

"He destroyed them. Jim could be a harsh critic of his own work and kept only certain paintings."

Nate shared the photograph with Arleen, and so the pictures slowly circulated the conference table.

"Oh, I remember this one! Jim tried his hand at impressionistic art. I bought him books that discussed the various art styles, so Jim experimented. See this one and this one."

Joe pushed more pages around the table. The room was quiet as the group watched Joe with fascination. Then it dawned on Joe that he was dominating the room. His school teacher instincts kicked in, and he regained composure.

"Oops. Sorry about that, Tony. I guess I got carried away. May I keep these?"

"The binder is yours to keep, Joe. You were correct; Jim's paintings are beautiful."

As Joe returned the pages to the binder, he noticed people nodding in agreement with Tony's declaration.

"When I meet with Jim's children, I'll impress upon them the desires of this group regarding ownership of the paintings. In the meantime, at least you have copies for memory's sake.

"Now, if everyone is ready, shall we move forward with our next speaker?" It was a rhetorical question, but Tony paused nonetheless. "Whenever you're ready, Doctor, you now have the floor."

Dr. Nolan made eye contact with each person. "Thank you, Tony." He opened his manila folder and pulled out several typed pages of notes and scanned the pages.

"James Kreider came from a small family of all boys. James' parents were Paul and Jane, and they had four sons—Joseph, Jake, James, and John. Joseph was born in 1946. Jake was born in 1949, and James was born in 1955. Their youngest son, John, was born on Christmas day in 1958. When I reflect back on being present for all their births, I sometimes feel rather old because so much time has passed.

"In 1958, Paul, James' father, took his life, which was just five years following the Korean War. His death was hard on the family, but Paul had served in the military at the end of World War Two and then was recalled to duty during the Korean conflict. Depression consumed the man until he could no longer handle the various battles inside his head. I tried working with Paul, but he withdrew from most outside influences. I was beginning to feel like he and I were making headway when the unfortunate incident took place.

"Jane, James' mother, was devastated and eight months pregnant with John. Raising four boys alone, she assumed the responsibilities of Paul by earning income through multiple part-time jobs. Through her heroic efforts, she was able to send her sons to college. Initially, when Jane became pregnant with John, she thought the child would help Paul focus on something other than his depression, but it was John who actually saved Jane from falling apart after Paul killed himself."

"How tragic, Doctor," interrupted Arleen. "I had no idea. James never discussed his family details."

"You're absolutely correct, Arleen. To look at this family, one would never know they endured such pain, but it didn't end there.

After Paul's death, I decided to help be a role model for the boys. Their oldest son, Joseph, was drafted into the army and sent to Vietnam. He died within the year, which was 1965. He was only nineteen years old."

Nate stared at the doctor is disbelief. "Jim was such a positive influence at work. He never discussed any of this information about his family."

Tom nodded in agreement. "After Joseph died, I aggressively worked to keep the Kreider family together. On Sunday mornings, my wife, Susan, and I would collect Jane and the boys and take them to church. In my opinion, James received his positive attitude from Jane because she was a resilient woman, who remained upbeat, despite her circumstances.

"Even though Jane raised her sons alone, she did a fantastic job. All the boys are worthy of a parent's pride. Jake owns several car dealerships. James, as we all know, became a high-level executive with Nate's advertising firm, and John is an insurance executive.

"For reasons I cannot explain, I had been particularly close to James, and I treated him like he was my son. When I started teaching James how to play golf, I realized how much I cared about the Krieder family.

"Many of you may remember our former mayor, Ron Golden. He was a rather tall gentleman with a prominent bald head. To Ron's consternation, the TV camera crews often applied large amounts of makeup to the top of Ron's head to reduce the glare." Tom produced a grin. "How many of you noticed the large, round bump atop Ron's head?"

"It always looked like he had a golf ball buried beneath the skin."

"That's nearly the truth, Joe. One afternoon, James and I were playing a round at the country club. James was just a young teenager then and learning to play the game. What he lacked in skill, he made up for in strength. Accuracy was not his strong suit, but he could smack a ball down a long fairway. We were teeing off at the fourth hole, which is a par six because the fairway makes an 'L'-shape turn in the middle."

"I'm familiar with that particular hole, Doctor. It has ruined many games and cost me far too many strokes," Tony groaned.

Tom nodded in agreement to Tony's declaration.

"James wanted to avoid the turn by sending his ball over the trees, separating our tee-off spot and the cup on the far side of the forest. I advised against James' plan because the trees are tall, but, nonetheless, he retrieved his largest club and squared off over the ball.

"I figured this would teach James a lesson about avoiding shortcuts when he would need to search for his ball. In retrospect, I wish I'd listened to that little voice inside my head and asked James to play the hole normally, but I did not.

"To our amazement, the ball lifted off like a rocket and sailed over the trees. Frequently, James would send his ball in a large, right-hand arc, called a slice. On this day, his slicing skills paid off. We stood in silence as we watched the ball vault into the sky, disappearing over the trees. Seconds later, we heard a man scream out in pain.

"Without thinking, James threw his clubs onto the golf cart and jumped into the driver's seat. Moments later, I followed his lead and sat in the cart. Instead of following the fairway, James drove straight toward the trees, plunging where no golf cart should ever venture. We bounced through trees and shrubs, over rocks, and emerged from the forest like an aircraft taking flight. Just on the other side of the trees, we were unaware that the landscape dropped off, by nearly six feet.

"As we flew off the hillside, plunging for the ground, I could see several men standing in a circle over Mayor Ron, who was sprawled out on the green. His hat and club were several feet away. By a miracle, the golf cart managed to careen down the embankment and skid to a stop just inches shy of Mayor Ron. The other players standing there were gripped in shock. I instantly jumped out to check on Mayor Ron's condition.

"James' immediate concern was for Mayor Ron, and he wanted to know if the mayor was still alive. Thankfully, the mayor was all right but received a rather nasty concussion. I sent a few of the other bystanders to fetch an ambulance. In the meantime, Mayor Ron remained unconscious. En route to the hospital, the mayor finally regained consciousness but complained of a massive headache."

"If I remember, Mayor Ron had a penchant for being impatient and volatile. What happened to Jim when the mayor found out what happened?" Nate asked incredulously.

"Actually, Nate, the mayor was quite pleasant about the situation. Unfortunately, his chief concern was missing the hole at number four. It turns out that the Mayor was just one stroke under for a birdie. Somehow, Mayor Ron was nicer than expected. Meanwhile, James was so distraught over the incident, that from the onset, he visited the mayor in the hospital and confessed his errors.

"Mayor Ron forgave James and requested he perform community service as punishment for his misdeed. After the unfortunate incident, Mayor Ron demanded James play golf alongside the mayor because Ron felt safer knowing where James was hitting his ball."

"Keep your friends close, but keep your enemies closer," Joe exclaimed.

Tom chuckled. "Exactly, Joe. Over time, James improved and played a decent game, beating my scores on many occasions.

"In 1980, James' mother, Jane, was diagnosed with ovarian cancer. She struggled through five unpleasant years. She was a God-fearing woman who deserved to see her sons grow old, but unfortunately, this choice does not belong to us. Her ability to stay positive, despite her circumstances, personally inspired me. Still, to this day, I strive to maintain a positive attitude and mirror Jane's fortitude.

"James was a middle child who classically played the peacemaker and jokester role all too well. His brother Jake taught James how to fish. I taught James how to play golf. Unfortunately, their younger brother, John, was several years their junior and saw his older brothers go off to college.

"When Jane died, Jake brought John to stay with his new family and provided John with a stable home environment. The family income was modest, but Jake managed to see John attend college. Thankfully, none of the other Kreider boys ever served in the military.

"When the boys were still young and Jake was ill with the mumps, I had Jane corral the boys together, so they could get sick as a group. Whenever one of the boys would get sick, Jane would be in my office with at least two of her sons."

"Did Jim ever get into mischief, Doc?"

Tom smiled and looked down. "Joe, they were typical boys. I remember one summer when the boys disassembled their roller skates to make these scooters. It was quite clever, really. In those days, children had clamp-on, metal roller skates for their shoes. The boys took them apart and nailed the skates to the bottom of a flat board, like a two-by-four. The boards were about two feet long, and they would ride them all over town, scaring folks to death on the sidewalks.

"They're called skateboards now, and I'm sure some genius has made millions selling these devices to unsuspecting parents. For doctors, such as me, these contraptions represent many scraped knees, stitches, and broken limbs. The Kreider boys were no exception and had their fair share of injuries. Eventually, the town police became involved because the lads were getting rather brazen with their skateboards.

"Our local university has an administration building located on a considerable rise overlooking the school campus. As many of you know, the school is divided by the boulevard, which runs into town. There is a long, circular drive from the street up to the administration building and back.

"Opposite the circular drive, two roads lead to the far side of the campus, where there is another circular road linking the two lanes. Before the boulevard was widened to handle vehicular traffic, this pair of campus roads all connected together, forming a large oval, which was used for track meets many years ago. Over time, the dirt track became paved roads, and the university expanded.

"The Kreider boys—James, in particular—decided to use their skateboards on the administration hill and race across the boulevard. Their goal was to see how far they could get to the opposite end without their feet touching the ground. As you can imagine, they didn't thoroughly develop their plan.

"To their credit, they did display enough common sense to watch for cars traveling down the boulevard. Unfortunately, they failed to consider cars entering the boulevard from the campus and well out of their line of vision.

"When the boys took off, it looked clear from their vantage point, so they sailed down the hill at full speed. How none of them were killed during their foolishness is beyond me, but they managed to navigate the hill with skill. At that very moment, a college lad, showing off his new red convertible, drove out from a side street and rocketed down the boulevard. The driver was distracted by trying to impress the girls and not looking forward.

"As the Kreider boys entered the boulevard, they faced an oncoming convertible aiming for their position at high speed. Thankfully, the driver turned his head at the last second to see three boys on skateboards crossing his path. The lad over-corrected to avoid striking the boys, and the car slammed into one of the massive oak trees lining the boulevard.

"It's a miracle, but the lad was unharmed, and his new red convertible was a total loss. Being highly competitive, James won the contest, but then the police arrested all three boys for nuisance. Since they were minors, they couldn't keep them in jail, but the police chief was hoping to scare the boys, which I believe worked. Their tomfoolery resulted in a pair of traffic lights being installed on the boulevard and a ban on skateboards for the entire university campus."

Tom sipped his wine and looked over his notes once again. "I won't bore you with too much more, but I do have one more story I wish to share. James was always a compassionate child, caring about other people in need. In addition to donating blood at our local Red Cross, James would volunteer his time at Thanksgiving and Christmas to help in the shelter soup kitchen. One year, James read in the paper about someone needing a kidney in our hospital.

"After discussing the situation at length, I suggested to James that he contact the hospital directly. The screening process was lengthy, and, despite his earnest desire to donate a kidney, he was eventually ruled a mismatched donor. In retrospect, knowing what I know now, it was a godsend he didn't donate a kidney because of his cancer diagnosis."

Nate raised his hand just off the table.

"Yes, Nate," said Tony.

"The doctor reminded me of an incident I'd like to share later."

"Thank you. I've made a note, and we'll come back to you when Dr. Nolan is finished."

"I'm almost done, Tony. I just have some personal observations. James was a good person with a great heart. As a doctor, it is always difficult to lose a patient. In my career, I've had my fair share of deaths, but James was more troubling than others. The ecstatic joy of watching a baby take its first breath cannot be described. But watching that same child grow up, seeing him become an adult, and then watching him take his last breath—"

Tom bowed his shaking head, pausing to gain composure. The others waited in silence, observing a man in pain. Finally, Dr. Nolan raised his head, took out his handkerchief, and blotted his eyes.

"It is sadness beyond words. It reminds me just how fragile our lives are. I thank God for the time I did know James and for our journey together."

Tony stood and rubbed his palms together. "This seems like a good time for a break." He looked at his watch. "Let's meet back in, say, fifteen minutes. Is everyone in agreement?"

His question was met with blank stares. Everyone was still processing Dr. Nolan's words.

"Excellent. Thank you."

Slowly, the room emptied, except for Dr. Nolan, who sat reading over his notes. Pastor Mike hesitated to leave and decided to join the doctor. He waited until everyone left the room.

"Are you okay, Doctor?"

Tom looked up and gave him a weak smile. "Perhaps. You know, my wife, Susan, just said something yesterday that I keep rolling around inside my head. She said, 'Why is it that one family has been visited with so much pain?' I couldn't answer her question. In my spirit, I'm sure God has a plan, but the mystery of it escapes me."

Michael reached out and rested his palm on the doctor's shoulder. He then quoted a scripture verse from the Bible: "It says in Isaiah 55:8, *'For My thoughts are not your thoughts, neither are your ways My ways,* declares the LORD.'"

"Thank you, Pastor. Now, if you don't mind, I think I'd like some time alone."

Pastor Mike slowly stood up and stared at the doctor. "Absolutely." Mike felt dismissed, but he then turned and walked out of the room.

Dr. Nolan waited until Mike was gone. He then bowed his head, folded his hands on the table, and began to silently pray, pouring his heart out to God.

CHAPTER FIFTEEN

"ARE YOU READY, OR WOULD you like more time, Dr. Nolan?"

Very quietly, Betty had opened the conference room door and saw Tom with his head bowed and his lips moving. He wasn't saying anything, so she assumed he was praying.

Tom looked up and gave Betty his grimace-smile. "Is it time already?"

Betty smiled. "If you need more time, Mr. Toncetti says the group can wait a little longer."

Tom frowned as if to process his thoughts. "No, of course. Tell Tony we may start whenever he is ready."

Betty nodded and left the doctor alone. Two minutes later, the team reassembled in the conference room. The group was subdued, and as each person walked in, they went out of their way to touch the doctor—a touch on the shoulder, a light pat—everyone except Mr. Martin. After everyone had sat down, Nate reached across the large conference table with both hands toward Tom and held his palms up. Dr. Nolan placed his hands on top of Nate's.

"Tom, I need to tell you what an incredible doctor you are. Jim was fortunate to have a physician of your caliber. Your religious beliefs, your care—they speak volumes about your character, and you must know, I'm not easily impressed."

"Thank you, Nate."

"I meant what I said. I'm not the kind of man who displays emotions publicly, but I can see the love you had for Jim, and it has touched my cold heart."

Tom let a small smirk creep into the corner of his mouth. "Careful, Nate. You might find yourself joining me for church on Sunday."

Jerking his retreating hands from the table, Nate said, "Okay, Doc, let's not rush into things here or jump to conclusions."

Nate was mildly defensive, but, at the same time, it was obvious he was thinking along the lines of the doctor but couldn't admit it in front of the team. Both men lightly chuckled and exchanged a nonverbal communication stare, trying to read each other's thoughts—the way men do when playing a game of poker.

"Well, thanks for sharing your stories about Jim. The more I hear in this room, the more appreciative I've become of the man," Tony acknowledged each person around the table.

Tony needed to have the team move forward, so he cleared his throat. "So, Dr. Nolan, are we ready to move to the next speaker, or did you have anything further to add?"

"I was nearing completion, Tony, but one more thought came to me during the break. If I may, would you folks be kind enough to indulge this old man as he wanders down memory lane just one more time?"

Tom and Tony both searched the conference room, checking to see if anyone objected. The room was in agreement.

"Thank you. I assure you, this won't take long. When James' oldest brother, Joseph, died, it took a toll on James. He was frustrated and angry, especially with God. First, his father and now his older brother were deceased. James was only ten years old at the time, and he couldn't understand why a loving God would be so mean—at least that's how he explained it. Those were his words.

"For nearly two years, a rebellious spirit arose inside James, and it affected his grades in school. His mother, Jane, complained to me on several occasions. The poor woman was dealing with her own losses and couldn't seem to handle James on top of everything else in her life. It was nearing the end of a school year, so Susan and I invited James to spend the summer months living with us.

"Our daughter, Charlotte, was almost eleven years old and wasn't too keen on sharing our home with an outsider, especially with a boy. Our situation became complicated when James decided to develop a crush on Charlotte; and, as he put it, he 'fell madly in love' with our daughter. Charlotte was kind at first toward James, knowing the circumstances that brought him into our home; but, eventually, the boy-crush was a little over the top for her.

"So now, Susan and I are not just dealing with a rebellious young man grieving the loss of a parent and brother, we now have the unfortunate pleasure of coaching our daughter on how to let James down gently but also helping James get through his first heartbreak. If my wife, Susan, had not stepped in with great wisdom, I was certain we were headed for a severe breakdown.

"Susan and Charlotte worked out a terrific plan and executed it with wonderful finesse. Quite often during this period, James would come to me in private and explain his dilemma and what he and Charlotte discussed. I, of course, would listen and commiserate with James by asking the questions Susan had prompted me with earlier. I must admit, initially when James developed the crush on Charlotte, his anger and attitude shifted, and I saw this as something positive.

But, as the summer progressed, I could quickly see disaster looming and feared the situation would soon worsen. Fortunately, I was mistaken. The magic these two women worked on James was having the desired effect.

"Remarkably, by the end of the summer, James and Charlotte had become good friends, and, much to my relief, the crush was soon forgotten. James seemed to emotionally move past his family's loss and was beginning to act like a typical boy—if there is such a thing.

"During that same summer, I spent a lot of time sharing my faith with James. Naturally, he was inquisitive and probed with deep questions about God and why I thought his father and brother were taken from the family. His questions caused me to rethink my own relationship with God, and I articulated my feelings as best I knew how at the time.

"One particular Saturday, James came to the breakfast table with his usual flair of tomfoolery and started teasing Charlotte. His timing was off the mark, and, in short order, Charlotte was in tears and running up to her room. Susan gave James a tongue-lashing that would bring a Marine to his knees and dashed after our daughter.

"James sat dumbfounded at the breakfast table, completely unaware and baffled by the performance of the two women. I asked James to stay seated while I checked on Charlotte and Susan. When I returned several minutes later, James was staring across the empty table with tears staining his cheeks.

"Unfortunately, James' mistake was not the insensitive teasing— the poor boy had just chosen the wrong day and displayed bad timing. Unbeknownst to James and me, earlier in the morning, Charlotte had begun her first day as a woman. She was emotionally upset, sensitive, and I'm sure, more than slightly ashamed.

"I attempted to explain the situation to James, but as you can imagine, I was in uncharted territory. I could tell by his glazed expression that James wasn't grasping my horrible explanation. In a desperate attempt to rescue the poor lad, we retreated to my study, where I had volumes of medical books. He slowly grasped the concepts and displayed a remarkable interest. I felt proud of my accomplishment.

"We became close, and somehow, our conversations eventually shifted to my relationship with God. James was genuinely interested in knowing about God. Taking my time, I explained the plan of salvation . . . "

"Excuse me, Doc, but what does 'the plan of salvation' mean?" Joe used his fingers in the air to denote starting and ending imaginary quotation marks.

"Excellent question." The others in the room shifted in their seats and leaned forward, anxious to hear Tom's response. "I explained how Jesus came into the world and died on a cross. Jesus died but came back to life three days later to prove He was God's Son and to save humanity. When we sin, break the law, make mistakes, we are destined for punishment, and all of us make mistakes. Originally, man was created perfectly; but, because of his free will, he chose to ignore and operate as if God doesn't exist. These actions by man separate us from having a relationship with God.

"When Jesus died, He took all the sins and mistakes we have ever made, or ever will make, and died for them on the cross. When He arose the third day, He conquered sin and death, granting us this same liberty if we will do one simple thing."

Arleen blurted out, uncharacteristically, the same thought the others were thinking. "Please tell us, Doctor. What is this simple thing?"

Tom scanned the room, making eye contact with each person. He had captured everyone's attention, and Tom was savoring the moment. "We must believe that Jesus is really God's Son, that Jesus died for our sins and arose on the third day alive, and then confess with our mouth these facts by telling other people."

Smiling, Tom sat quietly, watching the various expressions in the room shift. He waited for the information to sink in. Then suddenly, Nate jerked upright in his chair with an expression of disbelief.

"Wait a minute. You can't be serious!" Nate looked at the only real expert sitting at the table. "Reverend, is what the doctor telling us true?"

Everyone in the room intently turned and faced the pastor.

Michael smiled out the corner of his mouth because he had not held the attention of a group with such intensity in a long, long time. "What Dr. Nolan is telling you is true. It really is that simple."

Nate stood to his feet. "Then why does every preacher make it sound so complicated?"

Tom motioned with his extended arm. "Have a seat, Nate." While Nate slowly sank into the leather chair, Tom continued his conversation. "Man has complicated the simple message because it sounded too good to be true. But I assure you, the message God has for all of us is really very easy. God wants to have a relationship with us, be our Friend, save us from our mistakes, and have us live with Him in heaven. We just need to do what I explained."

"And then our lives will be perfect, right, Doc?" said Joe sarcastically.

"No, Joe. We still encounter the same difficulties, joys, and death as before."

"Then, why? What's the point?" asked Nate.

"So we may spend eternity living with God in heaven," Tom said beaming with pride.

Tony cleared his throat, "Ahem, excuse me, but I believe we need to stay focused on our task."

Nate cut him off. "Hold on a second, Tony. So, you're telling us that Jim made this simple decision—the one you're talking about?"

It was apparently clear to everyone in the room that the pastor was also unaware of this information, so Michael sheepishly deferred to Tom.

"Yes, Nate, James accepted Jesus into his heart that day and became what we frequently call a Christian."

The room fell silent. Blank expressions faced the doctor as he sat smiling. Without being choreographed, the eyes in the room slowly shifted their attention on Arleen. Tony spotted the activity and instantly jumped to his feet. Rubbing his flat palms together, Tony deftly redirected the conversation.

"This seems like a good time for a break. Shall we?"

A long, pregnant pause hung in the air as if those sitting there were waiting for the ceiling to collapse. Then, slowly, the conference room emptied in silence. Arleen sat staring into space, refusing to make eye contact with anyone, her eyes fixed on the far wall. She was angry. Dr. Nolan hesitated and closed the door, remaining behind with Arleen. He then reached out and touched her shoulder.

Arleen twisted her head, "I know what everyone was thinking. They accuse me of corrupting James and blame me for—"

"No one is judging you." Tom sat in the nearby chair and took Arleen's hands. "And in the words of Jesus, 'neither do I.'"[3]

"I'm not blind, Doctor!"

"I assure you, Arleen, they are curious. You must admit, James was a complex individual. We each have our concept of who this man was, but we're rapidly discovering aspects of his life that none of us knew. The pieces of the puzzle, called the life of James Kreider, are coming together, and a complete picture is emerging about who James was. So, I, for one, am anxious to hear your side of the story."

Arleen smiled. "You are ingenious, Doctor." Arleen knew exactly what Tom was doing, and she was not amused. She didn't resent Tom's tactics, but she hated that some people judged her without knowing the facts. She could see Tom was redirecting the conversation.

Tom stood and held out his arm. "That being the case, care to join me?"

After a lengthy pause, Arleen stood, hooking her arm into Tom's. Unmoved, she stayed silent, boring holes into the side of Tom's head. Tom continued to produce a pleasant expression and waited patiently. Finally, Arleen surrendered and gave out a heavy sigh.

"But, of course." She decided to let the issue pass for the moment.

---

3   John 8:11

CHAPTER SIXTEEN

"THANK YOU VERY MUCH FOR keeping your break short," Tony said, while still standing. Upon their return, folks were in better spirits, despite their previous exchange, which pleased Tony. He rubbed his flat palms together.

"So, shall we begin again?" He looked down at Mary, the stenographer, to ensure she was also ready. She curtly nodded in her usual sober, professional manner. "Excellent. I believe we will now have Arleen speak."

Nate lifted his hand off the table to signal he wanted to talk.

"Oh, I'm sorry. First, we'll let Nate have the table because he had an additional comment." Tony extended his arm toward Nate, and then sat down.

Shifting in his chair, Nate leaned forward. "When the good doctor was telling us about the time James wanted to donate a kidney, it reminded me of a story I'd like to share." Nate looked at Arleen. "I'll be brief, Arleen, if this is okay with you?"

Arleen was still mildly upset but displayed a perfect smile and nodded her approval. Nate smiled back.

"Thank you. Jim had been working at Tynedex a number of years. I had just been promoted to vice president, and Jim was a mid-level manager at the time. Our founding board meets annually on the top floor of our building, and to be invited to one of their meetings can be both a blessing and curse at the same time. It is a group of wealthy business individuals with little tolerance for wasting time or money.

"Jim was anxious to move up the management ladder and was our current sales rock star. I wanted to give him a chance to shine before the board and impress them with his amazing skills. With the company president's approval, I invited Jim to present our departmental business sales forecast. When I gave Jim the task, I warned him in advance that he would have one shot to impress these people; and, if he performed well, it would bode well for his career at Tynedex."

Nate folded his hands and looked down. "To tell you the truth, I was worried. Jim was too eager and young, but he proved himself time and time again. So, I took a risk and pushed him onto the biggest corporate stage he'd ever experience." Nate looked up and smiled. "And you know what? Jim knocked it right out of the ballpark. When I looked around the boardroom, the once dour, serious, stuffy, old board members were smiling and engaged with Jim. He blew their socks off and made me proud. A few even clapped when he finished his presentation.

"The company president was so impressed that he invited Jim and me to dinner that evening. As I escorted Jim from the boardroom and was congratulating him on a job well-done, the president came out of the boardroom and caught us by surprise. Well, the back-slapping abruptly halted when the president announced that the chairman and vice-chairperson would be joining us for dinner as well. Suddenly, it was like jumping from a burning building and surviving, only to find out you landed in quicksand.

"I spent a long time with Jim going over proper protocol and manners when attending a dinner such as this. When we arrived at the restaurant that evening, it was a ritzy and private club on the north end of town. As we disembarked from our cab, an elderly, homeless woman was sitting on the curb. Disheveled and dirty, she mumbled nonsense while attempting to place a child's pair of bright yellow rubber boots on her own dirty feet. Her feet were far too big, but that wasn't going to stop this half-crazed woman.

"She struggled and swore obscenities under her breath as we walked past, but Jim paused and looked down with compassion. My heart instantly caught in my throat because when I looked up, I saw the president and board chairmen sitting at a table near the window overlooking the street, just a few feet above our heads. They were intently watching Jim as he proceeded to bend over and assist the homeless woman, who was probably an insane asylum escapee or worse—a drug-filled nut job willing to do us harm.

"I tried smiling up at our hosts and tugged feverishly on Jim's arm, but he brushed me off. I was aghast as he finally attempted the impossible and stretched those child's yellow boots over her soiled feet. Relieved he had accomplished his task, I immediately pulled on Jim and said, 'Let's go now.' To my amazement, Jim helped the woman to her feet and ensured she was stable enough to walk. She smiled and then reached up, took Jim's face in her calloused, filthy hands, and kissed his forehead, thanking him profusely. She reeked of sewer and alcohol.

"Prying Jim free, we ran up the steps to the restaurant, all to the chagrin of the doorman, who witnessed our tragedy. My face was beet red. Meanwhile, the old street woman was waving at us like a little girl and beaming a smile that was missing many of her original teeth. I immediately pushed Jim into the men's room, just inside the main door. 'What are you thinking, Jim?' I screamed. He sheepishly grinned and asked, 'A random act of kindness, Mr. Martin?'"

Nate started chuckling. "I was embarrassed, but Jim was so honest and genuine about his act of charity that it actually humbled me. We freshened up and headed to our waiting dinner guests. Unfortunately, the evening's comedy didn't end. I can laugh about it now, but at the time, I was appalled and regretting I ever hired Jim to work at Tynedex because I was watching his career and mine ending in horrible flames.

"Drinks were served, and dinner ordered. The meeting was going as planned. Just as Jim was coached, he sat quietly, engaging randomly when called upon, and I started to relax and enjoy the evening. Outside our window, on the sidewalk below us, the lunatic homeless woman panhandled and accosted pedestrians for money. Periodically, she would stop, give us a toothy grin, and wave at Jim, blowing him kisses. I, of course, used my eyes to convey to Jim that he should ignore her. The homeless woman continued her antics throughout our dinner.

"Then, without warning, Jim looked at the vice chairwoman and asked if she would mind if he purchased the homeless woman some food. The staunch Mrs. Blanchford never flinched but nodded somewhat imperceptibly. Her expression looked as if she had swallowed lemon juice. Jim jumped from his chair and dashed outside. In true bewilderment, our guests watched Jim proceed to usher this crazy woman into the restaurant and to our table as if she were the very queen of England! The entire restaurant fell silent, including the kitchen and staff. Jim handed the homeless woman a menu and told her to order anything she wished.

"Looking around our table, I saw open mouths as they witnessed an unbelievable and surreal event just inches from us. The woman proceeded to order the most expensive steak and lobster dinner with all the trimmings and a glass of sherry. Sherry, mind you! And, how this homeless woman was to eat a steak with just three teeth was beyond me.

"She mumbled nonsense throughout her dinner and made loud noises as she ate. I chanced a glance at the president, and he actually looked ill. Sucking the red juice from the meat, the woman would spit a lump of gray mass into her plate, then begin attacking another bite. The only saving grace, if one could call it that, is she devoured her plate with the speed of a starved dog. She occasionally grinned at Jim and mumbled thank you.

"At the pinnacle of her engorgement, I could have crawled under the table and slinked out the door, changed my name, killed Jim with my bare hands, or killed myself. Perhaps I wanted to do all of the above." Nate took his finger and thumb and then drew an imaginary line across the air like a ticker tape scrolling on a sign. "I could see the headlines. Retired military colonel kills corporate members, co-worker, and self at fancy restaurant—film at eleven."

The table erupted in laughter. Nate shook his head.

"Unfortunately, there is more."

Joe blurted out, "Are you serious?"

"I wish I weren't, Joe, but yes. The woman proceeded to ask our waiter for three burgers and fries to-go. Mind you, those items are not on the menu. Jim jumped from the table and escorted the woman away, explaining to her that he would arrange for the burgers from another restaurant. I then realized that I had actually stopped breathing for an extended period of time and gasped. Then I noticed Mrs. Blanchford. She had retrieved a kerchief from her purse and was dabbing her wet eyes. When we made eye contact, she abruptly left the table for the lady's room.

"The remaining time was spent waiting, with the president boring holes into the side of my head with his eyes, but I refused to face the man for fear I'd crumble on the spot. When Mrs. Blanchford returned, she sat down, staring directly at me. I'm certain the blood drained from my face because I suddenly felt a chill run down my spine, and I shivered. When she began to speak, I was certain it was to terminate my service with Tynedex.

"Her voice was a little shaky; but when she spoke, she caught everyone's attention. She said, 'I have never witnessed such charity in my entire life.' She made an awful face and continued, 'The woman was disgusting and filthy.' Her kerchief covered her mouth as she lightly coughed. Then she said, 'I have two sons. I have sent them to college, paid for their weddings, bought them homes and cars, yet I cannot get them to even remember my birthday, much less have time for holiday visits.' She then pointed a well-manicured but wrinkled finger at the president and said, 'This young man was so compassionate to this homeless woman and treated her as if she were his mother. Promote that man. What was his name again?'

"All decorum was gone by this point, so I blurted out, 'Jim Kreider, ma'am.' She allowed a small smile to creep into the corner of her mouth and said, 'Tell Mr. Kreider I applaud his charity but would appreciate him avoiding such actions in the future, should they involve my company.' My simple response was 'Yes, ma'am.' The amazing part about this story is Jim paid the homeless woman's bill from his own pocket, even after Mrs. Blanchford insisted the company pick up the tab. I learned a great deal that day about Jim and myself."

Nate's voice trailed off as he stared at the conference tabletop. Everyone waited for Nate's answer. Finally, Tony spoke up.

"What did you learn, Nate?"

Nate's face was serious. "To never, ever invite a rookie employee to dinner when it involves the higher-ups."

Everyone laughed.

Tony looked around the room and saw relaxed faces. "Okay, folks. Now we have saved the best for last. Arleen, if you are ready, the room is now yours."

She smiled and made eye contact with each person, lingering for a long time with Pastor Mike, as if she were making a point.

"Thank you, Tony." Arleen pulled a small booklet from her purse and leafed through several pages before she began speaking. "A good place to start is when I met James Kreider. Almost thirty years ago, James walked into my office, making introductions. Something about the man was different than any other I had met.

"Most men make complete fools of themselves whenever they are around me. It took me years to accept myself as attractive. When I was younger, I did not understand the attention of boys or even young men, but as I grew older, I noticed the interest only worsened. One builds a tough exterior, and I shunned men because they were only interested in my outward appearance."

When Arleen looked around the table, several of the men were grinning.

"Eventually, I learned to use my beauty as an advantage in business. Most men I met were interested in my beauty, but not James. From the moment our eyes met, I could tell he was a kind person and genuinely interested in me as a person."

"Arleen, in an earlier conversation, you said the same thing about Jim. Can you be more specific?" Nate asked.

Her reserved smile indicated she appreciated Nate's discretion in the way he phrased his question. "A woman knows. Their body and eyes convey more than men realize."

Out the corner of his eye, Nate watched the stenographer, Mary, smirking and nodding as she typed away on her machine.

"Men of any age think they are cute or funny when they approach a woman, but soon they start acting like high school teenagers."

Mary snickered.

"James was pleasant but also respectful to me. He treated me like an equal, never moving his eyes away from mine. His blue-gray eyes locked onto my own, and I found myself drawn to him. When I saw the wedding band on his finger, I was surprised. Married men, especially, will play their stupid seduction games on women, so they may brag about it later to their buddies or to satisfy their inflated egos—but not James."

Mary was gleefully typing away and broadly smiling at the same time. Arleen looked around the conference table, and every man was staring down at the conference table because they knew she was correct—but not Dr. Nolan. Unlike the others, the doctor was fascinated because in the weeks this group had met, the stenographer never displayed any expression, other than her dour, business-only face. Meanwhile, Pastor Michael looked uninterested. Almost bored.

"I instantly trusted James and never regretted my decision. I liked his professionalism and character. For the first ten years, I randomly saw James visit our company for presentations and business meetings. When my employer decided to diversify our product lines, I was promoted to project manager over one of the new products. At that point, James and I started working closely together and more frequently.

"Our new products were being developed for a younger market, and this involved commercials for television and radio. James and I would work long hours and share dinner often. One of the things that impressed me about James was his genuine interest in me, my family, and my life. At first, I was suspicious because all the men I had known previously had ulterior motives, but James never made any advances toward me. I felt safe and secure that our relationship was strictly business.

"Occasionally, James and I would go see a movie, or, whenever I was visiting America, we would see a show or a play. We had many things we shared in common. Over time, our working relationship developed into a strong friendship."

Pastor Michael snorted. Tony silently hoped everyone would ignore the minister, but Arleen could not.

"Excuse me, Reverend—did you have something to say?" Arleen asked.

Mike looked around the table and saw everyone glaring his direction, including Mary, the stenographer. "Well, didn't you see that Jim was married and wonder why he was spending his evenings alone with you?"

"Tell me, Mike, do you have only men attending your church?"

"Oh, of course not, but what I meant is—"

"And do you talk to women in your church, perhaps even privately in your office?"

"Yes, well, that may be true, but the difference is someone else is with—"

"The difference is nothing, Mike. In the workplace, I interact with men and women, just like you. You're assuming we had an affair because we worked so close. Is that not it?"

Mike tried to laugh, but it was apparent he was nervous. He maneuvered to have the others take his side in the argument.

"The letter from James that Tony read to us on the first day was quite clear. In fact, everyone at this table knows exactly what I'm talking about."

"And you must know that you are completely mistaken, Mike. You are flatly wrong because I met James nearly thirty years ago. The letter from James was written recently. As a result, your assumptions are erroneous."

Everyone at the conference table was moving their heads following the conversation, like spectators watching a tennis match. Arleen did not wait for Mike to defend his position. She immediately went on the defensive.

"Tell me, Reverend—based on your relationship to James—did he ever disclose an intimate relationship with me?"

"No, but I assumed, based upon his letter—"

"Your assumption was wrong—the same as your thoughts that he and his wife were happily married. Now, if you will show a little restraint, I'll share with you when James and I became closer than just friends. We all sat patiently while you droned on about your boring relationship with James, so please show me the same courtesy."

Mike shifted in his chair uncomfortably. "Certainly, Ms. Chenair." It was clear Mike was embarrassed. Arleen smiled.

Nate was impressed with her bluntness.

"Since Mike has been so forward in his assumptions, let me explain something to everyone sitting here."

Tony stuck his hands out. "Arleen, I don't think that is necessary. No one sitting here is making any assumptions." Tony stared at Pastor Mike. "Isn't that correct, Reverend?"

Mike nodded silently, hoping the attention would move in another direction.

The room was silent for a long pause, and then Arleen continued to speak. "James was married. He knew that. I knew that. We acted like adults and showed respect to one another. Over the course of several years, one develops a friendship with the folks in their workplace, be it a woman or man. James was no exception. We would share our lives with each other. I learned about his three children, and he learned about my family.

"I was an only child, and I was obviously interested in James' family, since he had siblings. James was proud of his brothers and told me many stories about his childhood. Even with our years of sharing, James only provided me with the information that his older brother died during the Vietnam War, and his father had passed away many years earlier. Until Dr. Nolan shared intimate details of his story, I had no idea of the tragic events in James' life. Initially, he kept many particulars from me, speaking only in general references.

"Over the years, our friendship grew as we learned to trust each other. When his mother, Jane, was ill, James was apparently overtaken with grief because he was close to his mother. In fact, he canceled several European visits because of her illness. As his friend, I tried to show support and listen, but James took her death rather difficultly. He loved his mother.

"Emotionally, James was like a roller coaster—up one day, down the next. Jane fought hard to overcome her cancer; but, unfortunately, cancer eventually won the battle. The moment I found out about her passing, I flew to America to be with James. At her funeral service, I watched the poor man sob like a baby. It was the first time I saw the emotionally sensitive side of James, who generally displayed a controlled presence. During my visit and the funeral service, James even introduced me to his wife, Samantha, but the woman was chilly when she spoke with me. During the service, she stood next to a young man, apart from the other family members, and held the young man's hand. James said the man was her boyfriend."

"Were you shocked by James' comment?" inquired Dr. Nolan.

"No, Doctor. I was more shocked by the calmness of James as he explained her relationship with the man. As he disclosed details I didn't want to know, his feelings were absent, almost robotic."

"And did he explain what happened?" Joe asked.

"No. I think he was looking for someone safe to share his feelings with and without judgment. We had shared similarities regarding our secrets, so James needed someone who understood his dilemma. The day I met Samantha, I suddenly knew why James was always reserved and careful regarding his private life. Yet, somehow, the shared experience bonded us closer.

"Most men don't know this, but a woman understands the character of a man by how he treats his mother, his wife, and his daughters. James was an amazing father and son, but he felt like a failure when it came to his marriage. I had no intention of being a surrogate, and James never made me feel that way either. But I did try to be a supportive friend when he was grieving."

Arleen looked at Nate with intensity. "Originally, I wasn't going to share my personal story, but now I feel differently. I think it's important."

Nate shifted in his chair and leaned forward, wondering what Arleen might disclose. Arleen was usually reluctant to share intimate details of her personal life. Years of repressive feelings surfaced, immediately reminding her of the pain she had suffered years earlier and the judgments people rashly made of her life. As she sought the rationale for disclosing her story, she finally decided that if she were going to give meaning to the life of James Kreider, she needed to be honest. Even the idea of being honest about a hidden part of her life seemed almost terrifying. She was finally finished worrying about Pastor Mike because she had lost all respect for the man, but the others were another story. She would choose her words carefully.

Taking a breath, she began. "When I was a very young teen, I made a grave mistake."

Pastor Mike shifted in his seat, and, despite all efforts to avoid eye contact with the man, Arleen sensed he was about to interrupt again. Taking a brief glance his direction, she witnessed Tony wrap his hand firmly around the wrist of the outspoken minister. Satisfied she could proceed in safety, she continued her story. Mike looked wounded—like a boy caught red-handed stealing candy—but held his tongue nonetheless.

"I was only sixteen at the time, and I had a crush on a man in college, who was twenty-five and many years older than I. Through very poor choices, I foolishly became pregnant. On the day I was to give birth to the child, my embarrassed and horrified parents took me to a far-away clinic, where I gave birth to a child I never saw. While I slept under the administration of potent drugs, the doctors removed the child, and I was allowed to recover without ever knowing the gender of my baby or any other specifics.

"Embarrassed, my parent refused to discuss the matter and eventually sent me to a special school run by nuns. Years later, they sent me to finishing school and, eventually, off to college. No one in my family or the town I grew up in would ever discuss the matter of my child or acknowledge it existed. Eventually, I gave up trying to find the child and worked to forget I ever experienced anything at all."

"Arleen, what a devastating experience it must have been for you," expressed the doctor.

"You are correct, Doctor, but as you said earlier, we all make mistakes."

Arleen looked directly at Pastor Mike. "Like the nuns told me in school, Reverend: 'All of us have sinned and fallen short of God's ideal.'"[4]

Using his brain finally and not his mouth, Mike casually and slowly nodded in agreement.

"My experience created very negative feelings towards men, and I felt I could not trust them. As I grew older, men continually

---

4   Paraphrased from Romans 3:23

reinforced my mistrust. I have never been married and had no desire for marriage either. I saw less need for a man in my life the more involved I became in my career. Then I met James, and my whole idea of men changed."

"And what about the father of the child?" asked Joe.

"Tragically, he was killed in an auto accident a year following our illicit encounter. I never told him about our child and never spoke to him again."

"That's awful, Arleen. I'm so sorry," said Joe.

"Thank you, Joe. It was a long time ago, and, with time, the feelings fade—but not the memories." Arleen glanced down at her notes briefly. "James was a sensitive and caring man. During our times of sharing, I disclosed the knowledge of my child to James. He was sympathetic and a good listener. We shared tears and laughter concerning both our lives. Completely unknown to me, James began to inquire concerning the whereabouts of my child.

"Additionally, I discovered that James hired a private investigator to locate my child. Over the course of a year, James worked diligently to find the child I gave birth to. After an exhausting seven months, the private investigator located my daughter. It wasn't until James was certain that my daughter had been found before he disclosed this information. Unfortunately, we could not contact my daughter directly.

"The government requires many documents to approve direct contact between a birth parent and a child. The government writes the child, requesting permission for the contact. If denied, then our energies would have been wasted. But my daughter agreed. During the next ten months, with government bureaucratic paperwork, I was finally granted the approvals to initiate contact with my daughter."

Arleen smiled. "Not only did I discover I had a daughter, but I also learned she was married and that I have two grandchildren."

The room erupted in cheers and mild applause. Arleen nodded approvingly.

"I now have a reason to smile and be happy."

Arleen pulled her cell phone from her purse and scrolled to the files she wanted. She then showed the pictures to Tony. As the pictures traveled around the table, Arleen continued to describe her new family.

"My grandchildren call me Memau. It's a French colloquial word for grandma. The children are five and seven years old. My daughter's husband works for the diplomat corps of France and translates documents from English and Russian into French. He is brilliant, and so are the grandchildren. My daughter was working as a secretary, but she quit working after her children were born. My daughter, Nicole, says one day she might go back to work, but, for now, she is happy being a mother."

Nate smiled. "Arleen, with all the emotional pain you've suffered in your youth, it is wonderful to see such joy on your face. You must be very proud."

Choking on her words, Arleen nodded in agreement and said, "I have James to thank for my family. I didn't know where to start, but he took the initiative and pursued my daughter until he found my family. His gift is very precious."

"Sounds like love to me," the doctor said kindly.

Arleen chuckled. "You are correct, Doctor. And although it is too late, I now realize how much James loved me in so many ways."

Tony watched Mike shift in his chair, and he could tell Mike was about to say something insensitive, so Tony broke into the conversation.

"Tell us, Arleen, when your relationship with Jim changed and, perhaps, the circumstances allowing this to occur."

As Arleen continued to speak, Tony glanced at Pastor Mike, who had his face down, staring at the conference table. Without raising his head, Mike slowly lifted his eyes and glared at Tony. Without blinking, Tony gave Mike his best courtroom smile, knowing he had beaten many men in fierce courtroom battles before and without drawing blood.

"James was a very cautious and kind man, intelligent, but sometimes humble. I have observed him assisting elderly to board a train while he stood in a downpour. Everyone around him seemed to like James, and my colleagues were always teasing me and telling me I should marry the man. Because he was already married, I didn't pursue the relationship, and we remained good friends.

"It was during his mother's funeral that I learned why James was careful and protected his relationship with Samantha. He wanted his children to experience two parents, even though their marriage was horrible. I met all three of his children at the funeral, and everyone was polite and kind. When Stephanie observed her mother and the young man together, she immediately confronted her father.

"James and I were casually speaking when Stephanie walked up and began criticizing her father for being weak. She demanded that James fix the situation, stating that Samantha was embarrassing the whole family. James guided Stephanie away from the group of people, and the two of them talked. I watched from a distance and could see they were in a serious disagreement.

"In the meantime, Samantha and her boyfriend, along with most of the guests, began leaving and driving away. Before she left, Samantha came over and thanked me for being there. Then I stood with Staci and Robert while we watched James and Stephanie argue. Robert said they would be okay, and Stephanie was just overreacting. Staci called her mother an awful name and stated she hated the woman. This was my introduction to the Kreider family.

"When Stephanie and James walked back, I could tell she had been crying. I offered some facial tissues from my purse, and at first, she declined. As we walked back to the cars, she put her arm around my shoulder and said she would take me up on my offer after all. We lingered behind, while James and the others walked ahead. Stephanie thanked me for being there to support her father, and then we hugged.

"A few days later, James called me and asked me out for dinner. We met, as usual, at our favorite restaurant, Le Cardon. Throughout the dinner, James smiled continuously; so, eventually, I asked him why he was smiling so much. He told me he was beginning to have feelings for me and that he loved me."

Mike blurted, "The man was married, for heaven's sake!"

"Listen, Mike, you be patient. This is my time to talk, not yours. Let me tell my story."

Mike closed his eyes, holding up his hands in resignation.

"Thank you. I was flattered by James' confession and confused at the same time. His marriage to Samantha complicated our potential for a relationship, and I stated this to James. He agreed, but he also said he could not deny his feelings any longer. With Samantha's boy-friend and their relationship, James felt the marriage was reduced to a piece of paper. He had no feelings for Samantha, other than the fact that she was the mother of his children.

"That evening was the turning point in our relationship; and for the first time in my life, I actually allowed myself to love another man. Our time was spent discussing how our relationship might advance in the future, and he openly discussed divorce. He stated that Stephanie was supportive of his decision and encouraged James to finally enjoy life. Unfortunately, James was frightened of the idea of divorce.

"Apparently, Reverend, you and he did discuss the idea of divorce, but—"

"Yes, Jim and I did discuss the idea of divorce, but he said he was asking questions for a friend of his. I explained—"

"You told him it was wrong, and the Bible is against divorce. You said to him that a man who remarries openly commits adultery—"

"Well, he does!"

"But that's not the total truth, is it, Reverend?" Arleen overemphasized the word *reverend*. She didn't give Mike a chance to respond. "You see, Jesus said that when one of the people in the marriage commits adultery, the other may be granted a divorce!"[5]

Mike was taken back. The Jezebel was now quoting Scripture. He sat up straight. "Now you listen here—"

"No! You listen to me. You filled James' head with inaccurate information and half-truths. Dr. Nolan is correct; you should spend more time reading your Bible and less time talking about it."

5   Matthew 19:9

Mike began to stand up, but Tony grabbed his arm and pulled Mike back down.

"Sit down, Reverend."

Tony looked squarely at Arleen.

"I think this part of your conversation should be taken somewhere else—separate from the group. Wouldn't you both agree?"

Tony scanned back to Mike and then to Arleen. Meanwhile, the others in the room sat in silence. After waiting a minute or two, Tony pushed the meeting back on target.

"Mary, please be kind enough to read Arleen's last productive statement, so she may proceed with her story."

Without hesitation, Mary pulled the paper from the tray and began reading. "He stated that Stephanie was supportive of his decision and encouraged James to finally enjoy life. Unfortunately, James was frightened of the idea of divorce."

Tony still gripped Mike's arm but looked at Arleen with raised eyebrows, as if to say, "Well, go on."

"The issue of divorce for James was one he could not resolve. As time moved forward, he and I ignored the subject, and we let our love flourish."

Mike could not contain himself. "This is unbelievable. I can't listen to this trash."

Nate jumped to his feet and slammed his fist on the conference table. The telephone conference devices bounced up off the surface. Nate leaned over and pointed a finger at Mike.

"Do me a favor, Reverend, and stop talking, please. I, for one, want to hear what Arleen has to say, and I'm sick to death of your interruptions. I think I understand your position. In fact, I think most of us in this room understand your predicament. But please stop judging. You're not helping your cause of Christianity with this attitude. This may come as a shock, but I actually want to understand how this mess works out. Can we be adults here for once?"

Nate stuck his hand out and held it, waiting for Mike to take it. Mike reluctantly grabbed Nate's hand.

"Let's be big boys here and agree to disagree. You're a decent person, Mike, and I think you genuinely believe what you preach, but please try and be open-minded for once. If you continue with your judgments, I will lose all my respect for you, and I don't want to do that. Do you?"

A range of emotions swept through Mike like a tornado. As he processed the feelings, all he could see was devastation in the wake. Still, Nate refused to let go of Mike's hand and held on in a death grip. Breathing deeply, Mike could not win, and he knew it. He hated defeat, but at the same time, no one was on his side either.

Tom reached out and placed his hand on top of Nate's and Mike's.

"Jesus asked us to show compassion and not judge. Nate is asking for the same thing."

Tony placed his hand on top of the other hands.

"Reverend, you're intelligent and passionate. We're asking you to be compassionate."

Mike hesitated but appeared as if he would explode. Arleen stood and placed her hand on top of the hands.

"We are a team, Reverend. We are in disagreement, but I think we can maintain respect for one another."

Tony could see Arleen was genuine and hoped Mike would see it as well. When Arleen smiled, it melted Mike's cold heart.

"You all are telling me the truth and not blowing smoke up my backside?"

Everyone nodded in agreement. Mike let his shoulders slump.

"Okay, I accept."

"Thank you, Reverend. That took courage, and I'm proud of you." Nate squeezed his hand.

Mike sheepishly grinned. "Thank you, Nate." It was truly difficult for Mike to accept his defeat, but he had to admit the people in the room were genuine and honest.

"Mary, could you help me out again?" Arleen smiled at the stenographer.

The stenographer quickly grabbed the paper from the tray and read Arleen's last statement. Mary's voice was confident. "As time moved forward, he and I ignored the subject, and we let our love flourish."

"Thank you, Mary."

The stenographer smiled and nodded.

"James and I lived apart and nearly halfway around the world from each other. Whenever we had the chance, we connected. I started flying to Asia for Chanel, and we tried to coordinate our trips, so we could be together as often as possible. Despite our efforts, James and I were only able to be together four or five times a year. Each time we met, we immediately started where we left off. Our love for each other grew almost as fast as our passions.

"Two years ago, James began his quest to find my daughter. Then, tragically, Samantha and her boyfriend were killed in an auto accident. Because I had to appear in court regarding my daughter's paperwork, I could not attend the funeral. We talked by telephone, but

I could tell James felt guilty for her death. He stated that God was punishing him for having an affair with me.

"In a courageous move, I visited the Catholic nuns where I went to school. I wanted some answers; and, although I feared the nuns, I had nowhere else I could turn. Sister-Mother Antoinette was amazingly kind and compassionate with me. She invited me to stay a few days at the convent as their guest while she prayed and asked God for guidance. Reluctantly, I agreed.

"For three days, the whole convent took a vow of silence and prayed with Sister-Mother Antoinette, fasting from all meals, except bread and water in the evening. I was truly frightened. On Sunday, the third day, the convent bells began ringing. I assumed it was the start of morning Mass, so I joined the others in the chapel."

Arleen opened her notebook and thumbed to a particular page. She then took her palm and pressed the pages flat. She then began reading from her notebook.

"Sister-Mother Antoinette started quoting Bible verses, and another sister copied them down for me. Here is what she spoke. 'Second Chronicles 7:14—'If My people, who are called by My name, will humble themselves and pray and seek My face and turn from their wicked ways, then I will hear from heaven, and I will forgive their sin and will heal their land.' Luke 15:7—'I tell you that in the same way there will be more rejoicing in heaven over one sinner who repents than over ninety-nine righteous persons who do not need to repent.' Romans 12:17-18, 'Do not repay anyone evil for evil. Be careful to do what is right in the eyes of everyone. If it is possible, as far as it depends on you, live at peace with everyone.'

"She then quoted Mother Teresa. 'I am not sure exactly what heaven will be like, but I do hope that when we die and it comes time for God to judge us, He will *not* ask, how many good things have you done in your life? Rather, I suspect He will ask, how much *love* did you put into what you did? We cannot do great things. We can only do little things with great love.'

"I asked Mother Antoinette what all these words meant, and she smiled and said, 'Guilt comes from man and the devil. Love comes from God, and God loves you, my daughter. Dedicate your life to His love and in all areas of your life, do little things with great love.'"

CHAPTER SEVENTEEN

"I HAVE A QUESTION, ARLEEN." said Tom.

"Yes, Doctor?"

"Do you understand the information that Sister-Mother Antoinette shared with you?"

Arleen paused, thinking about Tom's question. "Are you asking me if I believe what she explained to me, or are you asking me if I believe in God?"

Tom was surprised by Arleen's response. It indicated she had given more thought to his question than the few moments she paused. Tom suspected Arleen anticipated the inquiry and had given it considerable thought. "At first, I asked because I wanted to know if you actually understood what Sister-Mother Antoinette shared with you. But, after hearing your response, I think I'd like to hear your answer to both questions."

Arleen looked down and folded her hands, pondering. She smiled and looked directly at Tom. "Yes, I believe in God. My knowledge is limited by the education I received from the Catholic sisters. James frequently shared his own beliefs with me, and we discussed them at length. To be honest, although I do believe in God, I'm confident it pales in comparison to your convictions. I understand what Sister-Mother Antoinette shared, and her message was very clear. There is the matter of whether my life matches her wisdom. I must confess—I think not."

"When you're ready, I'd be delighted to sit and discuss these things with you at a later date."

Arleen nodded her approval. "I think I would like that, Doctor. That would be terrific."

For a small time, the people in the room sat in silence. Then Tony asked, "Was there more, Arleen?"

Glancing down at her notes, she looked up and continued. "James and I met only three more times following my visit to the convent. I shared the words of Mother Antoinette, but I am unsure if James accepted my words of comfort.

"During our last meeting, I explained to James that I would finally be able to meet my daughter, her husband, and their children. James was filled with joy for me. He said he would be unable to travel for the next few months due to a particular project at work. It was an unusual visit, and for the first time since we had known each other, I felt James was withholding something from me. At the time, I dismissed the thought, saving the discussion for another occasion." Arleen paused, staring into space.

"We cried, and we kissed goodbye. It was the last time we shared an intimate moment, and the last time I saw James. And now . . ." Her voice trailed off.

Tears began to roll down Arleen's cheeks, and Tony again pushed the tissue box closer. Snatching a tissue from the box, Arleen blotted her tears and briefly laughed.

"I'm sorry. I miss James and love the man so much."

The group sat in honored silence, waiting for Arleen.

Leaning toward Arleen, Tony gravely asked, "Were you finished, or did you wish to add anything further?"

Arleen shook her head.

Tony looked at the stenographer. "Thank you, Mary, for your hard work and patience. Do you have an idea when we could expect a transcription?"

Mary smiled. "I should be finished by tomorrow evening." She started packing her equipment.

"Wow, that fast?" Tony was impressed.

"I have been transcribing every day. I will only need to finish today's work."

"Excellent work, Mary, and again, I can't thank you enough."

Mary smirked. "You'll be getting my bill."

Mary started for the door but stopped next to Arleen. After setting her bags down, Mary hugged Arleen and whispered in her ear.

Arleen smiled. "Thank you, Mary. You're very sweet."

Tony rubbed his flat palms together. "Okay, folks—are we ready for phase two?"

When Tony surveyed the room, the participants looked worn out and tired, but he ignored them and plunged forward.

"I know our meetings have been challenging for each of you, but now I have my own struggles. Tomorrow, I will be meeting with Jim's children. The topic of Jim's will is on the agenda. Once Mary sends me the transcripts, I'll have an email copy sent to each of you. Doctor, did you get a chance to find out if your pastor will be speaking at Jim's services?"

"He feels it isn't necessary; but if you'd like, he says he will prepare something. He indicated that once he initiates our introductions, he will remain available but in the background."

"Excellent, and thank you, Doctor. I think our group should meet the day before the service to go over any last-minute details. I believe we can accomplish our objectives in less than an hour. Are there any objections?"

After waiting a length of time, Tony wrapped the meeting up.

"Excellent job, folks. Please call my office if you have any questions. We will meet again in just over a week."

The participants slowly stood and stretched. People were interacting with each other as they made their way to the door, but their mood was subdued.

*   *   *

Back in his office, Tony picked up his telephone and dialed his secretary.

"Hello, Shelly, do me a favor and check with Jim Kreider's children. Find out if they have arrived and checked into their hotel. Please arrange for them to meet me in my office on . . . " Tony pulled his calendar up on his computer screen. "Hold one moment—Okay, it appears I have an opening in my schedule on Wednesday, between ten and one. Schedule an hour meeting and see if this time will work for them. If they need transportation, please ensure the company car and driver is available. Thank you, Shelly. Please hold all my calls for the rest of the day."

Tony folded his hands behind his neck and closed his eyes. Leaning back in his chair, he let out a long, slow sigh of relief. After a few minutes to collect his thoughts, he grabbed his cell phone and speed-dialed his wife's number.

"Hello, Mrs. Toncetti, are you busy?"

"I'm always busy, Tony. What's up?"

"How would you like to join me for a lovely dinner?"

"Would this date be with or without the children?" Rachel asked sarcastically.

"Your choice."

Rachel pondered the question. "May I make another suggestion?"

"Oh absolutely, my love. What did you have in mind?"

"Let's have an early family dinner, and then . . . you know that new spa that just opened near us?"

"Blue Lagoon?"

"That's it. How about we get a couples massage and soak in one of their private hot tubs afterward?"

"Excellent. I love the idea. I'll grab a nice bottle of champagne on my way home."

"Make it Dom Pérignon, lover boy—especially since it's a date night."

"I'm looking forward to this, Rachel. I love you."

"I love you, too. Bye."

Tony typed on his computer and quickly found the Blue Lagoon website. After perusing their beautiful photographs, he dialed the business and secured an appointment. Rubbing his flat palms together, Tony exclaimed out loud, "Excellent! After today, I need this." He then called the local liquor market down the street from his house and ordered a chilled bottle of Dom Pérignon.

"Whoa, Mr. Toncetti. A big celebration tonight?" The owner had a thick Italian accent.

Tony smiled. "Sort of."

*   *   *

When Robert Kreider walked up to Betty Thurgood's desk, he was wearing snug-fitting jeans and bright green tennis shoes. The pants were held up sans belt, and his youthful shirt was buttoned to the neck. A leather bag was draped over his shoulder, and he was wearing expensive dark sunglasses. He smiled down at Betty. She glanced up.

"Good morning, sir. How may I help you?"

"The name's Robert Kreider, and I have a meeting with Tony at ten."

Betty typed on her computer. "Yes, Mr. Kreider, please have a seat. Mr. Toncetti will see you in a moment. Are your sisters with you?"

Robert pointed his thumb over a shoulder. "In the lady's room, I'm afraid."

Betty nodded. "I'll escort you in when they arrive. Would you like something to drink?"

Robert smirked. "A dry martini—shaken, not stirred."

Betty's face was expressionless as she allowed the young man foolish airspace.

Robert coughed. "Do you have bottled water?"

Betty reached behind her desk into a hidden refrigerator in her credenza and then handed Robert the bottle. She barely let a smile form on her lips.

Robert sheepishly smiled. "Thanks."

Moments later, two young women of polar-opposite dress codes strode up to Betty's desk. The prim and proper receptionist unconsciously let a small gasp escape her lips. Stephanie was smartly dressed in nice black slacks and comfortable, low heels. She wore a colorful blouse and matching jacket. She was dressed professionally.

Staci, on the other hand, was actually frightening. Her head was shaved on either side, leaving a narrow mohawk, which she had dyed jet-black, and she had cemented her hair into evenly-spaced spikes that were sticking straight up—like a fan. Her makeup was tawdry, and her porcelain white skin was covered in brightly colored tattoos from her neck to her ankles. Metal piercings were placed into her tongue, ears, nose, eyebrows, cheek, and lips. Betty's imagination could only wonder where other piercings were placed on Staci's body. Staci wore a tie-dyed, loose-fitting shirt. Her tight-fitting, hip-hugging jeans stopped at mid-calf, and she wore old-fashioned lace-up boots with short, spiked heels. Lace ankle socks added the right flair to her ensemble.

Betty immediately pinched the bridge of her nose at the eyebrows, mimicking a headache. She was actually regaining her composure and needed a moment to gather her thoughts. Stephanie looked over her shoulder and spotted Robert, who was waiting to join his sisters.

"Robert! You're dressed like that?" Stephanie pointed at his clothes.

"Seriously? We're here to meet regarding our dead father, and you're gonna critique my clothing style? What about the freak standing next to ya?"

Stephanie made a wordless sound of disgust and rolled her eyes.

"Hey, freak," said Robert in friendlier tones.

"Hey back, Bobby."

The two siblings hugged, and then Robert held his arms open like a little boy for Stephanie. She started to lean forward and reluctantly hug her brother when he then taunted her with another joke.

"Come on, sis. Give me some sugar," he said, while grinning.

Disgusted, Stephanie pushed Robert away.

Robert shrugged, "Whatever."

Betty stood. "Please, follow me."

She ushered them through the frosted glass doors and into Tony's office. Two chairs were in front of Tony's desk, so Betty gathered a third from a small table in the back of the office.

"Please have a seat. I'll let Mr. Toncetti know you are here."

Betty closed the office door as she left. Stephanie took the center seat and got comfortable. Robert took the chair to her right but pulled it backward about a foot before sitting. Staci watched Robert and did the same with the seat to the left of Stephanie. Stephanie scowled as she glanced over her right, then left shoulder to see her siblings slightly behind her. She immediately thought they were being childish.

Robert had ulterior motives but wasn't about to share. Staci was curious, so she imitated Robert. Stephanie reached into her small handbag and pulled out a rectangular makeup mirror. Opening it, she inspected her face and then casually turned the mirror so she could see Staci. Pivoting the reflection, she saw Robert, who was grinning like a Cheshire cat. The mirror snapped shut with a loud click.

"Good morning, everyone. Thank you for meeting with me," said Tony as he burst into his office.

Robert stood to shake hands. "Counselor."

Tony slapped Robert's shoulder while shaking hands. "Good to see you, Robert. How is school?"

"Law studies are far more complicated than computer science."

Tony nodded. "And the pay is a lot better, too."

Turning his attention to Stephanie, Tony shook hands. "Why, Miss Stephanie, you are looking gorgeous this morning." Tony beamed a huge smile.

Stephanie produced a soft handshake and pursed her lips into a forced smile. "Mr. Toncetti."

"Tony, please! All of you should call me Tony."

When Tony looked over to Staci, his smile nearly vaporized. "Wow, Staci. You, ah, you've ah . . . my, oh my, you sure have grown up since the last time I saw you." Tony was struggling with his words.

Tony nervously shook Staci's hand, but abruptly ended the maneuver, retreating to his large, leather desk chair. He glanced up at all three of the Kreiders. Upon seeing Staci head-on, Tony immediately focused on the papers sitting on his desk. As he shuffled through the folders and papers, he mumbled aloud.

"Now, where did I put those papers?" Finding the correct folder, he exclaimed, "Ah, here it is." He set the folder on the top of the other work sitting on his desk and rested his hand on the folder.

"Tell me, how are your accommodations?"

"The hotel is comfortable," said Stephanie.

"Are you kidding me? It's fantastic. Thanks," quipped Robert.

"Like, what were you expecting, Steph? The Taj Mahal?" smirked Staci.

Stephanie glared at her two siblings.

Tony rubbed his flat palms together. "Excellent." He then opened the top folder. "First off, let me say again how terribly sorry I am for your loss."

Stephanie blurted out, "Oh, cut to the chase, Tony. Dad's been dead for weeks—no thanks to you for not telling us. I mean, we had no say in the arrangements, and I feel like I'm not important in this situation."

Behind Stephanie's back, Robert was making over-exaggerated facial expressions and silently mimicking his sister's speech. Staci giggled, which Robert found hilarious. Stephanie twisted her neck toward Robert, catching him before he could stop himself because he was showing off to Staci. Robert instantly acted normal with a "who me?" expression. Fuming mad, Stephanie bolted from her chair and aimed for the office door.

Tony jumped from his leather chair, "Stephanie, wait." But it was too late. By the time Tony rounded the desk, she was gone. Tony reached over the desk and snapped up the telephone, punching one of the buttons.

"Yes, Betty, is Stephanie there in the lobby?"

"Why, yes, sir. She's in front of the elevator."

Tony almost screamed, "Stop her immediately. Don't let her leave!"

Betty was flustered, "How shall I do that, Mr. Toncetti?"

Tony was frustrated. "I don't know; just stop her. I'll be right there." Tony slammed the phone down. Turning to face Robert, Tony pointed a fatherly finger at the young man. "Good grief, Robert. Grow up, man!" Tony dashed out the office. As he race-walked toward the elevators, he became aware of the attention of the other office personnel, so Tony tried to smile and act nonchalant.

Robert leaned over and whispered, "Wow, what a stick in the mud. She always gets her panties in a twist over nothing."

Staci gravely said, "Dude, you should, like, back off. You ticked off Tony."

Robert gulped. "You're probably right. I'll apologize when they get back."

"If she comes back, Bobby."

"Oh, she will," said Robert, but he wasn't too confident.

Tony arrived at the front lobby, finding Betty with her arm wrapped around Stephanie's shoulder. Stephanie was crying. Betty was trying to console her but failing miserably. She actually looked relieved when Tony appeared.

"Thank you, Mr. Toncetti."

Tony nodded at Betty and then tried to steer Stephanie back toward his office. Stephanie stood her ground, arms crossed.

"Robert is so immature. And he's exasperating!"

Tony was at a loss. "I harshly reprimanded him."

Stephanie glared at Tony, doubting his efforts would do any good. She made a wordless groan and rolled her eyes.

"Please come back with me?"

After a lengthy pause, she reluctantly agreed. Relieved, Betty weakly smiled as Tony escorted Stephanie back to his office.

When Tony and Stephanie walked into the office, Robert stood to his feet. "Look, Stephanie, please accept my apology. I was a jerk."

"Humph!" was her reply.

Tony was still upset with Robert. "You're supposed to be learning something at college, especially if you want to be a lawyer. I'm extremely disappointed in your behavior. I expected more from you."

Robert was embarrassed and tried to sound sincere. "You're right, Counselor. Again, I apologize for being a jerk to both of you. It won't happen again. I promise."

Stephanie refused to face Robert and stood behind her chair, staring ahead. She spasmodically jerked when Robert touched her shoulder.

"Come on, Steph. I apologized. Don't make this worse."

She shrugged his hand off. "Really? Do you think it's possible you could change?"

"I promise."

After waiting a long time, Stephanie conceded and sat in her chair. Tony waited for everyone to get comfortable. He lifted a page from the folder.

"I have your father's will. He wrote a short letter to be read before I disclose the contents of the will." Tony cleared his throat.

My dearest Stephanie, Robert, and Staci,

If this letter is being read to you by my attorney, Tony Toncetti, then I am no longer among the living on this earth. I know you will be shocked and probably upset, especially Stephanie because I chose not to involve you in my arrangements. There wasn't anything you could do to help me, and the last thing I wanted was having you stand around my bed as I lay there sick and dying.

All of you feel that perhaps your mother and I didn't love you or love you enough. I can assure you, your mother and I discussed our love and appreciation on many occasions. We are proud of all of you. Yes, your mom and I didn't see eye-to-eye, but we did agree one hundred percent that our children were the greatest gifts we ever received.

The panic and grief you're feeling will pass once Tony reads my will because I have made preparations and taken care of your college needs. I'm sorry I won't be around to see you get married or see my grandchildren. So many hopes and dreams don't matter when you're lying on your deathbed. No one plans to die; it just happens, and I thank God there was time to prepare.

To Stephanie: I know we disagreed on your choices, but guess what? I respect your decisions. Your fiancé, Charles, seems like a great man, destined for great things. I will be with you in spirit the day you walk down that aisle to get married and brightly smile from heaven.

To Robert: Yes, I bemoaned your career change after being so close to graduating, and I know Tony influenced your decision, but I'm proud of your goals. Do me a favor—don't become an obnoxious attorney who charges outrageous fees! No offense, Tony, but I want Robert to bring light into the world—especially in the dark world of the legal system. Robert, use your knowledge to help people and save them from the injustices they cannot fight themselves.

To Staci: You are and always have been my little bunny rabbit. Although you've decorated yourself, I still love you. Please think long and hard about your choices—especially when it comes to a partner or husband. You deserve the very best because you're worth it. Never forget that! Like you, I had hidden artistic talents, only I didn't know it until it was too late.

I've chosen five people to represent me at my funeral service. Listen to what they have to say because they will speak the truth about who I am. If either of you wishes to speak, please do so because I'll be there listening.

There is nothing else that matters more, in this life, than relationships. Hold on to the good ones, reject the people who steal or destroy your dreams, and brightly shine the inner light inside each of you. Leave this world a better place wherever you go.

One last instruction: Robert, I have a personal note, and Tony will give it to you today. It is a sealed envelope. It's something I'd like read at the end of my service. Thanks.

May God bless each of you and be your guide each and every day. He is the answer to everything. All you have to do is ask Him!

I love you very much,

Dad

When Tony set the letter down, he fought back the tears because the message touched his heart. He just hoped that his children would feel the same way about him when he was gone.

Tony looked up. Every one of the Kreider children was softly crying, so Tony waited in silence.

Stephanie pulled a small packet of tissues from her purse. She offered it to Staci and Robert. They each took one and dabbed wet cheeks. Being sensitive to the situation, Tony excused himself from the room.

"I'll be right back," he quietly mumbled.

For an eternity, the Kreiders sat quietly, absorbing their father's words. Slowly, Robert reached across the desk and picked up the letter Tony had just read. Stephanie and Staci scooted their chairs into a tight circle with Robert. In the quietness, they each reread the letter, focusing on the paragraphs addressed to them personally.

In a rare display of affection, Stephanie reached out with her arms extended and embraced her brother and sister. They locked arms and hugged tightly, like a football team in a huddle, sobbing uncontrollably. They touched their heads together, the same way they did as small children whenever they heard their parents arguing and fighting. A flood of long, repressed memories washed over the group, recalling the multiple times they repeated this exercise when they were still living at home.

Tony barely opened the door and spied on the trio. When they had recomposed themselves, he entered the office quietly, sitting behind his desk. Tony waited for the right timing. Reaching into his top drawer, he withdrew a yellowed envelope with handwritten notes.

"Is that the envelope Dad spoke of?" Robert asked.

Tony nodded and handed it to Robert.

Holding it like a treasure, Robert studied the handwritten notes.

"What's inside, Bobby?" asked Staci.

"I dunno. It says it should be opened for Dad's service." Robert looked at Tony. "Do I open it now or wait?" Robert's finger was poised under the envelope's sealed flap, ready to rip it open.

Tony shrugged. "What are the instructions?"

Robert read the words. "For my son Robert. To be opened and read at my funeral service. That's it."

"Well, you're studying to be a lawyer. How would you interpret the message?"

Robert let a small crack form in the corner of his mouth. "The first part is easy and direct. It's addressed to me. The last part is tougher because there are two instructions."

"Are they separate instructions or co-joined?"

Robert's eyebrows narrowed as he studied the writing.

"Is there a comma in the last sentence?" Tony asked.

Shaking his head slowly, Robert said, "No. It's one sentence with two instructions, co-joined by the word and."

"Which means what, my young lawyer?"

Robert looked disappointed but felt proud that Tony would call him a lawyer. He took the envelope and stashed it in his leather bag. "I'll wait, as instructed."

Tony smiled. "Excellent."

Staci was very disappointed. "Seriously, dude?"

Robert shrugged. "Sorry. I wanted to know myself, but it'll have to wait."

Retrieving the will from Jim Kreider's folder, Tony explained why he wouldn't be reading from the beginning. "The actual will starts on page two because the first page is perfunctory clauses found in all wills. I am of sound mind, et cetera, blah, blah, blah. Is that okay?" Tony made hand gestures.

The three Kreiders nodded.

"Excellent." Tony started reading the will from page two:

> I, James W. Kreider, have disposed of all assets (home, furnishings, autos, time-shares), amassing my wealth into three separate and equal trust accounts. There are accounts for Stephanie, Robert, and Staci Kreider.
>
> All outstanding debits, credit cards, and loans are settled without burdens set aside for my heirs to deal with. Costs for cremation services have been paid for in advance, which also includes funeral service expenses.
>
> Hospice care for my remaining days is settled and paid for.
>
> All that remains of my wealth is divided into three equal, remaining shares with the following caveats:
>
> The college fees for Stephanie and Robert have been previously paid for and will continue to be paid for the remainder of their current degrees.
>
> Staci has not received any college tuition, and I wish to reimburse her for tuition and her remaining fees toward her current degree.
>
> Therefore, Staci will get a portion over and above the equal parts for Stephanie and Robert for her college tuition.
>
> The shares will be distributed in the following manner:
>
> Each semester year, each child will receive a check from their trust for $23,000 for college expenses.

The amount will be deposited in their personal bank accounts.

Because they are each at different college levels, any remaining balance in their trust will be distributed in annual installments until all trust funds are depleted.

Each installment shall not exceed $25,000 per year.

This will shall not be modified in any manner.

Signed, James W. Kreider.

Tony set the will down and looked up at the Kreider children, who were absorbing this new information. He could see they were processing, calculating, wondering what was next. Tony knew he must be prepared for their reactions because this is usually where world war three would break out. Even among semi-placid families, who swore allegiance and love for each other, they would turn on each other over the reading of a person's last will and testament.

CHAPTER EIGHTEEN

"STACI HAS REFUSED TO ACCEPT any money from Dad for college before now. Why should she get more than Stephanie and me?" Robert was agitated and angling to pull his older sister into the argument to join his side.

Staci's response was sharp and fast. "Because, Bobby, I watched you and Stephanie constantly argue with Dad about college and tuition. Like, you know, Dad claimed he was going bankrupt dealing with our education, so I didn't want to be a burden. I refused, but knowing what I know now, I guess I was, like, wrong about Dad."

Stephanie turned toward her brother, placing her body between Staci and Robert. "I have no problem with Staci getting paid for her college. You and I have had it pretty easy monetarily. Give her what's due."

Staci interjected one more comment. "Besides, Bobby, you're getting two degrees, and we only got, like, one. So, quit complaining."

Sulking, Robert shrugged. "Whatever."

Tony hated this part of his job, more than anything else. Perfectly ordinary families experienced earth-shattering fractures whenever money was involved. He watched level-headed individuals quickly turn into rabid animals, scavenging a carcass bare—until every morsel was stripped from the dry bones. Seeing this happen to Jim's children was disappointing.

Pulling additional papers from Jim Kreider's folder, Tony placed them in front of the trio.

"This document indicates you have witnessed your father's will and acknowledge the terms and conditions. It also states you agree." He handed a pen to Stephanie. "There is a place for each of you to sign. Please sign all four copies. You will each receive an original. The last copy will be filed in the probate court, unless . . ." Tony stared at Robert. " . . . unless someone wishes to contest the will. If that happens, there will be no trusts or checks until the matter is settled in court, and I'll get my fees from your trusts for defending your father."

Tony knew he was stretching the truth because Jim had already agreed on Tony's payment in advance. Still, Tony was trying to avoid probate court and the headache it causes. He hoped his tactics were working, and Robert wasn't wise enough to know Tony was mildly bluffing.

Robert slowly nodded his head, indicating mild resistance, but was also in agreement.

Before her brother could change his mind, Stephanie placed her signature on the pages and pushed them toward Robert. She held the pen for him to sign and was hoping her gesture was convincing.

"I don't know what got into me. Sorry." Robert quickly signed the papers and pushed them toward Staci. "Still, I don't think it's totally fair."

Trying to put Robert at ease, Stephanie reassured her brother. "We're all dealing with the loss differently, Robert. Thank you for agreeing."

After Staci had signed the documents, Tony snatched the papers up and tucked them into the folder. He then rubbed his palms together. "Excellent. I will be meeting with the guest speakers for about an hour on Friday to discuss any last-minute details. All of you are welcome to be here, and I would recommend it. This will give you a chance to meet them before Saturday's funeral service." Pushing them toward a commitment, Tony added, "I'll send the limo by the hotel and pick you guys up."

"Where will the service be?" asked Stephanie.

"Dr. Nolan's church. It's called Bread of Life Church."

"Why not our old church?" inquired Robert.

Tony's expression became serious. "It wasn't convenient." Tony quickly moved to the next item on their agenda. "Now Friday, the driver will pick you up for our last meeting, and he'll also pick you up on Saturday. Are there any questions?"

All three gravely nodded their heads in response.

Staci raised her hand as if she were a kid in school. Her voice was timid. "I have one."

"Yes, what is it, Staci?"

"In Dad's letter, he, like, said something about discovering his inner artist—or something like that. I don't remember his exact words. Like, what did he mean?"

Stephanie and Robert shifted in their chairs. This question caught everyone's attention. Tony smiled.

"It seems your father was a painter. The only person aware of this was your neighbor, Joe Langley."

"School teacher, Uncle Joe, our old neighbor?" blurted Robert.

Tony continued to smile and nodded.

"Are we talking paint-by-numbers artist or something else?" asked Stephanie.

Staci sat upright and leaned forward. "Dad painted oils, water-colors, charcoal? Like what medium are we looking at, Mr. Toncetti?"

Standing, Tony indicated they should follow him. Resembling a bunch of grade school students on a field trip, the trio tagged behind Tony as he led them to a room in the back of the office complex. He held the door open and motioned for them to enter. The room was dark, but the moment Robert stepped into the blackness, a sensor detected movement, and the lights flickered on. The area was an empty room large enough for a small conference of one hundred people.

Surrounding the room's walls were various paintings on stands. Above each painting, individual lights illuminated the canvases, displaying colorful images. The Kreider children stood dumbfounded, staring. Staci immediately walked around the room, examining the displayed images. She stopped in front of an impressionistic painting, which demonstrated artistic skills similar to Claude Monet.

Her clashing shadow juxtaposed the soft pastel colors of the painting. She reached out and gingerly let her fingers dance and caress the rough texture of the oils. When she turned to face the others, tears were streaming down her cheeks.

"Do you, like, see it?"

Robert shrugged and shook his head, totally uninterested.

"That day in the park. I was so sick. Like, we went to the park, Dad said, to cheer me up."

Stephanie walked alongside her sister and stared at the painting. "You're right! Robert, come here. You remember that day, don't you?"

After joining his sisters, Robert stood staring at the image. It was a typical impressionism with blurred colors, no distinct edges—as if the picture was out of focus or from a fading dream.

Staci traced out a dark patch of color. "That's me, sitting by the river." She moved her hand to the left. "Like, that's you, Bobby, skipping stones across the water." She moved her hand to the far right. "And see, this is Mom and Dad, and that's you, Stephanie. Like, you guys were sitting on a blanket getting lunch ready. It was a beautiful day. We laughed, ate lunch, and . . . " Staci's voice trailed off.

Lifting the painting from the stand, Staci pulled the frame to her chest as if it were a precious child. She slowly slumped to the floor and began rocking.

"I miss you, Mommy and Daddy." After a long pause, she looked up at Stephanie. "Like, you know, this just isn't fair."

Robert bent over and gingerly took the frame. "May I?"

Staci let go, and Robert set the painting back on the stand. He studied the image carefully. Then, as if an imaginary light bulb went on, he smiled.

"I remember now. I was maybe eight or nine years old. Dad packed our lunch and made us peanut butter and jelly sandwiches."

Staci smiled. "Yes, and you were, like, crazy that day. You took your sandwich apart and laid potato chips on the inside, then squished it all together."

"I think I remember you asking me to do the same for you."

"It sounded awful at the time, but it was really good."

Robert's face contorted. "Mom refused to eat and was mad because Dad didn't fix something wholesome. They got into a serious argument over stupid sandwiches."

Stephanie glumly added, "Yeah, *Father Knows Best* meets *Mommy Dearest!*"

Staci stood facing Tony. "May I keep this one, Mr. Toncetti?"

"Of course. In fact, all of the paintings belong to you three. You may do with them as you wish, but—" Tony paused to ensure he had their attention. "Would you mind if we displayed them at the funeral service? I think other people would like an opportunity to view them."

It took only a moment for the Kreiders to quickly agree.

"I would like to add another request, if I may. The five people your father chose to speak have also requested an opportunity to purchase a painting. I've made no commitments but merely said I would make the request known. Before you answer, you must know that initially, Joe Langley volunteered the knowledge concerning the paintings because they were at his house."

"Why at Uncle Joe's?"

"Joe set up the studio for your father, bought the equipment and teaching material, and made sure your dad had a retreat."

Staci cheerily responded, "Then he should get one."

"Hold on a sec, freak." Robert faced Tony. "Didn't you say they were willing to buy the paintings?"

"That's what I said, yes—"

"Robert Kreider, have you no shame?" Stephanie had her hands on her hips.

"Oh, knock it off, Stephanie. You're not our mom. If the paintings have value, let them buy one."

"Dude? Like, where is all this greed coming from?"

Tony stepped in to abate their arguing. "Please, please, listen to me. Take a day or two before you decide. Talk among yourselves, and, when you have a plan, let me know. This doesn't require an immediate decision."

Tony picked up a black, three-ring binder and extended his arm. "There are color photographs of all the paintings inside. We cataloged them. Take this back to your hotel and talk it over first."

The Kreiders were in a somber mood as Tony escorted them to the elevator to say goodbye. He watched the doors quietly close.

* * *

When Tony returned to his office, he dialed his wife.

"Are you interested in another spa date, sweetie?"

Rachel paused. "Bad day, hon?"

Tony loudly sighed but didn't answer.

"Same time and place?"

"I'll get the Dom Pérignon."

"I love you, Tony."

"I know. And I love you, too. Bye for now."

When Tony dialed the liquor store and made a second request for the chilled champagne, the owner was shocked.

"Twice in one week, huh? Does Mrs. Toncetti know about dis?" His thick Italian accent distorted the words.

"As a matter of fact, she does. It's her favorite!"

"Whoa, Mr. Toncetti, you've gotta let me in on your secret."

Tony snorted, "Stress, my friend— seasoned with loads of drama."

* * *

For the next two days, Tony was relieved, appreciating the break from the Jim Kreider mess, when Shelly pensively stepped into his office. She waited. Tony looked up and smiled.

"Yes, Shelly?"

"Sorry to bother you, Mr. Toncetti, but a Robert Kreider is on the phone asking for you. Are you in a meeting?"

Tony contemplated long and hard on the question, then sighed noisily. "Put him though, Shelly."

"He's holding on line one, sir."

"Thank you."

"Oh, and Mr. Toncetti?"

After picking up the phone, Tony's finger hovered above the keypad.

"You were right. The Kreider children didn't match up when I met them in person— especially the youngest, Staci."

Tony nodded in agreement.

As Shelly walked out, she closed Tony's office door.

"Good afternoon, Robert."

"Counselor. Please tell me you're not allowing Staci's teenage boyfriend to attend the funeral. Dad would be livid if he knew."

Tony's patience was exhausted, and he showed no inclination to shelter Robert from his wrath, yet he tempered his comments. Tony's voice was firm as he chastised Robert. "Listen very carefully to what I'm about to say, Robert. Are you listening?"

"Yes, sir," sputtered Robert.

Tony knew he was about to tell a little lie, but he was tired and no longer wanting to deal with spoiled children who felt sanctimonious. "Your father was very specific concerning who would attend his funeral. Unless you can produce documentation to the contrary, I suggest you reconsider your position in this matter."

Robert was quiet.

"Just as I suspected. I also know you telephoned your sister earlier and proposed this same argument, and I must tell you, Robert, I'm quite disappointed in your attitude. Please cease and desist. Otherwise, you're bordering on destroying all respect I have for you and ruining our relationship. Besides, please understand that our firm controls the trusts for all three of you. It would be such a shame to have clerical errors delaying your payments or school tuition."

"Tony? Are you threatening me?"

This time Tony went quiet, waiting for Robert to process the conversation.

"Well?"

Tony had to control himself. He was enjoying the situation too much. Tony spoke softly, with confidence.

"Robert?"

"What?"

"Stop being a jerk. What's eating at you, son, because honestly, I don't understand where your attitude is coming from?"

Robert was breathing hard into the phone, but not talking. He knew Tony was correct and could make his life miserable. Robert hated Marcus and what Staci was doing with her life. He held Marcus responsible for the condition Staci was living in.

Suddenly, Tony saw with clarity what was happening. He felt compassion for the confused young man.

"Robert, the pain of losing your father must be awful. You feel the responsibility to keep your small family together. But you cannot fill your dad's shoes, nor can you fix any situations you deem unsuitable in your perfect little world."

"So, you think this is about perfectionism?" Robert seethed.

"No, I think you're overcompensating for the pain of your loss."

Robert bit his lower lip and fought back the tears. Tony could hear him sniff into the phone.

"Listen to me carefully, Robert. You are not in charge, and this isn't your funeral service or is it about you. It's about your father, whom I respect. In fact, after hearing from the team your dad chose to represent him, I have even more respect for the man. So, do me a favor and drop your pretense."

Robert groaned loudly. He attempted to defend his position from several perspectives, but with each start of a sentence, he quickly realized he was boxed into a corner. Like a chess game, when one opponent forces the other to yield, Robert suspected Tony was about to call out "checkmate."

"If it makes you feel any better, I was surprised by Staci's appearance as well; but as a lawyer, I'm taught to not judge a book by its cover. You must learn to do the same if you want to be a successful lawyer."

It was a no-win situation, and Robert knew it. Reluctantly, he conceded Tony's position.

"Okay, Counselor, you're correct, and I was wrong."

Tony could hear the resignation in Robert's voice. "You mean that?"

"Yes. You win."

"Robert, it's not about winning. It's about doing what is right. Hopefully, you'll come to understand the sensitivity required for this whole situation regarding your father."

"Well, I don't, but I'm going to quit now."

"We don't always get our way, Robert. Sometimes we negotiate for the best possible solution, even if the results aren't perfect."

"So you say."

After a period of silence, the line went dead as Robert disconnected the call.

Frustrated, Tony stared at the phone receiver in his hand. A flat tone was heard, but eventually, it gave way to a pulsating busy signal, followed by a monotone female voice making the usual declaration. Tony cradled the receiver, wondering if it would ever get easier.

* * *

The conference room of Toncetti, Silva, Barnes, and Smith was cramped and noisy early Friday afternoon. In addition to the five team members chosen to represent Jim Kreider at his funeral, the three Kreider children were now present. Tony requested his secretary, Shelly, join the group.

Various refreshments dotted the credenza, along with beverages; and when Tony entered the room, he could feel a shift in the mood. Everyone was casually chatting and intermingling, but Tony's presence brought the group to an abrupt halt. The participants stared at Tony, waiting.

Tony hated that his position created such tension. He pushed his way toward the credenza, greeting folks and shaking hands. As soon as he started filling a china plate with food, the room immediately returned to its loud conversations.

The three Kreider children were comfortably mixing, and even Staci had dressed in casual attire. Her Mohawk hair was not spiked in its usual fashion but lay relaxed. Other than the tattoos and piercings, Staci appeared normal.

Setting his plate at the head of the conference table, Tony poured himself a cup of coffee and sat down. Moments later, the various team members slowly threaded their way to their customary positions and sat down. Joe deliberately sat next to Dr. Nolan, leaving the far end of the conference table open for the Kreider children.

Stephanie selected the armed chair at the end where Joe Langley had initially sat during their meetings. Robert and Staci sat on either side of Stephanie. Slowly the room quieted, and Tony waited for a natural break to occur before addressing the group.

Wiping his mouth on a monogrammed, white, linen napkin, Tony took a moment to initiate eye contact with each person. "First off, I want to thank all of you for being here today. Your commitment to honor Jim Kreider is admirable. The work accomplished in this room was not an easy task. We've all experienced emotional upsets and challenges. Yet I believe we've also grown to understand each other and appreciate Jim Kreider better. Personally, I know I've learned more about the man than I ever knew and this was made possible because each of you has been honest and open. I can clearly see why Jim chose you to represent his life.

"As I'm sure most of you have already introduced yourselves to the three Kreiders, let me formally welcome Jim's family. Stephanie." Tony extended his hand to the far end of the conference table, and Stephanie nodded to the group. "Jim's son, Robert," who then raised his hand slightly. "And Staci." She softly smiled at the group, looking nervous.

"Now, I'll introduce the team—starting with Nate." Tony extended his hand.

"Hello, I'm Nathanial Martin, vice president at Tynedex Corporation. Your father and I have worked together for nearly forty years. Please accept my condolences for your loss."

"My name is Arleen Chenair, and I work for Chanel S.A. of France. I have known your father for almost thirty years. We met before, but I'm not sure if you remember. I can only imagine the sadness you must feel. James was a wonderful man. He will be terribly missed."

Tony turned and faced Pastor Mike.

"You already know who I am. Oh my, look how much you three have grown. I'm sorry for your loss. Jim was a great father." He turned and faced Tom.

"Of all the difficult tasks in this world, witnessing the death of a young father is monumental. Mere words cannot express my grief, much less yours. I pray the fond memories of your dad will sustain you during this time," said Dr. Nolan. He looked to Joe.

"Hey guys, great to see you," began Joe. "It's been a long time. I just wanted to tell you how much your dad bragged about all three of you. Your dad loved you very much, and he was proud of you—yes, even you, Staci."

"Thank you, Uncle Joe," said Stephanie.

"Yes, thank you, Uncle Joe, and all of you for your kind words," agreed Robert.

"We're really touched by your words. Thank you," Staci mumbled.

"Excellent. Now, Stephanie has indicated she wishes to speak tomorrow, as well as Robert. Staci has declined." Turning to his secretary, Tony said, "Shelly, if you please."

She stood and began handing out a printed document.

"As Shelly hands out the papers, please note that this is a draft for Jim's service tomorrow. We are open to discussions, suggestions, or changes. Please take a moment and look over the agenda."

Dr. Nolan raised his hand slightly. "Tony, our pastor, Ken, has indicated he will introduce everyone and then give a closing prayer at the end of the service."

"Thank you, Doctor."

"If it's all the same to you, Doctor, I'd be honored to give the opening prayer," Rev. Mike requested.

Tom smiled. "Excellent, Mike. That's a splendid idea, and I'll let Ken know."

Shelly made notes concerning the changes.

"Okay, are there any other comments?"

The room was silent.

"How about any changes to the itinerary?"

Several individuals shook their heads.

Tony rubbed his flat palms together. "Excellent. This was supposed to be a draft, but it appears everyone has signed off carte blanche."

"Excuse me, Tony." This time Robert lifted his hand.

"Yes, Robert."

He set the black, three-ring binder with the color copies of the paintings on the conference table. "I was thinking," he glanced over at Stephanie and Staci for approvals. "What I mean is, we thought that if this group is interested in any of the paintings, they may like to let us know by—"

Staci interrupted. "We wanted individual paintings for ourselves. The rest, we put sticky notes on each picture with a number. Look through the book, and, if you'd like one of the paintings, put your name on the sticky note."

Stephanie assumed the lead. "We all feel Uncle Joe should get to select his painting first. It's a family thing."

"Thanks, guys. You have no idea what this means to me. I figured they were for sale. At least that was my understanding," said Joe, humbled by their generosity.

"They were originally, but after my sisters and I talked about it, we came up with another idea." Robert motioned for Staci to finish.

"We'd like you to pick out your own picture. Then, whatever you think it's worth to you, we'd like you to donate the money to the local food bank. It was daddy's favorite charity. Everyone will donate something, except Uncle Joe. And that's because he got daddy painting in the first place."

Nate interrupted, "Are you sure? The paintings are valuable, and we're all willing to pay whatever price you set."

Stephanie closed the book and pushed it toward Joe. "No, we've discussed this at length and feel this is what our father would want. The remaining paintings will be priced and made available for sale to the general public after the service."

Tony was dumbfounded. He didn't think they had it in them. He would have loved to have been a fly on the wall for *that* conversation.

"Stephanie, I'll make sure the paintings are marked accordingly when they go on display during the service tomorrow. Also, please provide the food bank contact information to Shelly, and we'll have it printed in the service handout. There may be others who'd like to donate as well." Tony looked at his watch and then stood.

"Excellent work, folks. Please stay as long as you'd like and talk. I said we'd be finished in under an hour, and I'm afraid I have work calling me. Thanks again and see you tomorrow. Shelly will show you out when you're finished."

CHAPTER NINETEEN

"EXCUSE ME—MISS CHENAIR?"

Arleen turned away from the painting she was viewing. She regarded the young woman standing in front of her. "If I remember correctly, you must be Staci. Please, call me Arleen."

"Yes, ma'am."

After shaking hands and a moment of awkward silence, the two women stood staring at each other. Arleen initiated the conversation.

"Is everything okay?"

"I'm sorry. I don't mean to stare, but you're so beautiful. Even dressed in all black, you're so, so pretty."

Dismayed, Arleen struggled with her words. "Why, thank you. And you, you look very nice as well, Staci."

Staci's black hair was spiked in a razor Mohawk, and she had painted the ends bright purple. She was dressed in solid black pants and a long-sleeved, turtleneck top, the collar wrapped tightly around her neck. It did the job of hiding most of Staci's tattoos. She wore lipstick to color-match her purple-tipped hair. Staci rolled her eyes. She recognized the shocked looked on people's faces.

"Ah, thanks," hesitated Staci. "Can I, like, ask you a question?"

Arleen nodded and smiled.

"You and Daddy had something going on, didn't you?"

Arleen scanned the room, making sure no one was within ear-shot. She acted as if she didn't understand. "Whatever do you mean?"

"You and Daddy were an item. Am I right?"

Arleen frowned and felt a tight knot in her throat. "Why would you say that?" Arleen was still pretending to not comprehend the young woman.

"Yesterday, there was a sparkle in your eyes when you talked about Daddy," Staci smirked. "Look, it's okay with me, and I didn't mention this to the others, but I'd like to know."

Arleen stiffened. "Your father and I were very close friends. That's all."

Staci knew otherwise and rolled her eyes. "Like the impressionistic painting you were staring at just moments ago, the one with your name tag on it—you totally selected it for a reason."

"Yes, of course. It's beautiful."

"Well, for one, that painting matches a photo I found on Daddy's cell phone. In the photo, it's clear you and Daddy were kissing, but I suspect someone else took the picture."

"Your father's cell phone?" Arleen faltered, shocked to hear this information.

"Look, Arleen, like I don't really care about what you and Daddy did. I just want to know the truth. Daddy was lonely after Mommy went off with that stupid young man from her job. And it only got worse when they were killed. I mean, like Daddy deserved better. And now, here I am talking to this beautiful woman that I suspect was Daddy's girlfriend. So, tell me, what's the truth?"

Arleen stammered with her words. "Was there anything else on your father's cell phone?"

Staci reached into her purse and thoughtfully pulled out Jim Kreider's cell phone. She extended her hand toward Arleen.

"It was among his stuff from the hospice. Like, the battery was totally dead, of course, but I recharged it."

Arleen wore a look of concern.

"Look, do me a favor. If you want me to send any pictures to your phone, that's okay. But I'm going to delete certain ones when you're done. And don't worry—I haven't shown these to anyone else."

Arleen's hands were shaking as she took the phone. She muttered, "Merci beaucoup."

As Arleen viewed the images stored on Jim's phone, she quickly found herself embarrassed. Jim had saved some very intimate photos. She had no idea he had kept the images or how he took them.

"If it's okay with you, I would like to have them all."

Staci took the phone, and, in a matter of minutes, she typed with her thumbs. "Done! Like you want any of the texts or emails, too?"

Nervously looking around the church foyer, Arleen nodded.

Again, Staci rapidly tapped on the cell's front screen.

Arleen was almost in tears from embarrassment and the joy of finding the new information. "Thank you so much, Staci. How can I repay you?"

Staci shoved the phone into her purse. She then surprised Arleen by wrapping her arms around the woman, giving her a huge, child-to-parent-type hug. Since Staci was at least a foot shorter than Arleen, her actions required Arleen to bend over at the waist to accommodate the shorter woman. Staci whispered into Arleen's ear.

"I'm just glad Daddy found someone like you to love. I hope you two were happy."

At that instant, anyone walking by would see two women crying and hugging. It would be natural, especially since they were attending a memorial service. Dr. Nolan and Pastor Mike were standing in the foyer of the church and spotted Staci and Arleen sobbing.

* * *

The entry foyer of the Bread of Life Church was enormous. The vast, open space was lit with modern lighting. A visitor's welcome station was located in the middle of the foyer and manned by several eager and smiling teens. A coffee and beverage kiosk dominated the right side of the entry area. A crowd of people milled around the counter, ordering drinks and chatting with friends. The foyer was now crowded with people examining the paintings and greeting one another. The paintings were arranged in a large arc behind the welcome booth and on easels, with individual lamps illuminating them.

"This place is huge, Doctor. It's bigger than a movie theater."

"Our congregation is growing fast, Pastor Mike. Unfortunately, I only have the opportunity to know the individuals who attend the same service my wife and I go to every Sunday morning."

Astonished, Mike blurted, "You have more than one service?"

"In truth, we have three on Sunday morning and one on Saturday night. Each service has about 1100 people."

Sounding annoyed, Mike exclaimed, "You have nearly 5,000 members?"

Dr. Nolan nodded. "How large is your church, Mike?"

Dismayed, Mike shook his head. "Perhaps 600, maybe."

"Come, let me show you around."

The church quickly filled with arriving guests, and the noise was now decibels higher. As ushers unfolded padded chairs from several carts and filled the aisles and empty space around the sanctuary, people immediately sat in the new seats.

When Joe Langley entered the foyer with a slender, attractive woman on his arm, he was dressed in black slacks, a white shirt, and a dark tie. The black sports coat was too big for Joe, but Joe strutted through the crowd and exclaimed, "Good grief, this place is enormous!" Upon hearing his thunderous voice, Staci disconnected from Arleen and immediately ran toward Joe.

"Hey, little bunny. You doing okay?" said Joe.

Staci wrapped her arms tightly around Joe as if he were a lost relative discovered after years of searching. Joe kissed her on top of her head, laboring to pry his body free.

"I'd like you to meet my lady friend, Sandra."

Staci smiled and shook hands. "Any friend of Uncle Joe's is a friend of mine." Staci looked past Sandra and saw Marcus wandering through the foyer. "Hold on a sec. I'll be right back." She dashed off.

"Uncle Joe?" asked Sandra.

Joe gave her a sideways grin. "It's a long story."

The foyer lights dimmed, and soft music punctuated the air. At the same time, guests quickly headed for the main auditorium. The front center two rows of seats were cordoned off with rope, and the ushers escorted the team and family members into this section. Just below the speaking podium, on a long, black-draped table sat a brass urn and a gold-framed photograph of Jim Kreider. The image, taken years earlier, made Jim appear even younger. Two colossal floral bouquets sat like bookends on the table.

The team members introduced their respected partners and families to each other as they maneuvered to their seats. When Arleen appeared, the team shifted in their seats, allowing her a single spot on the end of their row. The Kreider children and their partners sat in the first row, along with Jim's brothers and their families. The ushers removed two chairs on the end of the first row so that Jake Kreider could park his wheelchair. Again, the team began a new round of personal introductions for the new arrivals of Jake and his wife.

On the podium level, which was two steps higher than the main floor, a group of young adults arrived and positioned themselves near instruments. The pianist began playing a moving song, which was soon joined by guitars and a drummer. The musicians started singing, and the words appeared on several large screens across the front of the church. The people in the audience stood and joined the players, and soon the room was filled with a throng of impassioned voices. The song filled the auditorium.

Since most of the team did not know the music, they stood mute, reading the words being flashed across the big screens. For all intents and purposes, the singers could have performed in a foreign language, and it would have the same effect on the team seated in the second row. When Nate scanned the room, he saw multiple individuals with their eyes closed, their bodies swaying to the music, and some people had raised their hands in the air.

After the fourth song, the music stopped, and everyone sat down. A man in his mid-to-late forties walked on the stage to the podium. Wearing jeans, sports shoes, and a long-sleeved sports shirt with no tie, the man stood momentarily, intently surveying the room.

"My name is Ken, and I'm one of the pastors here at Bread of Life Community Church. We welcome you here—especially those of you who are visiting for the first time. We are here, of course, to celebrate the life of James Kreider. During this service, we will have an opportunity to hear select individuals speak about Jim's life. But before we begin, I would like to introduce Pastor Michael Richards. He is the lead pastor of the downtown First Baptist Church, and he will lead us in an opening prayer."

Wearing a dark suit, white shirt, and low-key tie, Mike walked onto the stage, taking his position behind the podium. He gave a surprisingly minimal prayer, followed by amen, which was repeated by many in the audience. When he was finished, Ken stepped up to the podium.

"Thank you, Pastor Richards. I will now turn the service over to Mr. Tony Toncetti."

When Tony walked to the front of the room, it was clear he was nervous. Years of courtroom battles in front of the city's toughest judges could not prepare Tony for the discomfort of standing in a church auditorium filled with almost 1300 strangers. Tony rubbed his palms together and coughed, which echoed throughout the large room.

"You know, I think the last time I stood in a church was on the day of my wedding. I was just as nervous that day as well."

Small laughter could be heard throughout the audience.

"Jim Kreider came to my office nearly six months ago. We sat down to discuss his will and plans for the event of his death. As a lawyer, I perform this procedure multiple times during the year with my clients as if it were a normal routine and don't give it a second thought. I had no idea of Jim Kreider's motivation but followed the man's instructions as I had done on many occasions.

"That day seems like it was just yesterday, yet here we are to celebrate the life of a friend, father, brother, work colleague, boss, neighbor, client, and significant partner who has been taken from us. We're left with fading memories of a man, whom I've learned was larger than life. It gives one pause—to think about our own legacy and the impact we might have in the world and on those around us. Every life has significance—touches other lives, makes a difference— and it's up to us to keep their memories alive.

"Out of the countless people we encounter on a daily basis, Jim Kreider chose five individuals to represent his life in today's service. The following individuals will be sharing in this order: his work supervisor, Nathanial Martin—vice president of Tynedex Corporation; his neighbor, Joseph Langley, a retired school teacher; his pastor, the Reverend Michael Richards; his personal physician, Dr. Thomas Nolan; and a woman who was a European client, Arleen Chenair. None of these individuals knew each other before their appointment by Jim Kreider, but they will be sharing their perspective on the man's life with you today.

"After the five representatives speak, we will hear from Stephanie Kreider, Jim's oldest daughter, and then Jim's son, Robert Kreider. Please listen carefully as each of these individuals shares the story of a fascinating man who changed his world—not in the way a famous author or politician, a scientist or technology guru does. No, James Kreider impacted many people and left his mark for us to appreciate his kindness, compassion, and generosity. Today, we will learn about the whole story of this man. Then, finally, at the close of this service, there will be a private graveside service to inter Jim's ashes. The family has respectfully requested that only immediate family members and those personally invited attend this part of the service. Thank you for your understanding. So, without further delay, I welcome Mr. Martin to the podium."

Tony took a seat in the front row while Nate eased his way to the front. Nate paused to survey the room and make eye contact with as many people as he could. Nate opened a narrow binder he had carried and glanced at the audience. He immediately made eye contact with several co-workers, including his secretary, Katherine, and Jim's assistant, Michelle. Nate was about to begin reading from the binder when he spotted board member Mrs. Blanchford, plus the president and CEO of Tynedex and the CFO, Jonathan Pendergrass, seated in the center of the auditorium. He wondered who had invited them, especially the CFO.

He suddenly felt agitated as Pendergrass scornfully stared in Nate's direction. Ignoring his feelings, Nate sighed and then plunged forward.

"My name is Nathaniel Martin, vice president of sales and marketing with Tynedex Corporation. For almost forty years, I have worked with Jim Kreider. In that time, I have found Jim to be a reliable and resourceful employee who was loyal and honest. In addition to being a rising star in my sales and marketing department, Jim also produced a bulk of the company's revenues because of his expanded client base."

Nate smiled and stared at Pendergrass when he made this last comment. Nate wanted the CFO to know that Jim's work ethics were top-notch and should not to be questioned by the CFO's department. Nate believed he saw Jonathan nod his head slightly.

"When I met Jim Kreider, I thought he lacked the qualifications and references of the kind of team I was building. But Jim challenged me— no, almost dared me—to hire him. Jim was bold and lived up to his promises and exceeded my expectations. From that day forward, our working relationship was solid. I found Jim to be competitive and a sports enthusiast. When he formed a softball tournament between various departments, Jim used the event as a way to encourage other workers to perform better.

"Several years ago, I expanded his territory to cover Asia and Europe. Again, Jim excelled, increasing company profits. When news of Jim's demise reached our company, several employees could not imagine the loss. I'll admit, I was initially concerned about the loss of income for the company, but I have recently realized that employees are more than just a number and revenue dollars. Jim's death awoke a renewed awareness of who my employees are and the value they bring to our company as human beings, rather than just the dollars they represent on the bottom line. Thank you, Jim, for reminding me of the importance of the individuals we work with.

"By the photos in Jim's office, one could quickly discover the appreciation and love Jim Kreider had for all three of his children. He shamelessly bragged about their achievements and proudly displayed their pictures prominently on his desk. It didn't matter if you had heard his story more than once, Jim would intimate his pride with raw passion every time. He adored his children. Sure, he complained about the costs to educate his children—and who wouldn't—but there can be no doubt about the man's dedication and love for his offspring.

"A little over a year ago, Jim's wife, Samantha, was tragically killed in a motor vehicle accident. Now we're here to bury my friend and colleague, Jim Kreider." Nate choked on his words. "If there is a God, I wonder why so much tragedy occurs in one person's life. Other than today, like Mr. Toncetti, I have never set foot in a church. But as I stand before you and proclaim my novice standing in church, it is because of Jim's life that I find myself questioning the existence of God and desiring to understand more. These are questions that have never before crossed my mind. So, you see, Jim's life has influenced me in other areas."

When Nate looked up, he saw the face of Dr. Nolan. Tom was smiling and slowly nodding his head.

"Jim Kreider was a decent, compassionate human being. Because of his generosity, I now readily dig into my pocket and share a buck or two with homeless strangers. Jim has changed my attitude in ways I wasn't aware of until our team began sharing in Mr. Toncetti's office. For example, many years ago, as a reward for an excellent presentation, he and I were invited to dinner with individual board members of our company. All of the company members had arrived ahead of us and were seated at a table overlooking the street. To my absolute horror, when Jim and I exited our cab, Jim compassionately assisted a homeless woman sitting on the curb. She was struggling to fit a pair of child's yellow rubber boots over a pair of filthy adult feet—which seemed like an impossible task. When I looked into the window, the CEO and board members watched in consternation as I desperately tried to pull Jim away from his mercy mission and out of the glaring stares of the restaurant.

"I can laugh at this story now, but at the time, I was convinced we both would be fired for Jim's lapse in judgment. I was wrong, of course." Nate looked up at Mrs. Blanchford and could see the woman subtly patting her cheeks with a handkerchief. "At some point in the evening dinner, Jim requested permission to assist the homeless woman. I, for one, thought he was going to purchase food for her and then send her down the road, but no. Jim invited her to join our table."

The room roared with laughter.

"This is obviously a small sampling of Jim's humanity, but there are much more. In a moment of time, when we least expect it, we lose dear friends or loved ones. It is the memories we hold in our hearts and share with others that keep these loved ones alive. There will never be another Jim Kreider, and there will never be another you. Cherish each moment you have. Treasure the people who are close to you, for none of us are certain when our journey in this life will end. Most of all, let the life of Jim be an example to us all. Thank you."

Nate returned to his seat, and Tom gave him an approving nod. Joe stood and took his place at the podium. He pulled some folded papers from his jacket pocket.

"Good afternoon, everyone. My name is Joe Langley. I'm a retired school teacher and a neighbor . . . What I mean is, *was* a neighbor of Jim Kreider. We were great friends, and I even became a babysitter for Jim and Sam's kids from time to time."

Joe looked up at Stephanie, Robert, and Staci and smiled.

"Poor Staci was always sick when she was little. Jim and Sam would rush her to the doctor or hospital, leaving Stephanie and Robert at my house until they returned. I became their Uncle Joe. Since I worked with kids in school anyway, it wasn't hard to have them around. Of course, there was that time when Robert, without permission, attempted to cut the lawn by using the riding mower."

Robert shifted in his seat uneasily and coughed loudly. Joe chuckled.

"We better save that for another day. Suffice it to say, Mrs. Miller, our other neighbor, wasn't too happy, but Robert and I patched things up eventually.

"Jim would frequently visit my house, and we would watch a game on the television or even share a few beers. During one of our discussions, I shared a desire to become a writer. Nate said Jim was a humanitarian, and I can attest to that. Without my knowledge, Jim went out and purchased several writing workshops for me and presented them as a gift.

"I discovered Jim yearned to be a painting artist. So, one day, I cleaned out a study in the back of my house and turned it into an art studio. I purchased an easel, paints, and canvas boards and presented it to Jim. Well, the man nearly cried; he was so happy. He struggled with his painting skills and would often roast his paintings in a barbecue pit in my backyard. I eventually purchased some DVDs by Bob Ross and gave those to Jim.

"If you remember, Bob was a smiling painter with a huge afro hairdo, who could crank out beautiful paintings in an hour. Well, in no time, Jim was duplicating Bob Ross' work and even getting better. In fact, many of the paintings I was able to save from the barbecue pit you will find displayed in the lobby of this building. I bought Jim more books, and he would study the painting styles. Then he would try to copy them. I think if you look out there at the paintings, you'll see Jim's work is impressive." Joe's expression turned serious.

"Home life wasn't easy at the Kreiders' because Sam and Jim didn't see eye-to-eye very often. Many times, the kids were at my house more than at home. After the kids started moving out and going to college, Jim changed his work patterns and started traveling more. The once-busy Kreider house suddenly became quiet.

"When Sam, Jim's wife, was killed by a drunk driver, Jim sort of spun out and was depressed. Unlike the funeral we're having here, Sam's was dreary, and I think it bothered Jim." Joe became circumspect. "It really makes one question life, and like Nate mentioned, wonder about why one family would deal with so much tragedy. Sadly, I didn't find out Jim had cancer until it was too late. I lost a really great friend and a terrific neighbor, and the world lost a fabulous artist.

"But you want to know what the worst part is?" Joe pointed to the three Kreider children. "These guys have lost both their parents. That's not fair, and I feel sorry for them." Joe looked intently at the three Kreiders. "But I want you to know, you still have a family, guys—me, your Uncle Joe."

Stephanie, Robert, and Staci all independently nodded to Joe and mouthed words indicating their appreciation.

"My heart and home are always open to you guys."

Joe pulled a handkerchief out and loudly honked into the white material, the noise echoing throughout the auditorium. He wiped tears away and then looked up, abruptly ending his speech. "Thanks for listening." Joe shuffled back to his seat where his lady friend, Sandra, quietly comforted Joe.

CHAPTER TWENTY

"PASTOR RICHARDS? ARE YOU READY?" whispered Tony as he leaned over several people.

There had been a long, uncomfortable pause because Mike forgot he was the next speaker. He quickly stood, reverently walked to the podium, and opened his Bible.

"In John 14, verses one through four, it says 'Do not let not your hearts be troubled. You believe in God; believe also in Me. My Father's house has many rooms; if that were not so, would I have told you that I am going there to prepare a place for you? And if I go and prepare a place for you, I will come back and take you to be with Me that you also may be where I am. You know the way to the place where I am going.'

"The Bible tells us that we have a home in heaven for those of us who are Christians. Our friend Jim Kreider is now in heaven, where he joins his mother, father, older brother, and wife, who preceded him in death. Jim is no longer with us, but he is in a better place with Jesus."

Nate leaned over to Dr. Nolan and whispered, "What on earth is he talking about?"

Tom shook his head. "It's complicated. I'll attempt to explain it later."

"When Jim and his family joined our congregation, the downtown First Baptist Church, it was just Jim, his wife Samantha, and Stephanie, who was just a baby then. In no time, they added a son and another daughter. I've got to say, it's good to see the Kreider children here with us today—even if they are all grown up now." Mike looked at Stephanie, Robert, and Staci with a downcast expression. "I just wish we were meeting each other under better circumstances, but we will one day see your parents again in heaven.

"When his children were in Sunday school, Jim started assisting their teachers. It was great to see Jim actively involved in the lives of his kids at church. Many of their friends were fond of Jim and looked forward to seeing him there on Sundays. In fact, he was well-liked by many in the church. As the children grew up and went off to college, I saw less of Jim and even less of his wife.

"Jim started visiting me shortly afterward for personal counseling, where he and I would walk together and talk. When his wife was tragically killed, I believed the man would go to pieces. I sensed he really loved his wife. After her funeral, I saw less of Jim, but I prayed for him every day. I'll tell you, though, that man loved his children. Jim would sit for hours and tell me about their schools, their relationships, and how proud he was of all three of you.

"Robert, when you decided to change your major in college, just before graduation, your dad blew a gasket. He got over it, of course, and, in the long run, he was proud that you're becoming a lawyer. Stephanie, I'm delighted to finally meet your fiancé. Your dad was excited to have a doctor for a future son-in-law. Staci, your dad would share your art with me and proudly proclaim you were the next Picasso.

"We're calling this a celebration service today, but for some, it may not feel like a celebration. We lose a father, a brother, a friend, or colleague, and we're sad. Their voice is silent, and memories fade, leaving grief in its wake. That's why we have Matthew five, verse four, which says, 'Blessed are those who mourn, for they will be comforted.' So, the Lord comforts us when we are sad.

"Therefore, as Christians, we are not only comforted now when we're grieving, but also in the future, where we have heaven to look forward to. We will miss our friend Jim Kreider, and even though he suffered in his last months on earth, I think he's looking down from heaven and smiling on us."

The room sat in utter silence, staring at Pastor Mike like deer staring into bright lights. Mike suddenly realized he knew so little about Jim Krieder, and his experience with the man paled in comparison to the other team members. He felt embarrassed and ashamed for not developing a closer relationship. Mike's words sounded hollow and robotic—as if he had just spoken the same words funeral after funeral for over forty years. After an uncomfortable pause, Pastor Mike walked back to his seat. A wave of guilt washed over Mike as he sat down.

Sensing Mike was troubled, Tom placed his hand on Mike's shoulder. Mike looked up, and Tom smiled warmly. Dr. Nolan then walked to the front and took his place behind the podium. His usual grimace-smile greeted the folks sitting in the auditorium. Clutched in his hand were his notes, folded length-wise, so Tom spread them on the podium, attempting to smooth the folds of the paper. Tom scanned the auditorium, recognizing many friendly faces. Unfamiliar faces scattered throughout the room reflected anticipation as they waited for Tom to speak. The doctor cleared his throat and began hesitantly.

"Many folks in here know me. For those who don't, I'm Dr. Thomas Nolan—or just plain Tom is fine with me. I've been a doctor for a very long time, and I remember the day James Kreider was born—so, yes, I guess I'm very old. As a child, James was headstrong but sensitive, talented but also kind. Like all boys, he got into trouble because he was a boy. It didn't matter if he were careening his skateboard down a hill, which caused an accident I might add, or trying to win a girl's heart, James Kreider was one hundred percent all-American boy.

"Not only was I present for James' birth, but I was also present for his brothers as well." Tom looked down at the man sitting in the wheelchair on the front row. "It's great to see you again, Jake. When you're up on your feet, we'll have to plan a marathon."

Jake chuckled, waved, smiled, and nodded back.

"Their father, Paul, was a veteran of World War Two and the Korean Conflict. When a man witnesses that much death, it can produce horrific effects. Tragically, their father took his own life, leaving the family broken. A few years later, during the Vietnam War, their oldest brother, Joseph, was killed in action. Jake was the second oldest, followed by Jim. Just before Paul ended his life, their mother, Jane, became pregnant with another child, John.

"Jane was a hard-working woman of deep convictions. Through prayer and incredible resources, she singlehandedly raised four boys, producing amazing men that any parent would be proud of. For a while, I had James stay with my wife and me. He was dealing with the loss of two members of his family and acting out his frustrations—as anyone would. Unfortunately, being a maturing boy and reaching puberty, his hormones kicked into overdrive, and his affections fell upon our daughter, Charlotte, who was a number of years older.

"That summer was one of the most difficult I've ever experienced, but somehow, a miracle happened, and we avoided a severe crisis. Eventually, Charlotte and James adjusted their relationship and became good friends, but there were moments when I could not see a positive outcome. I thank God I have a beautiful wife who understands and is full of wisdom."

Tom glanced at his wife, Susan, and they exchanged a silent conversation—as only married individuals can after many years of living together.

"During that same summer, I had the opportunity to share my faith with James. He asked a ton of difficult questions, but, eventually, he asked Jesus into his heart and became a Christian. During that summer, I watched an angry, confused young teen find peace and develop into the terrific man we all know.

"In his teenage years, James became fascinated with golf, and our friendship grew as we spent time hitting balls on the green. Most teenagers develop strength and stamina that we older folks are insanely jealous of, and James was no exception. As his skills in golf improved, his confidence also increased. One particular day, James' bravado peaked when he decided to tackle a par six, fourth hole by cutting corners.

"Rather than follow the golf course—which contained an elongated 'L' from the tee-off point to the hole—James decided to lob the ball over the tall trees and circumnavigate the bend in the fairway. Mind you, this hole required a par six for a reason.

"With incredible strength, James smacked his ball, lifting it like a rocket and launching it over the trees, where it was supposed to land near the fourth cup. Unbeknownst to us, standing over the fourth cup about to birdie his ball for a terrific score was our former mayor, Ron Golden. Unfortunately, when James' ball dropped from the sky, it landed squarely on top of Mayor Ron's bald head."

The room erupted into laughter. Tom smiled to himself.

"When James and I arrived, Mayor Ron was sprawled on the green and out cold. Fortunately, he recovered, but not without the prominent lump we frequently saw whenever Mayor Ron was on television."

Again, the laughter spread through the audience. Tom waited for the room to quiet.

"After this embarrassing incident, I lost James as my golfing partner because Mayor Ron wanted James by his side. Ron felt he was much safer knowing where James was hitting his ball.

"James was always a compassionate child, caring about other people in need. In addition to donating blood at our local Red Cross, James would volunteer his time during Thanksgiving and Christmas to help serve food in the shelter soup kitchen.

"One year, James read in the paper about someone needing a kidney in our hospital. He had his heart set on being a donor and saving a life. After discussing the situation, I suggested to James that he contact the hospital directly. The screening process was lengthy, and, despite his earnest desire to contribute a kidney, he was eventually ruled a mismatched donor. Acts of kindness, like this story, speak of James' character. He was a man of compassion—as seen in the story shared earlier by Mr. Martin."

Dr. Nolan glanced down at his notes and stared for a long time. Anyone close enough could see his tears cascading down his cheeks and landing on the papers in his hands. The room became uncomfortable in the lengthy pause. Suddenly, Tom looked up. He crumpled the papers in his hands and discarded them over his shoulder, papers floating to the stage floor behind him. Tom's voice was shaky and broken as he fought to deliver his next words.

"Why is it we wait until someone we care about is taken from us, to share our true thoughts? For weeks, the folks sharing today have sat and discussed James from a multitude of perspectives. We knew nothing of each other until we met in Tony Toncetti's office. During our meetings, I realized how little we actually know a person. Sure, we know someone, work with them, live next door to them, share a part of our life with them at church or at play, but rarely do we know a person thoroughly.

"I've discovered so much more about James from the other people on our team. Each person has a unique perception of James' life. It wasn't until we sat down and, in detail, shared what we knew about this wonderful man, that in doing so, we gained insight into the real James Kreider. Again, I ask, why did it take us so long?

"It's a sad commentary that we had to wait until James was gone before we could fully appreciate who this man really was—what kind of man he became—a vision of the real James and how he touched other people's lives. I stand before you ashamed—ashamed because I didn't take the time to find out more while James was still alive. I wish I had taken more opportunities to tell him how much he meant to me. I wish I had told him I cared and loved him like a son. He's gone, and I'll never have that opportunity again. This is the source of my shame today.

"This year, my beautiful wife, Susan, and I have been married sixty-five years. They have been the best years of my life."

Dr. Nolan looked at his wife and gave her one of his grimacing smiles, and she responded in kind by smiling back.

"Not a single day goes by that I don't take the time to tell her how much she means to me and how much I love her. Whenever I speak to our daughter, Charlotte, I do the same thing, expressing my love and appreciation. As I've gotten older, and hopefully wiser, I've come to the realization of how important relationships are—not just family, but all our relationships.

"Here we are today, trying to celebrate a life that is now gone from us. It's too late to express our appreciation and love for James. So how do we change this in the future?"

Tom looked around the room and let his words sink in. He could see somber faces and some who were wiping tears from their eyes.

"We start by telling each other today. We look at our friends, neighbors, co-workers, family, and we say to them we love and appreciate who they are—not just empty words of flattery, but meaningful words of truth. I'm serious! Look at the person next to you, especially if you know them, and tell them you care and appreciate who they are. And, if you don't know them, tell them anyway."

People sat dumbfounded, staring at the doctor.

"I mean it, folks. Turn right now to the individuals sitting on either side of you and tell them. Do it!"

Dr. Nolan watched with fascination as the room erupted in quiet chatter as people awkwardly attempted to follow the doctor's instructions. After a few minutes, the room quieted again, and everyone focused on Tom.

"That wasn't so hard now, was it? While you still can, make a promise to tell everyone around you how much they mean to you. Some of you call this a random act of kindness, but I call it being honest and human. We hide behind our insecurities, often covering them up with bravado, anger, coldness, judgment, condescending attitudes, even racism, but the truth is every one of you who heard another person share their love and concern was touched by the exercise.

"Why are we waiting until it's too late? It's time to stop hiding and share the truth. All of us want to be accepted and loved. If you disagree, then, just maybe, you may not be a human. Perhaps you're a machine or a robot. Humans need each other to survive, no matter how independent we feel or claim to be. Let us not waste another day by pretending we don't appreciate or need our fellow humans in our journey. We must share our true feelings and encourage one another. I urge you to do this each day and frequently—especially to strangers.

"When Jesus walked this earth, He spoke several times about this very subject when He said in Mark 12:31, 'Love your neighbor as yourself,' and John 15:13, 'Greater love has no one than this: to lay down one's life for one's friends.' I want to start by saying to my teammates—I love and recognize the value of each of you, especially in your sharing about James' life. I've grown to appreciate each of you. Do not let another day go by without taking the time to appreciate your fellow human beings."

Dr. Nolan paused to gather his thoughts since he was no longer following his script. He looked around and regrettably saw his speech notes scattered at his feet. Shaking his head, Tom dismissed his original plans.

"What I'm about to share comes from my heart, and I'm forgetting the notes I spent too much time preparing. You have no idea how difficult it is to stand before you today and witness the death of a friend, whom I helped deliver as a newborn just sixty years ago, seeing him take his first breath. When a baby cries out, catching the first gasp of air, they are breathing life into their body. To stand here and see that life now gone—especially when James was such a great person . . . Well, at my age, it weighs heavily upon my soul. There are so many dark and sinister humans who deserve to die—should die—yet, God chooses to let a terrific person like James die.

"If you're not asking why, then perhaps you should reexamine your compassion for humanity. There is far too much negative news bombarding us from the television. The only way we combat the negativity is to remember the good people, like James, and remind ourselves how much better we can act toward one another. As a doctor, I can easily tell you, life is too fragile. Cherish the moments you have and honor one another."

Tom folded his hands on the podium and looked down.

"Thank you for listening to this old man ramble on for so long." Tom looked up toward the ceiling. "Thank you, James, for giving me the opportunity to know you and to share our journey together. I know you're at peace and in heaven with our heavenly Father. Tell Him I said hi."

Tom produced his grimace and scanned the room in silence. He then stepped down from the platform, pausing briefly in front of the table with the urn. He took his hand and lovingly caressed the sides of the brass urn before returning to his seat. At the same time, Arleen stood. The two people briefly stood facing each other when Arleen reached out and gave Dr. Nolan a huge embrace.

Arleen whispered, "I love you, Dr. Nolan. James was truly blessed to have you as a friend."

"Thank you, Arleen. Now, do me a favor and share your truth about James and let us see a side of him which only you know."

Although Arleen was frightened by the idea and not confident what she would disclose, she assured the doctor. "I will do my best."

Arleen gracefully walked to the podium, clutching a small group of index cards containing handwritten notes. She casually but quickly glanced at her notes, then looked up and smiled.

"Like the good doctor just shared, I originally had planned to share something altogether different, but in lieu of what Dr. Nolan just spoke, I have decided to share from my heart instead."

Arleen gave a big sigh. "You're a difficult act to follow, Dr. Nolan. Your words were so moving." Arleen looked around the large auditorium. "When one is standing up here, one realizes just how many people are packed into this room. I wish I had spoken before the doctor because it is hard to follow a speech like his."

Soft laughter erupted in the room. Arleen took a deep breath.

"Rather than start from the beginning, I want to share the end part of my relationship with James. Dr. Nolan has given me the courage to be honest today, so thank you, Doctor.

"Although I worked with James in a professional relationship, he and I shared much more personally. I found James to be the most compassionate, loving, dedicated, and tender man I have ever known. James could make me laugh, and I loved how I felt whenever we were together. Our relationship may have started as work colleagues, but, eventually, we became lovers and passionate partners."

Nate smiled broadly and nodded his approval. He then glanced at Pastor Mike to see his reaction. Mike's face looked as if he had eaten sour grapes. Nate scanned the room and saw various expressions from shock to pleasure. Staci edged to the front of her seat and leaned forward. She appeared as if she didn't want to miss a word. Nate discretely gave Arleen a thumbs-up signal.

"When I was a young teen, I became infatuated with an older man, who was not really interested in me as a person but for my body and good looks. I made a terrible mistake and had a baby. As soon as the child was born, it was removed from me, and I never saw the child again. The whole incident doomed my future existence. Afterward, my parents arranged to have me spend years in a Catholic convent and private learning institutions so that I could not be around men. Once I became involved in my career, I had even less interest in men and viewed them as the source of my life's misery. But then, I met James.

"Everything I despised about men was turned upside down. James never used flattery or rude comments like all the other men I knew. James was compassionate, kind, professional, and a perfect gentleman. Very quickly, James and I became close friends. We went out for dinner, saw movies, laughed, and walked through the park. The whole time, James delighted in my company, and he never made any sexual advances. The more time we spent together, the more my heart opened to the idea of a relationship with a man. We saw each other often and frequently met during our various travels around the world. Then one day, James revealed he was married.

"My bad feelings returned, and I was devastated. When I pressed James for answers, he took his time and explained his situation.

James said he and his wife lived separate lives but remained married for the sake of the children. James told me his wife had a lover, and it was a very young man from her workplace. It seemed the more James shared about his home life, the more I grew to admire him. My shock shifted to compassion. James told me that as long as he was married, he could not be in an intimate relationship. He wanted to remain friends with me until then. So, we became the very best of friends. Our friendship grew stronger, and we enjoyed each other's company.

"Then a most unfortunate incident occurred. James' wife and her boyfriend were killed in a tragic car accident. I'm not sure why, but James blamed himself, and he felt responsible for their deaths. After several weeks of consoling James, I finally encouraged him to seek a professional counselor. I'm not sure he followed my advice because we never discussed the matter further. In three months, James started being like his old self again. Our relationship flourished, and we became intimate."

A few people in the room gasped at Arleen's disclosure.

"Before you judge me or James, you should know we entered our relationship by committing ourselves to each other and before God. We made a pact before God, and we honored our commitment to each other. Please understand, long before the government got involved in marriage, men and women made their commitments before God, and it settled the matter. Eventually, the government saw the chance to make money and established marriage licenses. Before that, marriage was a ceremony between people, not government entities. So please know, our commitment was sacred and honorable."

Arleen stood resolutely and let her statement permeate the room. As she disclosed her feelings, she was gaining strength and confidence.

She glanced at her teammates and received reassuring smiles from everyone, except Pastor Mike. She quickly dismissed his feelings on the subject and plunged ahead.

"One day, James surprised me by announcing he had found the child I had given birth to when I was so young. The news was welcoming and frightening at the same time. When I inquired, James indicated he did not know any details but had hired a private investigator to locate my child. It took me several weeks to arrive at a decision to meet this child.

"The private investigator took seven months to find my daughter; then the government paperwork consumed another ten months. Sadly, James never met my daughter, her husband, and their two beautiful children. He only had the opportunity to see the photographs of my daughter at an age when she was much younger. As I established relationships with my newfound family, James suddenly became distant. We spoke by telephone and shared emails, but he never returned to France for a visit. I ached to see James, but he would always tell me, 'Perhaps in the future.' That future never happened. I became so infatuated with my new family that I allowed time to slip by. Then, suddenly, all communication ceased between James and me.

"I feared the worst and could not reach out to anyone at his company without compromising James. When I discovered he had died, I was beset with horrible grief. Just as I was beginning to establish a fantastic relationship with this beautiful man, it was gone in an instant. I have spent much time trying to resolve my feelings and the circumstances of our friendship. I have questioned God and asked why. Eventually, I arrived at some conclusions.

"I think James was the catalyst to resolve my past hurts and allow me to reestablish a connection with a family I never knew. He provided me a chance to discover a part of myself that I thought was lost forever. He also opened my eyes to the possibility of love. Along our life's journey, we meet individuals who we spend a long time with and some not so long. Each person impacts our life in some way. James had an enormous impact on my life, and I regret it was far too short.

"It's important we look for the goodness in our experiences and not the negative—always seeking the contributions others made. We become better people for each encounter. James was instrumental in my future happiness, and, for that, I will always be grateful. I will always miss my James and wish we had many more years together, but it was not in God's plans. And, trust me—I have no idea what plans God has in store, for I am as confused as anyone else with regards to the subject. But I hope one day to meet James again."

Emotions quickly surfaced as tears began to roll down Arleen's cheeks, and she struggled to remain composed. For a lengthy period of time, she looked down, fighting her emotions. Staci sprung from her seat and ran up to Arleen, hugging the woman with all her strength. The two women began sobbing. Out of the silence, a single person began to loudly applaud. In no time, others joined in, and soon the room was filled with a deafening applause. It was Nate who started the response, so he stood to his feet and encouraged the room to join in. The whole church was applauding this woman's confession and rejoicing. Arleen was receiving a standing ovation.

Staci and Arleen looked up to see the display of affection and were astounded. As the room slowly returned to normal, Staci started to leave, but Arleen grasped Staci's hand and asked her to stay. They stood smiling and crying as Arleen attempted to finish her speech. Arleen made eye contact with Pastor Mike.

"I want to finish by saying that I loved James with all my heart and soul. He was my soulmate, and his loss has left a huge hole in my heart. I will never regret what we shared together."

Arleen looked down at Staci.

"Also, I now have an extended family and hope to connect with all of James' children. I hope you will accept me."

Staci began hugging Arleen, and the room started applauding again. Robert jumped from his chair, but Stephanie reluctantly got up. The two walked to the front. Without prompting, the three children group-hugged with Arleen and expressed their acceptance. Nate and Dr. Nolan both beamed with absolute pride as they exchanged private comments.

CHAPTER TWENTY-ONE

AFTER A LENGTHY TIME, THE room slowly returned to the peaceful, subdued state experienced earlier. Stephanie stood at the front, watching as the trio walked back to their seats. Arleen and Staci held hands as they walked. Staci was thrilled at the opportunity to have an extended family. Stephanie took her time and gathered her thoughts. She had not prepared notes and would speak from her heart. Looking up at the audience, she softly smiled.

"I'm a little overwhelmed at this moment, almost speechless. I'm sure my brother, Robert, would find this disclosure astounding. But, as I have sat in my seat and listened to five people share about my father, I've come to realize something. We really don't know a person completely. We are aware of a single facet of an individual from work, school, church, socially in our neighborhood, or through some other venue. But the truth is we only know the one side of an individual. It isn't until we sit in a room like this and listen to the various perspectives that we begin to see the whole picture about a person.

"I've learned more today about my father than I ever thought I knew. Dad was a generous man who cared. He made it possible for all three of us to go to college. He provided a good home for us to live in and made sure our needs were met. There was one thing Dad never provided, though. Despite all attempts by my parents to pretend that our life was rosy, we all knew he and our mother were not happy. They actually displayed more hate than love, but, at the same time, each of us knew our parents were staying together for the sake of us, the children. It was a sham, and we knew it. Mother and Dad individually expressed their love for us, but the idea of a loving family was almost a joke.

"It hurt even more when Mother decided to get involved with another man, while she and dad were still married. She tried to hide her relationship, but we knew. I wish they could have been more honest with themselves and us. Now they're both gone, and we'll never get the chance to resolve our differences. How tragic. Dad was always the one to look for the positives in life. He demonstrated as much love as possible, and for that, I am grateful. Mother was more self-absorbed, but don't get me wrong—I loved my mother.

"Growing up, I often would lie to my friends about our home life. I'm embarrassed to say—"

Stephanie paused, looked down, fought her tears, and took a deep breath. She shook her head.

"The notion of lying about one's feeling can be damaging. I've spent years in therapy, trying to resolve my issues surrounding the lies." She looked at her fiancé and smiled. "Thank you, Charles, for your patience and understanding." He warmly smiled in response.

"Despite the issues with our parents, I can confidently say we knew our parents independently loved us. For our dad, I learned how to challenge and question basic norms. I learned to not just accept something because someone said it was so, but to dig into the matter and arrive at my own decision. Dad taught me this lesson. Dad also taught me how to appreciate everything and take nothing for granted.

Even today—as difficult as this is—I'm learning something new and expanding my appreciation of Dad. By the stories we've heard today, you can only imagine that challenge.

"I remember once, when I was about six or seven, I decided I wanted to know what was in my Christmas presents. I waited until my parents were busy outside, and I snuck into the house and carefully opened several packages." Stephanie chuckled. "When you're young, you think you're so smart. No matter how careful I was, it was impossible to open the packages without some evidence. Some of the flimsy paper tore, and I did my best to hide the damage. I was sure I had gotten away with my deed when Dad walked into the room. I'm certain guilt was written all over my face.

"Dad surveyed the room and quickly spotted several presents askew. My heart sank when he picked up the packages and saw they were torn open. I excused myself, saying I needed to use the restroom, but Dad turned and sternly said, 'Sit down!' I suddenly felt sick. Mind you, our parents had never spanked us before, but I was certain, at that very moment, this policy was going to abruptly end. My bottom was feeling warm in anticipation. Dad sat on the sofa next to me and I just stared ahead, trying not to cry. I wanted to throw up.

"Dad didn't move a muscle but just kept staring, boring holes into my skull. I was certain, I would never see age ten. Then, suddenly, he asked, 'What happened here, Stephanie?' My mind raced for something to say that would prevent me from a punishment I knew I deserved. Just when all hope was lost, our cocker spaniel walked into the room. The dog was old and ambled into the living room, plopping onto the carpet, next to Dad's feet, looking up at me with his big brown eyes. I was instantly happy dogs could not speak because I was about to incriminate the dog for my sins.

"Taking a deep breath, I confidently told Dad, 'It was Sandy's fault. He tore into the presents, and I tried to stop him. I was afraid you and Mom would get mad, so I hid the damage. He was a very bad, bad dog, but please don't hurt him, Dad. He didn't mean to do it.' We looked down at Sandy, and the dog raised his head, perked up his ears, and was panting with a big grin. I was feeling pretty safe by this point. Dad smiled and reached down to pet the dog. Then he looked at me and said, 'That's terrible. I hope you didn't punish the dog.' 'Oh, no,' I said. 'I just told him he was a bad dog.'

"To my surprise, Dad said, 'Thank you for telling me, Stephanie.' I started to get up and leave when Dad stopped me in my tracks. He said, 'Tell me, Stephanie, do you see the video camera sitting on the coffee table?' To my absolute horror, I spotted the family video camera sitting on the coffee table, pointing at the Christmas tree. Ill feelings and guilt washed over me anew. Dad picked up the camera and held it in his hands. 'If we were to watch the video on this camera, what do you suppose we would see, Stephanie?' I was busted, guilty, and had no excuses. My face was beet red from embarrassment.

"Instantly, I confessed my sins and told Dad about everything. I started crying and blathered on and on about how sorry I was. Dad just smiled and hugged me, saying, 'Stephanie, never be afraid to tell the truth.' That's the kind of dad we grew up with. Although you thought you had gotten away with something, Dad was always one step ahead. Sadly, years later, Dad disclosed that the camera was sitting there turned off and not recording. He knew I was guilty of something but couldn't prove it. When Dad saw the video camera sitting on the coffee table, he instantly hatched his ruse to trick me. He and I have shared hours of laughter over the incident since.

"I'm grateful Mr. Martin shared the story about the homeless woman. Oftentimes, Dad would stop and assist homeless individuals. He wouldn't initially give them money when they asked; but if they were hungry, he would buy them food and meet their needs. I've seen him buy coats, sleeping bags, tents, and blankets for complete strangers. Mother would get infuriated with Dad's actions, but it left a permanent impression on me growing up. Once, dad spotted a woman and small child begging on a street corner. We loaded them into our car, and Dad took them to a nearby hotel. He paid for the room and had the manager order groceries. I found out later that Dad contacted a woman's shelter and moved them to the facility."

Stephanie looked down at Robert, who was smiling and nodding in agreement.

"The only time I ever saw Dad sad was when mom died. It was something I could not understand because they really didn't love each other that much. When I asked him about it, Dad said he was sorry for us and the loss of a woman who gave birth to his three children. He said he respected her contribution to the family, although he and Mom didn't see eye-to-eye on everything. Dad may not have liked Mom, but he respected her as our mother. Our father was a rare individual, and the world is less because of his death. I will miss him and the many times we talked, or argued, about various subjects."

Stephanie looked down at the urn and table containing her father's ashes.

"Dad, I hope you've found peace and are having a great time in heaven. Just wish we had you around a little longer. I love you, Dad."

Stephanie blotted tears, pausing at the front table. When she regained composure, she walked back to her seat. Robert stood and gave his sister a tight hug, whispering into her ear, "I love you, Stephanie. Thank you for a great eulogy."

Stephanie smiled. "Thank you, Robert."

When Robert walked to the front, he clutched a yellowed letter envelope in his hand. Taking a moment to stare at the envelope, Robert held the sealed envelope up with one hand.

"My dad gave this to me. I received it the day Mr. Toncetti read his will. I haven't opened it because Dad said to read it today at this service. I can tell you, I have been tempted to unseal the envelope just so I can see what's inside, but I learned something about this exercise. By having me—no, all of us—wait until today, it was a form of delayed gratification. It is a lesson I have always needed to learn. In our instant gratification society, we expect everything now, without waiting. Zap it in the microwave, and bingo—it's done minutes later.

"Yet, if there is one thing I've learned—as I am now entering another four-year cycle at college—is that patience is required to achieve the things we want. I nearly graduated with a computer science degree when I changed my major, and I'm now studying to be a lawyer. Dad was not happy about my decision because he was footing the bill."

Robert paused as a soft chuckle could be heard from the audience.

"Dad could be sensitive and voiced his strong opinion, especially concerning money. I can't blame him because it says he cared. I think that Dad felt his career turned out okay, and it gave him license to have a say in his children's. Don't get me wrong—I did appreciate his interest; but, at some point, we all have to make our own choices—good or bad—and deal with the consequences. In the end, it was Dad who provided the best wisdom, and I'll forever appreciate what he did for us.

"When I think back on my childhood, it was Dad who inserted himself in our daily lives. I'm grateful Pastor Mike shared the part about Dad working with us kids in Sunday school. I had forgotten about that. I got really jealous when my friends captured my dad's attention, and he paid attention to them. I didn't want to share my dad. When you have the best dad on the planet, you're not interested in sharing. I loved my dad and wanted my friends to know he was *my* dad, not theirs.

"Just when you think you know your parents and have them all figured out, they surprise you. I never knew Dad was interested in painting, much less thought he would be any good at it. But when I saw his work, I was shocked. His art is really, really great. Some of the paintings are spoken for, but if you're interested, the others are for sale. The ones with name cards are the ones spoken for. The paintings are being sold on a silent-bid basis. Please see someone at the greeting kiosk if you're interested. The money we raise will go to a good cause—feeding the homeless."

The people applauded.

"Now, the tough part. When an elderly grandparent dies, some-how, we can accept it. We grieve, of course, but we also recognize they lived a long life. I can tell you, I never understood the immense grief I witnessed when someone lost their child or someone who died at a young age. I don't mean to sound callous, but I thought, okay they died, and it's sad of course, but we move on. Then I lost my mom and shortly afterward lost my father. It felt like someone sucker-punched me in the gut."

Robert tightly gripped the lectern, fighting back his emotions. After a period of silence, Robert looked up. His eyes were red and moist.

"Nothing prepares you for the feelings. I was mad, distraught, angry again, glum, and incredibly sad. The feelings shifted quickly, and I couldn't understand why this happened to me. Yes, I know that's selfish, but why a great man like my dad? It doesn't seem fair. Over the last few weeks, I've had time to resolve my feelings somewhat. I now have tremendous sympathy for people who have lost their child or someone young. No, let me correct that. I have sympathy for anyone who has lost someone they love because it really hurts!

"The things we're left with are our memories, pictures, videos, and mementos—trinkets, really. They'll never replace the person we so desperately want to have one more conversation with, one more opportunity to laugh with. It's an empty feeling knowing that my parents are gone, and I'll never get to talk with them again. They'll never get to see their grandchildren. I'll never get to discuss my future with them. I'll never again get to say I love you. There are no more hugs. No more arguments. Nothing but my memories.

"I read something once by Mark Manson." Robert pulled a piece of paper from his pocket. "He wrote, 'Here's the truth. We exist on this earth for some undetermined period of time. During that time, we do things. Some of these things are important. And those important things give our lives meaning and happiness. The unimportant ones basically just kill time.'

"So, I ask you, which things are you spending your time on? The important ones? Or are you just killing time? I know for a fact that

Dad wasn't killing time. If you walk out of here with anything, you should have a sense that my dad never wasted time. He crammed a whole lot more into life than many of us combined. His was a wonderful life, and, I will horribly miss him."

Bowing his head, Robert couldn't hold back the tears, so he hung his head in silence. Both Stephanie and Staci jumped from their seats and ran to Robert's side. The three siblings knotted together and sobbed. Finally, Robert regained composure. He thanked his sisters and waited for them to return to their seats.

"Sorry, folks. I'm not sure what came over me. Now, where was I?" He looked down at his piece of paper. He wiped his eyes on his sleeves. "Dad's life begs the question—what are we doing with our lives? Dad cared for us kids, took care of the homeless, traveled all over the world, painted like Michelangelo, donated blood by the gallons, taught Sunday school, and excelled in his career. My efforts pale in comparison. How about yours? We all could take a lesson from Dad's example. I may be young, but I'm learning. I just wish I had noticed all this before Dad died.

"Thank you, Mr. Martin, Dr. Nolan, Pastor Mike, Uncle Joe, and Arleen. You have given us a wealth of knowledge about our father. I really appreciate you and what you shared with us today. I'm touched by your honesty and the intimate details you've shared. I know much more about my father because of your words. I also have a deeper appreciation for Dad."

Robert held up the yellowed envelope.

"And now the mystery envelope." Robert again dried his eyes on a sleeve. "Dad had this prepared for some time because it's old. I have no idea what's inside, except that he wanted it read today."

Taking his finger, Robert worked the flap of the envelope open, being careful not to tear anything. The room watched in anticipation. Robert scanned the page and smiled. He started to chuckle and then finally looked up.

"The following quote is copied from a book, titled *The Proud Highway: Saga of a Desperate Gentleman* by Hunter S. Thompson. I gotta tell you, folks, this really summarizes my dad because only my dad would choose something like this for his own funeral," Robert said as he pointed at the page.

Lifting the paper up, Robert kept a straight face and carefully read the excerpt. He cleared his throat. "'Life should not be a journey to the grave with the intention of arriving safely in a pretty and well-preserved body, but rather to skid in broadside in a cloud of smoke, thoroughly used up, totally worn out and loudly proclaiming *Wow! What a ride!*' This describes my dad perfectly."

The room stood to their feet and loudly applauded. Robert walked back to his sisters and embraced them. Nate, Dr. Nolan, Pastor Mike, Joe, and Arleen encircled the trio, forming a huddle of wet eyes and grateful hearts.

EPILOGUE

THE PAIN WAS EXCRUCIATING. EACH panting breath was like a fire stabbing in the lungs. The mind raced in and out of consciousness. Disconnected memories of the past, visions about the present, and toils over unfinished business played out in the mind. Throughout the body, the only sensory working was intense pain. It was impossible to focus on a single area of hurt, for the entire body was in complete overload.

Unable to distinguish between night and day, the seconds labored into hours, the hours stretched into endless days. Nearly delirious, the brain cried out in muted silence, screaming for it to stop, yet no one answered. The withered man lying in bed was certain that what he was experiencing was as close to a living hell as anyone could get.

God, why can't you hear me? James thought. *Please make this stop— even for one minute!*

If at that hour, someone was standing next to James, they would have heard nothing, except the raspy and rapid panting of a dying man. In his ears, James listened to the drumming of his fast heartbeat—the monotonous percussion compounding his torture.

One minute, a cacophony similar to an out-of-tune orchestra mixed with the glaring sounds of a harried city intersection was blasting in James' head, but then instant silence. No, not silence, but far purer—the absence of all sounds. Not what one would experience in the forest or mountain top because, even there, one will hear faint sounds. At this very moment, James heard nothing! It wasn't unnerving or frightening at all, but peaceful. Just minutes before the silence, James was confident he would go completely insane, but now there was tranquil solitude. It was a little confusing.

In the undisturbed peace, James became acutely aware he was no longer in pain. Wait! No, it wasn't that the hurting ceased; there was absolutely nothing. No pain. No feelings at all—just serenity and peace. Plus, his body felt weightless.

The room had been dark, but now warm, bright light began to consume the darkness—similar to when damp morning fog, thick as soup, hangs in the air, until the early sun rises and warms the earth. As the sun penetrates the sky, the fog retreats and vaporizes, vanishing into nothing. So, it seemed that the black abyss that surrounded James moments earlier was now disappearing and being replaced with soothing light. As the darkness faded, the light grew warmer and more intense.

James could see his bed beneath him. A withered, frail, dead, and gray corpse lay motionless. Rather than feeling disgusted, James felt immense compassion and love.

Was that me a moment ago? Did I look that horrible?

The weightlessness increased, and James began to ascend into more light. The intensity and whiteness were brighter than a thousand suns.

Surrounding James were points of light, swimming and swirling around. Like sparks flying above a fiery pit or fireflies dancing in the night sky, there were hundreds and thousands. James could sense their individual light as they moved past him. *Are you angels?* James thought. Suddenly, the scene changed, and picturesque, snowcapped mountains appeared, sweeping meadows. The images were more intense and beautiful than anything he had ever seen in a *National Geographic* magazine. The colors were pure.

Millions of blurry beings moved about, but then one prominent Individual came into focus and slowly moved toward James. Appearing as a collage of every picture countless artists had created, and yet unlike any of them at the same time, a Being bearing the image of a man approached James. Instantly, James plunged toward the Man.

"Jesus!"

There were no formal introductions, but James could make no mistake about the Man. Immense joy swept over James, and he and the Being blended together in what one might describe as an embrace.

"I love you so much, Jesus. You're more beautiful than I imagined."

In a smooth, velvet voice, Jesus greeted him, "Welcome home, James."

Their embrace lasted an eternity, and as impossible as it might seem, the light enveloping Jesus and James was even more intense and loving than anything experienced thus far. When the intimacy of this moment quieted, Jesus looked intently into James.

"There is someone who has waited a long time to see you. She's been asking me when you would be arriving. Come, I would like to introduce you to her."

From among the myriad of beings just out of focus, a beautiful, elderly woman appeared. Silver curls framed her smiling face as she moved closer.

"James, you're finally here." She embraced him with a motherly hug.

"I'm afraid you have an advantage over me, for I don't recognize you. Although I must admit, you do seem familiar." James frowned.

"Really? You don't recognize me at all?" she asked with a grin.

"I'm sorry, but I don't."

"But you're the reason why I'm here."

Jesus smiled. "Perhaps we should help him out, Ethel?"

She nodded. As if by magic, the woman was transformed. Her radiant smile was quickly replaced with a toothless grin, and her appearance resembled a homeless woman. She held up a yellow rubber boot. She giggled like a little girl.

"Oh! It's you!" James exclaimed. "You're the homeless woman, trying to wear the child's rubber boots."

Instantly, she changed into the beautiful woman again. They embraced this time with deep meaning.

"Thank you for your kindness and love, James."

As they embraced, James looked up at Jesus, Who was smiling.

"Ethel, is it?"

She nodded. "Yes, and because of your kindness that day, I met a street preacher who told me about Jesus. You see, your act of kindness prepared my heart to receive something new. I was penniless and dying. No one paid attention to me. I figured God had given up on me. Then I prayed and asked God to send me an angel. Just then, you appeared. You got out of the taxi and showed me great kindness. I cannot thank you enough." She began kissing his face.

With his soft voice, Jesus interrupted, "You had more influence than you imagined, James. Ethel is just the beginning. Many, many lives were altered because of your love. I have someone else I'd like you to meet. Like Ethel, she's waited a long while to see you."

Ethel released James, and he turned to face another blurry image coming into focus. Instantly, he ran toward the woman, so familiar and yet long gone from his life. James dropped to his knees and hugged her tightly.

"Mom, I have missed you so much. I am desperately glad to see you."

With a benevolent smile, she looked down and said, "James, my son, you look so much like your father. It's good to see you."

James wept tears of joy as he embraced his mother. "Oh, how I love you, Mom."

Their embrace lasted a long time. Neither spoke, but through their touch, they communicated what each felt inside their inner being. When James finally raised his head, he saw that they were surrounded by hundreds of beings. Some were long-passed relatives, friends, and people James had known throughout his lifetime. It was a reunion of many souls, disconnected through death on earth but reconnected in heaven. The sheer joy of seeing souls lost long ago made James incredibly happy.

When the grand reunion was finally at a close, James looked around for Jesus. "Where did He go?"

A tall being, clothed in a long white robe with massive wings attached behind his shoulders appeared, and James instantly thought he knew who this was.

"You must be Michael?"

The being rolled his eyes and sighed, "Everyone makes that mistake. We don't even look alike. My name is Raphael."

"Oh, I meant no harm. Sorry."

The angel smiled. "Have no fear. The Master, Jesus, went to greet other new arrivals. He asked me to guide you for a while. Come, there are others who would meet you."

"Great, Raphael, because I have a ton of questions to ask you."

The angel laughed. "I'm sure you do. They all have the same questions to ask."

As Raphael and James drifted into a crowd of beings, James locked arms with Ethel and his mother. Infinity of time passed, yet on earth, it would have seemed like mere minutes or even perhaps a thousand years. James asked a million questions, and everyone was patient, taking their time to answer.

"Why is it I feel nothing but absolute peace and love, unlike I've ever felt before?"

Every being around him began to laugh. Suddenly, the familiar voice of Jesus appeared.

"Because, James, this is how My kingdom operates. Here, we experience the pure love that my Father intended from the start of creation. But, enough questions for now; I need to show you something else. Come." Jesus extended his nail-scarred hand, and James stared at the holes. He slowly grabbed Jesus' hand.

Instantly, they floated far and away from the throngs of beings. As they drifted past mountains, lakes, and forests, James could see wild animals of various types mixing and gathering below. Lambs played with lions, while others who would regularly hunt and eat each other lazily slept alongside one another. Fear was absent from all the creatures, and they were content to enjoy each other's company. Finally, Jesus brought James near an endless horizon. Along the edge and behind him, James could see all of heaven; but when he looked over the edge, everything disappeared into a light blue haze.

"Keep looking, James; you'll see in a moment."

James stared into the hazy pool beneath, and as he looked, suddenly events on earth came into clarity. He saw a large room with hundreds of people. Music filled the space. It was as if he could reach out and touch the people below; it seemed so real. But when he tried, the scene returned to the hazy blue pool. After pulling his hand back, the image returned. He also could hear voices as if they were standing in front of him.

"Is that Nate? And look—there's Joe, my neighbor!"

Jesus and James lay on the ground, next to one another, looking over the edge.

"Where is this, Jesus? I don't recognize the place," James asked as he turned his head toward Jesus.

Never moving his head, Jesus stared below. "Keep watching."

Arleen walked into the room. The people seated in the row stood and moved down, so she could sit at the end. With an ache in his voice, James cried out.

"Arleen, my love, oh how I miss you." James turned toward Jesus again. "Even dressed in black, this woman is radiant. I miss her so much. Why are you tormenting me by showing me this scene? Why are all these people gathered together?"

Jesus smiled and put His arm around James, pulling him in close. "Just watch. It will make sense in a moment."

A smartly-dressed man walked to the front of the room.

"You know, I think the last time I stood in a church was on the day of my wedding. I was just as nervous that day as well."

"That's my lawyer, Tony Toncetti," James exclaimed. "Why is he there, and whose church is this?"

Then James spotted his own portrait on the table in front of the church. Large flower bouquets draped the table, and a brass urn sat in the middle. James turned toward Jesus.

"This is my funeral?"

Jesus continued to smile. "Keep watching and learn, my son."

One by one, James listened as each person walked up to the front and shared their encounter with James. When Arleen walked up front, James softly smiled.

"She's so beautiful; I just wish we had more time together."

"Ah yes . . . time," Jesus remarked. "You always have too much or too little and never value that which you have."

When Arleen finished speaking, he and Jesus watched the tearful exchange between Staci and Arleen, followed by the speeches of Stephanie and Robert.

"Tell me, Jesus, will my children be here in heaven, too? Will Arleen?" James pleaded.

"James, like you, each person has the choice to accept and believe in Me. Every person will decide. Their individual choice will determine their future."

"But I want them to make the right choice. Can't you send angels to help them or perform some kind of miracle? It happens in the movies all the time," pleaded Jim.

Jesus smiled, "James, I want everyone to make the right choice. You have a free-will right to choose your own destiny. It is My prayer that everyone will make the correct decision."

"You make it sound so effortless," said Jim.

"For some, it is. For others, there are distractions like power, fortune, popularity, fame. Sometimes, drugs or drinking get in the way."

"But didn't You drink wine?"

"Moderation, James—moderation in all things. By themselves, none of the things I've listed get in the way. When these things become a priority, there is no room for Me in that person's life, it is the path to separation and destruction."

"Then I hope they make the right choice."

"As do I, James."

Jesus and James lay there together, watching and listening to the scene below. When the funeral was over, Jesus stood and looked into James' eyes.

"Well, what did you think? What did you learn?"

"To tell the truth, those events seem so far away. I almost think the struggles don't really matter that much."

James looked puzzled.

"What troubles you, my son?"

"So, now what do we do?"

Jesus leaned his head back and let out a belly laugh. "Come and see, James. You are about to discover so much more."

THE END

ACKNOWLEDGMENTS

I owe a debt of gratitude to my wife, Emily, for her belief in me, her support, and her tolerating the long journey it took me to write this book. Your patience and love are unconditional.

To Linda Humes—the first person to review my manuscript—thank you for all your editing, critique, and wisdom. I value your friendship.

To David Hinman, a good friend and pastor, who provides prayers and support in my life journey.

To Fred and Diane Laura of America's Pie Company, for serving a delicious slice of heaven every Saturday with homemade ice cream. Thank you for your incredible support.

To Karleen Sucher, whose father provided the inspiration for the story.

To Kala Weinacker, Emily's daughter, without her, there would be no epilogue and for allowing me to use her childhood stories.

To my mother, who encouraged me—as a child—to always seek higher goals and taught me how to enjoy life.

To the countless family and friends who supported and encouraged me to write.

To Sam Lowry at Ambassador International and the excellent team, for believing in me as an author and making *Final Grains of Sand* a reality.

BIBLIOGRAPHY

In the last chapter, two quotes are referenced from outside sources:

Manson, Mark. *Mark Manson. Author. Thinker. Life Enthusiast.* September 14, 2014. https://markmanson.net/life-purpose (accessed November 18, 2016).

Thompson, H. S. *The Proud Highway: Saga of a Desperate Southern Gentleman.* New York: The Random House Publishing Group, 1997.

ABOUT THE AUTHOR

David Harder currently resides in the White Mountains of Arizona. In addition to writing, he is a featured clay artist. He grew up in southern California and served in the U.S. Navy during the Vietnam conflict. For nearly eight years, he lived and worked in Germany. From sales and marketing, he eventually became a CEO and business owner before moving to Arizona. A graduate of San Jose College with a degree in business, David also studied at Santa Clara University.

For more information about

David Harder
and
Final Grains of Sand
please visit:

http://www.DavidHarder.com
https://twitter.com/davidcharder
https://www.facebook.com/David.Harder.Author/

For more information about
AMBASSADOR INTERNATIONAL
please visit:

www.ambassador-international.com
@AmbassadorIntl
www.facebook.com/AmbassadorIntl

*If you enjoyed this book, please consider leaving us a review on
Amazon, Goodreads, or our website.*